NANDRIA'S WAR

A Novel by Mary Jane Nordgren

To Debby
All the best!
M Nordgren

Cover by William A. Helwig
Graphic Ingenuity

ISBN 978-0-9703896-8-8

TAWK PRESS
47777 Ihrig Road, Forest Grove, OR 97116

NANDRIA'S WAR is the first is a series of novels set in the early 1940's which grew out of Mary Jane Nordgren's respect and love for her three uncles who served in World War II,

Arthur (Bud) Page - Navy

William J. (Bill) Page - Army

Robert W. (Bob) Page - Marines

CHAPTER ONE

Boonetown, Missouri, January 1940

Nandria stepped from the train onto the long-ago paved main street of Boonetown, Missouri, and nearly into a pothole disguised by the layer of snow. The rhythm of the train's sway tingled in her feet almost as much as it had when she'd carried her infant off the hospital ship in Halifax. Her long, slender legs threatened to betray her and, clutching her baby to her chest, she staggered a step to keep from falling.

The elderly man behind her holding her paisley bag and his own battered satchel lurched forward to help her, but she had caught her balance before he could get to her.

A farmer in straw hat and bibbed overalls who had disembarked from the train turned to watch. The weather-faced woman who stood beside the hay wagon holding the reins of a pair of thick-legged, sway-backed horses peered at her, studied her farmer-husband's expression as he took in this stranger's youth, loveliness, some degree of wealth as evidence in her clothes—and Negro. The woman turned to flail Nandria with a look of hatred and disgust: No young colored woman deserved better than was the common lot of rural Missouri Whites.

Though no word was spoken, Nandria could watch the woman's slack lips contemptuously form the word 'uppity.'

Nandria looked away in sadness.

It wasn't more than she had expected, but it was far worse than she had hoped.

"What are your grandfather and grandmother going to say, Little One?" Nandria whispered to her infant in the sling at her chest. "I wonder if they know about us. Surely your daddy told them . . ." But she didn't know; not for sure.

Straining and blowing back steam, the engine ground forward, hauling cracked and crackling wooden passenger cars past in increasing increments of speed.

Nandria watched it rattle by with a panicked feeling that made her want to throw down all her luggage and grab a hold on a vertical railing to swing back up the steps to escape with her infant Rose. But, shuddering, she held her ground.

The end of the train rushed by, buffeting her with a whoosh of air pocked with dirty snow. She cowered a moment, then closed her eyes, shuddering. She inhaled, deliberately blew out the manure–and–wood smoke air, lifted her chin, and opened her eyes to check her sleeping infant. Sighing, she looked around.

The few who had come to meet the train scattered in their own directions. The elderly man who had helped her with her bag sidled up, smiling over tobacco–stained teeth the leer of any man sure of gratitude for a favor done. He opened his mouth near Nandria's cheek to say something, then, glancing at an approaching 1920's Packard, dropped the paisley bag at the ragged edge of the paving, and, without looking back, hurried toward the prim woman driver. A powdering of snow lifted and fell back into the dirt around the once–colorful paisley.

Chapter One

Nandria peered beyond the leaning shed beside the railroad tracks in toward what must be the business district center of this quaint small town. She had read about wooden porches in front of stores being joined side to side to form walkways above the mud. But until now she had not seen, or expected to see in January 1940, a boardwalk. It graced three storefronts in the center of the small town—'Boonetown General Store,' 'Ludwig Leather' and a tiny establishment squeezed between them. The middle doorway and window together looked barely wider than her own arm-span, but the sign on the narrow window read, with difficulty, 'Harriet's Cosmopolitan Hats for Discriminating Women.' Its crowded letters had been partially wiped over with whitewash and below the distinguished declaration, in crude, hand-painted letters, was the sign 'Old Soles—shoe repair, cheap.' Nandria smiled.

Shivering, she wrapped her baby's blanket closer around Rose as a blurt of cold air rushed at them over the tracks. The gust fluttered a red rag stuck into the cracks of the plank door of the leaning storage shed long ago painted in the railroad's hunter green. Nandria saw the rag for moment as a warning hand waving to tell her to go back. Leave this place. Take your baby and run.

Nandria twisted to turn her back to the fury of the gusts of wind. She now faced away from the town center toward a barn and livery stable with two sedans and a small truck waiting in its yard. Waiting for what? For whom? Nandria wondered. And for how long? Judging from the peeling paint and weathered frame shops and houses, her husband Will's hometown Boonetown was no boomtown. The Great Depression must have manhandled them, and it showed no signs of relaxing its pitiless grip any time soon.

No wonder that farming wife had resented her coming. Even the red cloth coat Nandria's father had given her while she was in college was more than that woman or most others in this town could probably afford. Nandria's being colored only added to the resentment, she knew. And, knowing the powerful urge to blame others if only to try to hang onto one's own dignity and self–worth, in a way she couldn't blame them. But she clutched her infant closer to her, also knowing the consequences of such scapegoating.

"Not you, little Rose," she whispered. "Not as long as I can do anything to protect you."

Standing there beside the tracks, Nandria became aware that most of the prying eyes from various parts of the town were turning away, no longer even curious. Nandria Brown Minnick felt as alone as she had ever felt in her life.

She cooed to her baby, wishing that just this once the war departments of her England and his U.S.A. had allowed her Will to keep his promise to her. Since they'd met in Ethiopia, and then again in Spain's civil war, the U.S. Intelligence Service had thrown Will at her and snatched him away again. Often when she needed him most. But to take him away on assignment even from the dock in Liverpool…

He'd been away when Rose was born.

He hadn't known of Nandria's family lost on the Athenia.

But how could she fault Will when her own mother, for all her university degrees in mathematics, had still been naive about the depth of Mussolini's and then Hitler's perfidy. She'd still thought she and her diplomat husband and son were safe in 1939. But at least she'd been willing to be talked into letting Nandria take Ned out of country. And now all three had been among those passengers killed outright or drowned by German torpedoes.

But Mother had been wiser than Nandria herself when Will, after saving Ned and her in Ethiopia, reappeared when they needed him in Spain's civil war. This time Ned's adoration of the lean, young farmer had kept Will close long enough for Mama to see in his green eyes what Nandria was not allowing herself to believe. Will Minnick, in both Ethiopia and Spain, was a white American and therefore hated. He would be massacred, whichever side found him protecting them.

"I know," he'd told her when she tried to get him to save himself. But he wouldn't leave them until she and Ned were safe in the arms of their parents.

"I know," he'd answered their mother when she tried to warn him against the prejudice he and Nandria would encounter were they to allow their attraction to each other to become serious.

"Son, you can't know," Nandria's mother had insisted.

"From the other side, I know very well," he'd said with a half–smile of deep sadness.

"But directed at you?"

He'd stood, head down for a moment, then had lifted his chin and peered at her with green eyes that told her he did know. Mrs.

Brown had said nothing after that, though she ached for them both.

A year later, he and Nandria had married quietly in London, but their honeymoon was cut short. Nandria had been left swirling her champagne in its stemmed glass until it went flat, and salty from her tears. The turmoil in Spain, and then Poland and Central Europe kept separating them. He'd leave without saying where he was going, and Nandria would hear nothing for days, or weeks.

"But you're safe here in England," he'd soothe her, resting his hand gently on the growing mound of her abdomen. "That's what matters to me. You and our baby are safe." He hadn't said it aloud, but Nandria could see in his eyes that the time of safety in England was growing shorter and shorter. He moved them to a village along England's northeastern coast. He said it was because it would be nearer where he went out and came back. Nearer the area where a fledgling air force was being assembled. But, she knew, it was also farther from London, which he seemed to believe would soon be the target of Nazi bombs.

She'd carried their baby nearly the full nine months with him intermittently there for support. She'd fretted as she neared her term, and then he'd gone again, this time even when she'd felt the first contractions in what did turn out to be false labor. She hadn't told him. He would have had to go regardless of her need to have him near.

She'd been doing what she could, helping with the British army's paperwork. It wasn't her life's dream work, but she was good at it. And as organizations of all sorts of shapes and sizes would find out about her skill, they would pursue her to help them, despite the growing obviousness of her pregnancy. She'd been organizing a supply depot's files when her water broke earlier than expected. She was in labor, but the depot was suddenly under siege. She'd found a small side room, probably sleeping quarters for the ranking officer. With so much going on, Nandria thought she'd go through early labor on her own and only call for help when she really needed it. But as she grew in need, enemy planes roaring strafing runs over them created chaos. She called for help, but no one heard. Rose Annelise Minnick was born with only her mother attending. Nandria was scanning the small room for something to use to clamp the umbilical cord when a young private entered on some sort of errand and surprised them both.

"I shall never forget the look on his face, little one. Or his kindness in helping us when he could finally take in what was happening," Nandria smiled as she whispered to the top her three-month-old's soft, fuzzy head. "There are such good people in the world, Rose. Be sure you remember them, too, when the others work to put you down."

"Well, Sugarlips," a leering voice close by startled Nandria. She twisted to face the man who had spoken and found two, not one. Both were shabbily dressed in heavy wool jackets unrelated to the size of either man. Both were shaggy-bearded. Both had lips pursed in lewd puckers and were making smacking noises. As they came near—they had to have been hiding behind the railroad shed or Nandria would have noticed them approaching—their loud and staccato smacking noises disturbed Rose's sleep. The infant lifted her head, her tiny face screwed up in what looked to be annoyance. She whimpered, opening that rosebud mouth and howled.

Nandria looked around quickly. Even the baby's cry did not seem to be arousing any interest in what was going on. There would be no help. The two scarecrow figures were nearly close enough for them to touch her, but no one was looking their way.

Nandria covered the baby with her blanket, swallowed once and set her feet to face the men.

"So, I take it you gentlemen have never been to New Orleans," she said in a husky tone that talked down to them and hid much of the fear that threatened to make her tremble.

CHAPTER TWO

"Huh?" the two scruffy men grunted in unison.

Their facial structure and high cheekbones were so alike, they had to be blood relatives, if not full brothers. Nandria looked into the rheumy blue eyes of the taller, what seemed to her to be the older man, but she couldn't tell his age, or his intelligence.

The younger, more compact man twisted his large head on his scrawny neck and peered down at her with watery blue-gray eyes.

"Whadya say, Sugarlips?" His breath on her neck was warm and stank of what had to be home brew such as she hadn't smelled except in a small village outside Addis Ababa. She'd been with her father, who had found reason to leave soon after the brew was shared.

"I said," Nandria told him after clearing her throat imperiously, "I take it neither of you gentlemen has been to New Orleans, or you would have known to keep a respectful distance."

"What from?" the older one asked.

"VooDoo priestesses do not enjoy being crowded."

"VooDoo?" they chimed.

"You mean that stuff where they keep dead men walking around and doin' stuff?" the younger gaped.

"And stick pins in them little straw dolls so the guy they wanna get back at is hurtin' all over?"

"Very painful," Nandria explained with what she hoped was a gleam in her eyes. She shuddered, not entirely from another chill blast. "Very, very painful."

The men looked at each other and then stared at her. Nandria's eyes raked up and down each of them, and then, cradling her baby against her, she turned away and stood looking out at the forlorn coupe in the car repair lot, deliberately ignoring them. When they didn't leave on their own, Nandria, with her back to them, began a slow, rhythmic swaying to a low chant of nonsense words.

One of them sneered, but the other hushed him. They stood, open handed and open mouthed, and then gratefully turned away as a battered, once–upon–a–time blue pickup truck rattled up and parked beside the railroad shed.

"Bodie," they informed each other.

Nandria felt rather than heard them shuffle away. She turned to watch a gimpy older white man whose limping skeleton moved his shapeless bib overalls and whose skull–like head held a wide–brimmed felt hat on bald pate, sheltering it from the film of snow. He clambered out of the truck and called, "Miz Minnick?"

Nandria nodded, surprised anyone knew her name. This couldn't be Will's father. There was no resemblance in stature or features. And his continual clucking and smiling as he approached did nothing to substantiate Will's reluctant description of his father as something of a bear.

"Howdy there. I's the Minnicks' handyman, Bodie."

Cuddly this man was not; too angular. And his deferent, sunny disposition was not likely ever to have been thought of as bruin.

"Sorry to be so late. I knowed it was you soon's I seen ya. Will Minnick would have only the purdiest, all right, all right." He paused for breath as he helped her out of her knapsack and picked up the paisley bag to carry them to the back of the truck. "The mister's so taken up with fixin' that blamed thresher, I said I'd fetch you, and, oh, ain't that young'un the spittin' of our Will? You got more to carry?" he asked when he'd gotten the bags set in the back of the pickup. "That's it? Well, come along then," he commanded, smoothing the woven blanket covering the worn front bench seat. She held the baby's sling close against her chest, and Bodie helped her up onto the running board and into the cab.

Tools of various sizes and shapes were crowded into a cardboard box between her and the driver's seat. Oil, grease and long wear had bent and folded the flaps so the box stood nearly full at half-height. Bodie unconsciously shoved it over against her with his hip as he climbed in under the steering wheel wrapped round and round with yarn.

"When's our Will gonna be comin', you know that yet?" he asked as he pumped the gas pedal and turned the ignition key with both hands. He let the engine rev a minute before fighting the upright gear stick.

When she didn't answer, he finally looked over.

Nandria's eyes were glistening as she stared straight ahead. Her head moved shallowly side to side.

"Well, no matter now. The thing is to get ya home," he said as he willed the truck to move forward and then executed a U turn that bumped over the railroad tracks and back again. They headed into the quaint town that Nandria had studied from a hundred meters away.

"Them Bratton boys give you a hard time, did they?" he asked low as they entered Boonetown. "Them boys kin be mean. Sorry I was late and they got to you."

She peered at her infant; so long as Rose was safe . . . "No harm," she muttered, closing her eyes to compose herself in the over–warm truck cab after standing in the cold for so long.

They were still in low gear when a stooped, scrawny man with a pot belly waved to Bodie to stop the truck in front of Ludlam's Leather. As he shuffled to the driver's window, he hauled his jacket lapel to one side, and Nandria saw what looked to be a hand–fashioned tin star pinned to his collarless blue shirt. The lawman crouched, brushing the edge of his felt hat at the window frame. Squinting, he peered in.

"Sheriff Yakes. Crank down your window," Bodie muttered to Nandria, barely moving his lips. "Hello, Sheriff," he said jovially as he rolled down the window on his side. "Just bringin' Will's Missus to the farm."

The sheriff stared her up and down, even craning around Bodie so he could see down her legs to her wet shoes. But Nandria had turned to her window where a pale, gaunt young woman, hardly more than a girl was shyly fingering the shoulder of Nandria's red coat. Nandria was sure what she really wanted to touch was little Rose. Multi-colored bruises ranged up the girl's thin, bare arms, and under her milk-chocolate eyes were healing smudges of greens and yellows.

"So purdy," the girl breathed. "You're goin' out to Minnicks, ain't you? We'll just near be neighbors. I live a couple miles up the dirt road, even shorter if'n you cut across the fields. "Here," she said, thrusting a small stone from her pocket into Nandria's hand. "I thunk this'un was real purdy."

"Emmy Lu!" a gruff male voice bellowed. The girl and half of the gathering crowd around the Minnick pickup cowered.

The girl snatched back her hand and, wrapping it in its mate, entangled both in the folds of her voluminous cotton skirt. "It's Horace," she whispered, eyes wide and fearful.

A huge hulk of a man with high cheekbones and beard matted with tobacco spittle yanked Emmy Lu away from Nandria's window. A tall, broad woman in frock coat and a girl, much larger and better fed than Emmy, caught her and kept her from being thrown to the ground. The woman glared at Horace, but his back was to her by this time as he bulled his head in at Nandria's window.

Drawing the blanket close around little Rose, Nandria cradled the baby's head in her left hand and strained left as far as she could go. She was leaning awkwardly over the box of tools but her right hand on Rose's back was ready to whip out and scratch at his eyes if he made even a gesture toward the infant. His breath was nauseating, but Nandria voiced no protest.

You would not be doing this if my Will were here, she thought. But Will was on assignment somewhere, probably Central Europe. Keeping her eyes on this brute of a man, Nandria exhaled slowly to regain control of herself. To her relief, he pulled back without making a move to touch the baby.

Horace popped his head back out and hollered over the top of the track cab. "Hey, Sheriff, Bodie's got a nigger in here! Whatcha gonna do 'bout that?" The man's spittle sprayed as he laughed and bent his head in again near hers. Bits glistened on the red shoulder of Nandria's coat, but she did not wipe them away. Not yet.

Shrugging, Yakes glanced sideways at the crowd before answering. "Bein' born shit ain't agin the law, Horace. Long as she knows her place, we gotta let her be."

Nodding quickly at the faint chuckle that murmured through the people pressing close around him, the sheriff slapped the pickup's door.

"Go on with you, then, Bodie. Mind you don't break no speed limits in this here junker." He went to slap the window frame, but yanked back his hand as the Minnicks' handyman was already cranking up his window with his left hand and reaching for the gear stick with his right.

Grinning at the crowd's reaction, Yakes elaborately waved Bodie on as people moved out of his path. Bodie lurched forward so Horace had to stand up fast.

"Uh–oh," Bodie breathed as he glanced into the side–view mirror. "Horace ain't gonna forgit that. You'n me best stay out of his way until after his next drunk. Likely he ain't gonna remember he's got a grudge, but sometimes he does. Best you just clean stay away from him altogether, Miz. Them Brattons got mean streaks a mile wide down their backs. Best never tangle with 'em a'tall, a'tall."

Pulling away, Bodie checked again in the mirror.

"See that fella in the turned-around collar comin' up to the sheriff?" he told Nandria. "That there is Pastor Dean Kylie. Thinks pretty high of hisself, he does. But Will's mama dotes on 'im." Bodie clucked the roof of his mouth and clutched the steering wheel in both hands now that he'd gotten the truck into second gear.

Had Nandria been able to hear the men, she'd have known what the town leaders thought of her. Lip-reading the conversation in mirror image from the moving truck was more than she could do as yet. But from what she could see of their body language she was fairly sure she already knew the gist, most likely.

"On her way to Minnick's?" the pastor asked, peering up the single main street at the retreating truck.

"Bold as Brass." Yakes hawked phlegm and spat, away from the pastor's feet. "Yeah. What you whore around with is your business, but Will sending her here," the sheriff spat again, this time a little less carefully, "that takes the cake."

"A cake with bitter icing, Sheriff," the pastor intoned. "Very bitter icing. I'll need to talk on arrogance, come Sunday."

Bodie rattled through town on what still felt to Nandria to be the wrong side of the road. They travelled between mostly brick-faced storefronts and strained clapboard single–family houses. The majority of the houses were tidy, but worn and in need of paint. Low shoveled mounds of snow were gray and peppered with soot. Late asters and the few leaves remaining on trees scraggly in picket–fenced yards bore their lace of snow as finery. In many of the front windows, curtains could be seen drawn to one side, but no one came out onto the wide front porches of their homes or even stepped into view to wave or welcome.

For once, Bodie was silent, biting his lip. Now and again he clucked with his tongue at the roof of his mouth.

Rose stirred and screwed up her face as though she would cry, but her threat was managed quickly as her mother bent to swaddle them both in blankets and gave her suck.

Bodie looked over once, then stared straight ahead.

Nandria had time to look out her window at how quickly the town faded behind them and the road's paving narrowed and roughened. Occasional farmhouses sat back far from the road, dominated by barns even more greatly in need of fresh paint. What had been the almost universal brick red was now faded nearly to gray pallor pink. Behind or beside almost every home lay the remnants of what had been huge gardens.

"Down that road is the swamp bog," Bodie told her when Rose was once again satisfied and breathing softly in sleep. "Don't wanna go there."

"Quicksand?" Nandria ventured. She'd done as much reading as she could from books at the library in London before coming with her husband, she'd thought, to the land where he'd grown up.

"Some," Bodie admitted, "but mostly snakes."

"Oh?" Nandria's voice sounded cowed, even to her.

"Yep. Moccasins. And rattlers."

"Oh," she managed, and that settled all talk again for miles.

The rolling hills, covered as they were in whiter snow than had remained in town, displayed rural beauty marred only by the evidence of even greater poverty. The farther they drove, the bleaker the picture. Each homestead showed greater neglect, though most still showed the residents' brave attempts to work with whatever they had left. It was not laziness which had conquered this land, but economics. Economics which these farmers had had no say in developing and were far slower in recovering from than the city banker types.

Nandria had seen it again and again in developing countries, particularly in Africa, but also in Spain. It was the real people who suffered. It was always the foot soldiers who had had no say in declaring war, who did the dying.

And still the land remained, rolling hills whose rhythms of line gave hope that man might some day gain the balance and forward movement of Nature herself. Beauty always gave hope, however contradicted by one's experience with greed.

After a long drive on a heavily tracked, dirt road paralleled by deep ditches on either side, Bodie turned the truck into a lane with one low point arched over by skeletal trees bending in from both sides. In summer, when the trees were in leaf, this must be a refreshing 'tunnel' of shade and coolness.

As they rose from the now leafless dip, Nandria could see in the distance a wooden farmhouse built, evidently, in three stages. What had obviously been the original house presented its entire south facing front wrapped in deep porch with its own roof held up by sturdy pillars.

The west face was plain except for windows on the first and second story, split nearly in half by a vertical line where the narrow clapboards met rougher, wider wallboards of a creamier, peeling white. The north face, differed yet again from the original front, in that its white was a pearly gray though the boards were only slightly wider so that their irregular matching only began to be noticeable nearly two thirds of the way up the side of the building. Nandria grew sadder and sadder as she studied its proclamation of poverty close to the eaves.

Bodie drove up beside the farmhouse and parked as near as he could to the last addition. It was a porch enclosed so it was now a room of its own. Two wide, wooden stairs led up from the back yard. Behind, across a deep yard, towered the once-red barn with a path shoveled through calf-high snow between the barn and the house steps. A smaller path, probably foot-worn, led to a chicken coop with a multi-limbed but squat mulberry tree hovering over it. A whimsical doghouse sat alone, peeling blue paint. On a clothesline strung between the back steps and an elm just north of the house long johns hung stiff, frozen and unclaimed.

Bodie clucked once more, turned off the engine and jumped out his side to hurry around to help Nandria and the baby ease from the truck. He watched her look around as he gathered the knapsack and paisley bag from the bed of the pickup.

With a swish forward of the bag, he indicated for her to walk one of the worn paths to the back porch steps.

"Yep," he said, "good land. When Minnicks had both strappin' sons here to help, this farm was sompin' all right, all right. Come on, Girl, let's get you in an' settled. Then I'll go and tell the mister that we brung you home safe and sound."

Nandria tightened her lips against the protest that rose within her. Home? Without Will, could this ever be home?

CHAPTER THREE

Nandria carried Rose across the enclosed porch and looked in at the doorway into the kitchen while Bodie kicked off his boots and set them at the entry to the porch. Realizing that outdoor shoes were not to be worn into the house, Nandria slid off her wet, patton leather Mary Janes and scooched them to one side of the door as Bodie, with an anxious look on his face and carrying battered leather moccasins, hurried by her in holey socks to the kitchen. It was only then that Nandria realized that the low tone she'd half-heard must be a woman's moan.

"Missus?" Bodie cried.

Nandria stepped quietly to the doorway of the kitchen and peered in. Obviously the Minnicks had electricity into the house since a low-hanging bulb dangled, lighted, over the scarred oak table to the right. But, instead of a refrigerator, an icebox stood bulky to Nandria's immediate left. Against the far wall loomed an ancient wood-devouring range. At the sink board under the window to Nandria's far left, a frail, gray, worn farm wife bent within her faded, floral print, cotton housedress and bibbed apron. A large men's handkerchief was tied loosely around her neck with the 'V' of cloth demurely covering her throat. She leaned against the lead-lined sink, swaying in heavy, thick-heeled, black, laced shoes. Her thick, white cotton socks, folded fat over her ankles did nothing to help hold her up.

"Missus?" Bodie exclaimed again in alarm, dropping Nandria's luggage on the floor partly under the oak table.

"Where ya been, Bodie? I been needin' ya. Can't remember where that paring knife skittered off to," the worn woman complained. She swiped back thinning hair from her eyes.

"Well now, Missus," Bodie said as he rushed over to pick up the paring knife on the sink board beside the woman. "Come on, now, let's us set a spell at the table. Come on, that's it." Gently he led her to a chair at the table and helped her lower herself into it. He gave her the knife, which she took in her left hand. "Just hold on one minute."

He hurried back across the dark linoleum floor to lift a pan of unpeeled potatoes from the deep sink and brought them over to set them on the table in front of her.

"Now, Missus, them potatoes don't worry none about whether you're standin' or settin' whilst you get 'em ready for his supper. So set a bit now. I brung ya company."

"Company?" The woman fussed again with her hair and wiped down her dress and apron with, fortunately, the dull edge of the paring knife. "My dress. My apron. My hair. No. No company, Bode. No company."

"Hesh now, Missus. It's your daughter-in-law. Will's wife and wee one to see ya. All the way from London in England, don't ya know."

The woman startled. Her pale green eyes widened and her mouth gaped open as she stared up at Bodie hovering over her. Her white cheeks brightened to rosy.

"Will?" she cried. "Will's here?"

Quickly Nandria slipped into the room and sat at the end of the table closest to the porch door where she could reach to stroke the woman's hand.

"Not yet, Mother Minnick. He wanted to come with me, but he could not get away yet. But he will come soon. He promised."

Doris Minnick lifted her chin and twisted to face Nandria and the baby. Seeming to forget her panic over her son, she smiled gently at the squirming infant. She reached with her right hand to pat Rose's cheek with the knife–less hand. Nandria had been watching.

"Such a cunning little one. So tiny. How old is he?"

"She is a girl, Mother Minnick," Nandria explained, still eyeing the paring knife Doris continued to grasp in her left hand. "Rose. Named after you. Rose is your middle name, is it not?"

Doris sat back, rocking so the paring knife clicked again and again on the oak surface.

"Funny name for a boy. But he'll be tough defending himself with a name like that. That'll be good. A man's gotta be tough, I'm afraid. Remember, Bodie, how many scraps our Will got into over his being Willard. Not William. Some of the teachers would insist he must be William to be called Will."

Bodie grinned and straightened wearily. "And not Wee Willie Winky."

But Doris was already interested more in the baby than in the conversation. She rocked forward again and caressed Rose's cheeks.

"Such purdy skin. I always loved brown. So rich, like good earth."

Without warning, Doris clattered the knife to the table and laid her face on the oak. The baby startled and screwed up her little face, ready to howl. Nandria soothed her, staring at her mother-in-law.

"Tired, Bodie," Doris whimpered. "Have the girl finish supper for me, will you? So good of the mister to get me some help 'til I feel stronger again. So tired."

"Aye, Missus, it's been a long day," Bodie whispered. He slid the paring knife from her hand and set it away from her toward the middle of the table. "Poor lady, good lady," he crooned as he gently turned her so he could help her up by lifting under her armpits. She stood swaying and he half-carried her out of the kitchen, deeper into the house. To her bedroom, Nandria surmised.

For a long time, Nandria sat rocking her infant and peering at the doorway through which this strange handyman had carried her mother-in-law. *Will's mother. The woman he adores, but has not seen in how many years? Does he know how unwell she is? But I cannot stay here, Will. I cannot. So much hate. How can I expose our tiny daughter to so much hate? Because it will spill over onto her. Hate always spills over onto the innocent. Even though she is half you, she is still half me, and that makes her anathema.*

"There is little but hatred here for us," Nandria said, unsure to whom she was speaking but needing to hear the words aloud. "I suppose I could ask the handyman to take us back to that train. It was a time getting to this mid-America purgatory. And it would be as draining to try to go back north. But at least in Canada I could do some good, working with the Sisters. So many wounded." Nandria closed her eyes, remembering how much more she had learned to do on the Canadian military hospital ship from Liverpool to Halifax than the paperwork to which she had been assigned. She'd learned far more about wound care and nursing that she would have chosen to. And she had seen more that she would gladly un-see, if that were possible.

Rose's whimpering in her arms made Nandria focus on the present, always a good place to focus in a crisis, her mother would say. Thought of her mother, now drowned and dead, brought Nandria to tears. She rose, crying, to root within the paisley bag for one of the few cloth diapers still clean. Sobbing, she laid her baby across the seat of one of the sturdy oak breakfast chairs to change her. As she lifted Rose and held the infant to her with her fresh-to-the-world smell and soft skin cheek to cheek against her own, Nandria wept as she hadn't since Will had had to leave her at the pier in Liverpool. And even then, she'd been pressed so quickly into service organizing the paperwork for the wounded Canadian soldiers aboard the hospital ship that she'd had little time for her own deep sorrows.

"The 'Salty Healer.' Is that not quite a name?" Nandria clucked to Rose as she settled her at the breast to nurse. A single tear slid unheeded from Nandria's chin and dropped onto her infant's forehead, startling her. "Oh, Princess, I am sorry."

But there was scarcely need for apology as Rose wrinkled her forehead in a frown but went right on with her task.

"You can focus, little one. Your grandmother would like that about you."

Your grandmother. Oh, tiny rosebud, your grandmother. Now you have only one and she needs us. How sorely she needs us, I do not believe even she knows. Your daddy would want us to stay and help, whatever the cost. Until it hurts you, my darling. That cost I will not pay. But until then, perhaps we need to stay. At least until your daddy can get here. We can decide together where . . .

Nandria watched her baby nurse, and when Rose was quietly sleeping again, Nandria wrapped her and laid her on her tummy carefully across her own thighs where she could feel immediately if the baby stirred. Nandria breathed deeply twice and reached across the table for the paring knife.

We shall be waiting here for you, Will. We will do what we can for your mother.

She was humming to Rose and peeling potatoes when Bodie tiptoed back out through the kitchen.

CHAPTER FOUR

Puffing visible vapor into the cold air, Grover Minnick marched across the slick path from his barn to the enclosed back porch.

"She's a quiet one, all right, all right," Bodie tried to explain as he hurried to limp behind his boss across the new layer of wet snow turning to ice. "The wee one, too. And she's quick to be gentle with the missus."

If Minnick slowed, it could have been merely a misstep on the slippery lower step.

"Supper ready?" was all Minnick wanted to know.

"Uh, I expect so," Bodie answered. "The gal was gettin' it in hand when I come back through the kitchen." He stopped as Minnick fumbled getting the porch door open. "She'd been crying, she had," he added under his breath, but Minnick, giving no indication of having heard, bulled onto the porch and sat heavily on the bench beside the door to wrestle off his boots. He stared a moment at Nandria's narrow, ruined, Mary Jane patton leather shoes, and then slid into moccasin–like slippers, rose and lumbered into the kitchen, leaving his boots helter–skelter across the floor.

Behind him, Bodie set Minnick's huge, scuffed boots as a pair on the oilcloth against the wall and sat on the briefly warmed bench to remove his own and line them up over against Mr.

Minnick's. He hurried into the kitchen to see Grover seat himself at the head of the table. For a moment, before he realized Bodie was at the doorway, Minnick had touched his wife's hand as she sat next to him at his right, closest to the stove. Seeing Bodie enter, Minnick whipped his hand away and tipped back his chair to stare at the slender, young, dark woman at the stove.

Even with that pickaninny hanging in that cloth sling on her front, the girl was pretty, although that luscious skin was too dark to be covering a true human being. "Exotic." That was a word Will had used when he was just a kid, Minnick remembered, frowning. That first-born boy of his had never been satisfied on the farm. Always thinking of something far beyond.

Minnick glanced at his Doris, for the first time in all those years wondering if . . . *Doris? Unfaithful? Never!*

Ashamed and uncomfortable with his own momentary loss of faith, Minnick looked back again at what was said to be his daughter-in-law at the stove serving up the meal. Nandria's face was flushed and glistened with sweat. He could guess she'd had quite a time trying to master the vagaries of the wood stove. He smiled, not realizing how many trips into the back country of African nations Nandria had made with her British diplomat father. Or how many variations of wood or dung stove she had learned to master.

Bodie settled into his usual place at the foot of the table, but realized that Nandria would need to crowd around behind him to get to the only other seat, which was behind the table next to the wall. With a silly grin at his boss, Bodie got up to shift to that wall seat at Minnick's left hand. Minnick looked at him and frowned, but said nothing.

Minnick exhaled slowly through flared nostrils. *Life is too complicated; always with the "what-if's" and the "oh, no's". Why couldn't things be simple? Peaceful. You should be able to work hard, make a decent living, sit back of an evening and just let the hurting melt away so you could sleep. He stared at his Doris, and looked down quickly. What's happening to this girl I married? She'd always been small, but strong. And strong-willed, feisty in her defense of him. Fun in following my lead, upright or even in our bed.*

Minnick bit his lip to keep from moaning. So many doctors they'd been to. So many asinine opinions. So many foul-smelling and fouler-tasting tonics he'd helped her down. But she wasn't getting better; she was getting worse. *Too young to be this old!* He caught himself, swallowing hard against betraying his despair. He'd nearly blurted it out loud.

He closed his eyes, then snapped them open as he felt the steam and smelled the aroma of the roast being set before him on the table.

Pot roast, it was. Then a large bowl of green beans and a crock of soupy, yellow-whitish slices of something layered in a sauce. It didn't smell bad, but then neither did the girl, though he'd always heard that niggers did. Smell bad. Maybe it was just the food aromas disguising her stench, he thought.

He frowned. For the first time, he realized that she'd set the plates in front of each person. How the hell could he serve them plates when they was all spread around to everybody already?

From the corner of his eye, Minnick recognized that Bodie was hand signaling the girl to stack the plates in front of him. Well, probably it was best to just let that go. If Bodie was teaching her, he'd have less he'd have to say to her, and that suited Grover Minnick just fine.

Besides, Doris was smiling. Pale, worn, weak as a kitten, but smiling like she hadn't done in some time, and that made Minnick lean toward letting the girl stay. *Where the hell was Will? How did he have the gall to write and say he'd married somebody we ain't even met? And that she was a nigger? If that wasn't bad enough, how could he send her here? He knows what Boonetown thought of coloreds. They're for workin' in the fields and domestic help. But who could afford to pay for either one of those with this Great Depression still squattin' over everybody?*

Nandria gathered the plates and stacked them in front of her father–in–law. She sighed when he merely scowled, but without saying anything, she went to sit at her end of the table facing him. Rose was quiet. The meal was made. She murmured her thanks to God that she'd arrived, but dared not question Him on whether or not she would stay, or for how long.

"Grace?" Minnick asked. He glanced at Doris, but her smile had faded with what color there had been to her cheeks. She was swaying in her seat, barely able to sit up.

"Well, we said 'grace.' I reckon that's enough," Minnick said. He began to ladle food onto each plate.

"Yeah, the Lord's heard it 'nuff times. He kin prob'ly fill in the rest for Hisself," Bodie agreed.

"Not much for me, dear Mr. Minnick," Doris sighed, leaning her head into work-gnarled hands. "I ain't very hungry this night."

"Now, Mother, you gotta keep up your strength," he urged.

She sighed again as Nandria watched her carefully.

"If you say so, dear Mr. Minnick, I'll try," she managed, but her lack of appetite was all too apparent to everyone at the table.

Minnick returned to doling out the food. He lifted the largest of the ill-matched serving spoons and tentatively set it into the bowl of yellow and white. Frowning, he let the spoonful plop back into the bowl.

"What the devil is this?"

Curious at last, Doris leaned forward to dip her own spoon into the crock. She brought the spoon to her lips and tasted. "Scalloped potatoes," she announced. Her eyes closed as though remembering. A gentle smile came to her lips.

"Around here," Minnick bellowed to no one specifically, "we eat our potatoes whipped with cream and butter."

While Bodie and Nandria sat in pained silence, Doris again leaned forward and dipped her spoon into the crock. She brought the spoon to her mouth and sighed with pleasure.

"Ummm. So good. I haven't tasted these since my mama used to serve these on special Sundays. I was always glad when our pastor'd come to our house after church."

Frowning, but more gently, Minnick peered at his wife.

"Good," Doris told Nandria. "Thank you, girl."

"Nandria, Missus," Bodie told her in a near whisper. "Her name is Nandria. Will's wife."

"So she says," Minnick growled, and Nandria started to rise in protest, then sat back, lips tight.

Doris did rise, swaying. "Will?"

Minnick lunged to his feet to catch her. "Mother, Mother," he crooned as he slid one large hand under her knees and the other behind her shoulders and lifted her in his arms to carry her to their bedroom.

"Oh, dear," Nandria cried and starting to hurry after them, but Bodie shook his head.

"Best leave 'em," he warned. "Too much for her."

Lips pressed together, Nandria finished serving Bodie's platter and set it before him.

"It's obvious he wouldn't want me near, even to help," she muttered mostly under her breath.

Digging in with his fork, Bodie merely raised his eyebrows above a brief nod of agreement. Nandria began to gather the food to set into the icebox.

"Does he ever take her to the doctor? Does he try to see what is wrong?"

Bodie shrugged. "It's happened before," he mumbled and went back to his eating. Eventually he rose, untucked his napkin from under his chin and set it beside his plate. He started for the porch.

"What happens now?" Nandria despised the fact that her question sounded like pleading.

"You kin see why we moved the Minnicks' bedroom down on this here floor. I sleep at my place, over yonder, beyond the west fence. I put your things in Will's room upstairs. You find 'em all right?"

Nandria sat, rocking her baby in her arms. She nodded in answer to his question.

"Well, I'll be back around dawn. He likes four bacons and two eggs, over real easy—just so they ain't runny 'til he forks into 'em. Three slices of toast, thick. Butter 'em, but leave the jam on the table for him to slather on hisself."

"Oh," Nandria murmured. Oh, Will. I don't want to be here. Lord, I do not want to be anywhere near your father. But how can I just leave your mother? She is so helpless.

Bodie shuffled to the porch in his stocking feet. Nandria listened to his grunts as he reset his feet in his boots, and then clomped back to the doorway to the kitchen. He poked his head back in to speak with her.

"Them slurpy potatoes? Pretty good, Miz. Not's good as whipped with butter, but fair to middlin'."

He withdrew and Nandria heard him clomp to the porch door and close it quietly behind him.

Nandria hugged Rose so close, the baby whimpered.

"Sorry, Love," Nandria whispered. She got up heavily to carry Bodie's plate and flatware to the sink and washed it with the rest. When the kitchen was in order, she snapped off the light and carried her daughter up to Will's room on the second floor. After changing Rose's diaper, Nandria settled into a wooden rocking chair next to the window looking out over the blue snow of the back yard and eerie blue shape of the barn in the light of the quarter moon. Nandria allowed the tears of grief and frustration to flow down her cheeks as she nursed her infant.

"This is the only grandmother you will ever know, my darling. How can I just leave her like this?"

She rocked and crooned and cooed long after Rose had fallen asleep before she settled her into the cushioned bottom drawer of Will's dresser.

With her infant secure, Nandria stole down the narrow staircase and out through the kitchen to the back steps. Drawing her arms around herself for warmth and strength, she stared at the myriad stars, intermittently veiled by meandering wispy clouds.

"Oh, Will," she spoke aloud finally, "I believe I must stay, at least until you come, and we think what is best to do. I cannot leave her in such a state." Hugging her upper body closer with her own arms, Nandria stared at the vanishing vapor witnesses to her words of commitment. "But that man," she vowed even more vehemently, "that man will not make me beg—even for common courtesy."

CHAPTER FIVE

Early the next morning, Nandria had washed and rinsed Rose's diapers, and cranked them as well as a load of Doris's unmentionables, through the wringer. She set a pile of large men's work clothes into the tub of the agitator to soak. A few dark stains—possibly grease or oil from one of the farm machines—she dealt with over the scrub board, hard as that was on her knuckles.

Outside, it was sunny and dry, if not warm enough to have little Rose rest in the yard for any length of time, so Nandria carried the second drawer of Will's dresser out to the enclosed porch and lined it with a flat pillow and blankets. She changed and nursed her baby and laid her in the drawer where she could hear her if she woke and cried. When Rose was settled, Nandria sat to pull on the oversized rubber boots Bodie had found for her. She slogged outside hauling the basket of wet things to hang them on the line that stretched from the corner of the enclosed porch to the elm about ten meters to the northeast of the house.

Doris's intimate apparel Nandria hung behind the thinnest of Rose's cloth diapers to dry without embarrassing the mistress of this house. A rough pole with an ingenious open hook arrangement of metal strips held up the line at two points in the middle so it would not sag. But Nandria, at five feet four inches, needed to lower the poles to be able to fasten the clothes with the long–tined, wooden pins. She was just lifting the second pole to stand more vertically when a dark, high–windowed Chevy chugged up the Minnick farm lane and parked in front of their battered blue pickup truck.

A slender man emerged awkwardly, lugging a frayed leather bag in which the black had worn to silvery in places. The man was probably in his early thirties, square–jawed, with a high forehead and nondescript, thick brown hair drooped into his pale, hazel eyes. He approached her with the mincing step of someone who prefers solid, dry flooring to irregular snow–covered paths across a farm yard.

"Ah," he said when he saw Nandria with the end of a clothespin between her lips. "Hello," he added as she was about to welcome him. "I'm Dr. Ricartsen. How is Mrs. Minnick doing this morning? You must be the new maid Minnick hired. Well, good to have you here to help. Lord knows Doris can use it," he said and turned away to make his way to the porch and into the house.

It took Nandria a moment to collect herself enough to remember to remove the clothespin from between her lips. She blinked, unsure whether she felt anger or amusement, possibly both.

"If you cannot change what is happening, then it is just right – for now," she recalled her father's oft–repeated quote from her childhood.

"For now," she muttered and gathered the unused clothespins, set them in the bottom of the basket and carried it into the house.

At the porch door she stepped out of the too–large rubber boots and into crocheted slippers she'd made painfully long ago under her mother's direction. There were no extra pairs of goulashes lined up on the oilcloth, she noticed. The doctor must have worn his on into the house. Nandria stared in at the plain, dark linoleum in the kitchen and noticed that the doctor had indeed entered without removing his boots. Tracks of mud and crusted snow led across the porch floor and into the kitchen. She sighed. The linoleum would be easy enough to clean, since she would obviously be the one to do it. She just hoped the oblivious physician would not walk too far into the living room. The carpet was threadbare along worn paths; it would not be easy to get the mud out of it.

Perhaps the brown mud will enhance what little color was left, Nandria chuckled to herself. *Momma would say there is a good side to every issue, if you look hard enough.*

But at times you have to peer pretty darn deep to see it.

After checking that little Rose was still asleep, Nandria walked into the kitchen to put the kettle on for coffee or tea, whichever the good doctor preferred. Picking up the drawer with Rose sleeping in it, she sidestepped through the door into the living room. Doris sat in the corner of the sofa just as Nandria had settled her with her needles and hook and yarn.

Dr. Ricartsen was sitting sideways to face the woman, listening with his stethoscope to her chest, through her housedress and light sweater.

When he'd finished listening and was folding the long tubes of his stethoscope, Doris peered at him quizzically.

"What do you listen for, Doctor?"

"Nasties, Mrs. Minnick," he told her and twisted forward to set the instrument into his bag on the floor. "I see Grover's finally gotten you some help." He nodded to indicate that Nandria had entered the room.

Nandria opened her mouth to explain, but, lips tight, she concentrated instead on her infant as she set the drawer that was her bed on the floor near the end of the sofa. Satisfied, she turned and rose to face him.

"Good morning, Doctor. I am Nandria Minnick, Will's wife," she said formally and extended her hand.

He rose, too flustered to acknowledge her offer to shake hands. His arched eyebrows accented his open mouth.

"Uh, good morning," he managed.

"I have water on to boil. Do you prefer tea or coffee, Dr. Ricartsen?"

"Uh, neither, thanks. I need to get to the Paislers. Just stopped here first as Bodie had told them Doris took another spell last night, and they called early to let me know so I could stop on my way to their place." He'd rattled all that off but was still shaking his head. "Wi . . . ?" he started, but Nandria interrupted to keep him from saying Will's name aloud in front of Doris.

"I shall be staying for a while, and helping with Mother Minnick. Is there something I should know about in taking care of her needs?"

"Uh, maybe you'll walk me to my car?"

"Of course, Doctor."

He stooped to gather the rest of his tools to stuff them into his satchel and buckle it. His movements had the long-limbed awkwardness of a colt or an adolescent, though he was obviously a decade or more beyond that age. He seemed so unsure of himself, Nandria found that, rather than being intimidated, she wanted to help him.

I could like him. I wonder, could I encourage him to like me? I need a friend. But she shook her own head, realizing that that process would probably take longer than she ever hoped to stay in the United States, let alone in Boonetown, Missouri.

Doris set her needles on her lap and laid her head against the sofa back. Her eyes closed. The soft scarf at her neck scrunched as her mouth dropped open.

"It takes so little to exhaust her," Nandria commented.

Dr. Ricartsen closed his thin lips and led the way out to the kitchen where the kettle was beginning a low, insistent whistle. Nandria hurried to lift it away to a cool spot away from the wood embers.

"Are you sure?" she asked as she held the kettle over the ornate teapot.

"Well, a moment, perhaps," he acknowledged and slid into the seat nearest the stove. "Tea, perhaps, if it would be faster. Sadie has me booked most of this morning and into the afternoon, and then I need to trudge out to see three farm folks, to see how they are coming along. Other side of town. Married to Will?"

The question came bald. Was she sure?

With a suppressed smile of amusement at his lack of sophistication, Nandria set the pot with steeping tea on the table and brought two cups, spoons, the sugar bowl and a cracked tiny crockery pitcher with a dollop of milk. She slid into her chair at the foot of the table.

"Yes," she assured him, "I am married to Will."

"That infant is his?"

She grinned at his directness. "Yes, the baby is Will's."

"But Will is not with you."

Her smile faded. The aching grief that rolled over her reminded her of how alone she was. But she sat up and straightened her shoulders to face the rude doctor.

"Will is in Army Intelligence. He was called to service just as we were to board the hospital ship to come to Canada."

"You came down through Canada?"

"Halifax."

"A hospital ship," he questioned as though it had just occurred to him what she had said. "Are you a nurse?"

"Oh, no, just someone experienced with paper work organization."

He grinned for the first time; the softened expression made him look as young as his actions implied.

"I bet the Sisters were glad to have you."

She nodded, smiling as well. Her memories of Major Kerwitz's gratitude were fond highlights from months of what had otherwise been heartache.

"When is he coming, then?"

"Will?" She shook her head. "I wish I knew. Little Rose and I are rather in Limbo for the time being."

"I can see where that might be." He frowned. "You're a Brit?"

"London born and bred."

"Tough over there?"

She closed her eyes. Talks with the troops on the ship and brief snatches of gossip from radio broadcasts fellow passengers on train rides south from Halifax had imparted to her had told her that things were worse now than before she'd left England.

"I got me a radio. For me to keep track, not that I can help. If you'd ever like to come and listen…" Dr. Ricartsen nodded, realizing her anguish. He changed the subject, but with little more finesse than he'd already demonstrated. "How in the world did you meet Will?"

"You mean . . ." she started, then realized her mentioning that she was a colored person when he had not was as rude as his blunt question had seemed to imply. He seemed naive, not mean. " . . .you are not in favor of war brides, doctor?" she redirected her question.

"Never knew one," he shrugged, "until now."

So you believe me. My father-in-law does not.

"To answer your question, we met in Ethiopia. A U.S. Intelligence junior officer, Will came to our rescue unexpectedly. I had just come from school in London to take my young brother . . ." Her eyes filled with tears and she looked away.

"Did something happen to your brother?" the doctor asked.

"Not then. Just recently. *The Athenia,*" she managed.

"That ship sunk by German torpedoes in, what? September?" His frown deepened in concern. "And the rest of your family, as well? Ahh, so sorry. Please, Nandria, is it? Come to my office some time when we can have a cup of coffee and sit and really talk. And hear the news. You ever get to listen to Gabriel Heatter? I want to learn about what is happening in Europe, and he seems to tell it straight. We Americans should know more than we do. I have the awful feeling we are going to be dragged into this, no matter how much we don't want to be."

He rose, picked up his bag, and went across the porch and out of the house before Nandria could pull herself together to walk him to his car.

Tears streaming, she sat there at the table after he'd gone until she heard Rose stirring and Doris talking to her as though she were a little boy. Nandria got up, wiped her face on a tea towel and hurried into the living room. But later, as she began preparations for the noon meal, scrubbed the last of the men's work clothes, peeled and sliced the last of the apples and set them on screening for drying, Nandria could not keep her thoughts away from those terrifying days when she had first met Will.

Momma, so naive about Mussolini. How could I believe you when you said you and father would be safe? Diplomats were always kept safe. You believed that. I guess everyone believed that.

"But it was 1936," she said aloud, exasperated. "Things no longer worked as they always had. The world no longer plays by the rules you thought you could always believe in."

Shuddering, Nandria heard again that terrifying staccato of gunfire and felt that tall figure from nowhere knocking them to the ground. Felt again the fear she had never believed could be so overpowering as they had crawled. Sweated. Panted. Held their breath until their hearts had threatened to burst within their chests. Such a long time to exist in terror. And Will, young, his face glistening with sweat and his green eyes narrowed in what Nandria realized was fear, refusing to leave them. *I loved him even then, although I would not admit that even to myself for months.*

Her mother had known before she did. And her mother was no happier about it than she was when she finally was honest with herself. *Oh, Mama, you were right to ache for us both. You and daddy made it through so much. Please help the two of us get through this.*

* *

By mid–afternoon, the clothes were as dry as the day would allow them to be. Nandria went out to gather them in to drape them on the enclosed porch so the heat of the house could suck out the last of the moisture. As she stepped into the already chilling air, Bodie trundled past her to the porch steps pushing a wheelbarrow. She stood aside a moment, clothes basket in hand, and watched him carry in long metal poles with their edges at right angles to make narrow 'L's. He came back out for a tarnished brass headboard and slats of wood. He lugged the pieces up onto the porch where she had planned to drape the clothes to finish drying.

"What are . . . ?" she started, and then decided she had only been in this country a matter of days and had no right to question him or anyone else about what they were proposing to do. She turned and went to finish her task in the yard. When she had gathered everything, she carried the basket onto the porch and stepped out of her large boots.

Bodie was tightening the last several nuts onto their bolts. He stood, surveying his work.

"Got to polish thet headboard a bit to spruce it up to what she has been, but she's good and solid, all right, all right. She'll sleep comfortable, I reckon."

He stood, wincing at knees that protested having been bent and carrying his weight too long. He brushed back thin wisps of hair and clapped his felt, wide-brimmed hat back onto his head. He set his tools into the metal box on the floor and stood erect again, hand on narrow hip.

"Yep, our Will was borned on this bed. And his brother Winfred. Freddy, we called him, but in front of the mister it was always Winfred. Both them boys watched their grandmother die on it, too, bless 'er."

Nandria set the clothes basket on the floor by the door.

"Why are you setting it up now?"

"The mister said to," he shrugged. "Yep, this here bed's seen lots. These brass rails has stood a lot'a grippin' for pain. Always put the help up here when a hand took sick or got hisself hurt."

"Is someone hurt?"

"Nah. Got no extra hands now, being spring's not sure she'll ever come. Got a whole rest a' the winter to git through first. This here's for you."

Nandria's eyes widened in surprise. "But we're fine in Will's room," she protested, feebly.

Hand testing one last nut on its bolt, Bodie didn't look up at her directly. He shrugged again, this time helplessly.

"I'll fetch the mattress down for ya, all right," he promised, gathering the metal tool box and moving toward the kitchen. "Don't need you fussin' over carryin' that."

Lips tight, Nandria stared at the skeleton of the bed, swearing the one phrase she allowed herself under her breath.

"Beaver dam," she whispered. A small washer like a flattened ring winked out from under the far foot of the bed, and Nandria bent to pick it up and stuff it into the pocket of her bib apron. "God loves a crikey beaver dam," she spat with little volume but a good deal of passion.

CHAPTER SIX

Rose was sitting up a bit now, for long periods less and less dependent on being propped with pillows in the corner of the sofa. She smiled when her mother met her eye to eye, but she grinned widely at Doris. Always. It delighted the older woman as nothing else did, whether or not Doris realized she was the child's grandmother. At times, Nandria wondered if the information might have gotten through the fog in which this woman lived. Most times, though, she was sure it had not.

Nandria sat in the rocker close beside the two of them on the sofa, suffering from twinges of jealousy at their deep joy in one another. Her long fingers were busy layering individual strands of colorful yarn through circles of wire she'd fashioned and twisted to make the loops that would be used to hang her yarn angels onto the Easter basket handle she planned for her daughter, whether or not the elder Minnicks planned to celebrate our Savior's resurrection. She had asked Bodie; there had been no attempt to decorate for Christmas, and Nandria wondered if her husband's family celebrated the birth of her Lord. Funny, Nandria had thought southern Missouri was part of what she had heard referred to several times as a "Bible belt." She'd chuckled at that description, picturing a tall, glowing figure with a halo and a wide leather belt with two holsters hanging down to carry the thick, holy books of Old and New Testament.

She thought of that again now, and chuckled within herself at the image in her head of less righteous figures in a pitchfork quick draw contest.

Nandria Brown Minnick, take hold on yourself. You are definitely withdrawing more and more into your own imagination and away from the reality of where and with whom you are living. But she could not blame herself. These weeks, and nothing much had changed except Rose. Nandria was still stealing old quilts and blankets from the backs of closet shelves to protect her baby and herself from the cold on the unheated, enclosed back porch, where they were sleeping in its total lack of privacy. Will's mother still called her "Girl" and mostly gave her suggestions and orders through either her husband or Bodie rather than address her desires to Nandria in person. Will's father gave orders through Bodie and rarely addressed her at all. When he did so it was always with a grunt of disapproval of a task she had not thought to do or had not completed to his satisfaction.

But no matter what Will's parents lacked in common courtesy or joyous spirit, Nandria was not about to deprive her daughter of the fun and excitement of holiday celebrations. If it had to be just the two of them, then so be it.

Nandria sat back, willing herself to calm down and make her determinations come true without regard to Will's family. She thought of Bodie. He was not a blood relative, yet he was far closer to being a part of this family than she was or ever would be. He was also as near as there was to a fellow human being, and many evenings like this one, he did not stay in this house but escaped to his own somewhere over beyond the west fence.

If either he or Will's father went into town at all, they did not invite the womenfolk to go with them.

There was no relief from the daily work routine. The days ground on and on.

And no word from Will.

Nandria closed her eyes. She had learned the hard way, the longer he was away without word, the more dangerous the mission he'd been on. He had not told her directly about any of that, but before she had left England there had been scraps of information from his staff and even from his fellow intelligence gatherers that had made it clear he was risking his life again and again. When he did come home he was so tired, she feared he might never awaken to himself again. But each time, when assigned, he went again without a word.

Europe was under ever widening siege. Dr. Ricartsen brought what little news she heard when he came to check on Doris after one of her bad spells. He came, he checked, but obviously had no idea of what was ailing Will's mother. At times Doris Rose would be almost spry. But mostly she was weak and confused. She just seemed far too young to be that old.

Nandria's thoughts were interrupted by a timid knock at the back door to the porch. Doris had heard it; she peered anxiously toward the kitchen. It was her reaction that confirmed for Nandria that the sound she was not sure she had heard was in fact real.

Minnick glared at Nandria when she rose to answer the knock.

"Someone coming, Mr. Minnick, dear," Doris whimpered, fussing with her clothes and hair. "Do I look presentable? Is the house sufficient?"

"Who the devil . . . ?" he started, but he did not stir from his place in the single easy chair.

"I shall see," Nandria said after re–propping Rose among the pillows. She was even less sure whether or not Doris would make the connection if Rose slumped and needed help to sit upright again.

The night was dark. Grover Minnick had no money to waste on electric lights that were not needed for an immediate task, and by now Nandria knew the layout of the kitchen and the porch by feel. She did not snap on the kitchen bulb or stop to light her kerosene lamp.

A slender figure was outlined darker even than the night at the doorway. For that moment, Nandria's heart rose in her chest. Could it be Will? But of course not. He would have let her know he was coming, and besides, he was far taller than the slight figure before her.

She opened the door and a girl tottered onto the porch.

"What…? Oh, my, are you all right? Emmy, isn't it?"

"S–sorry," the girl whispered, righting herself and turning away from what little light seeped onto the porch from the interior of the house.

In her apron pocket, Nandria fingered the "purdy" stone the gaunt child hand given her, the only friendly sign of welcome to Boonetown.

"I still have the lovely stone you gave me," Nandria told her, sure somehow that would be important for her to know.

White teeth were the only indication in the dark that the girl was smiling.

"Just come to see you was settled in, Miz Minnick." Emmy stepped deeper onto the porch as Nandria invited her in and closed the door behind her. Lowering her head, Emmy smiled again, shyly. "And to see the baby, mebbe?"

"Well, of course. Come in, come in. I'm sure the Minnicks will be glad to see you."

"Ain't Unca Bodie here then?"

"No, it was so cold, Bodie was afraid the weather would turn even worse so he went on home just after the evening meal. But do come in . . ."

With another backward step, Emmy made it clear she did not want or dare to enter the house.

"With or without Bodie, you are always welcome here," Nandria assured her, finally understanding her reluctance.

"Not with the mister," she whispered and turned away.

"With me, then. Always. Welcome. If you cannot come in, will you sit with us here on the porch, then? At least for a minute? I shall fetch," and here Nandria smiled to herself at her own use of the quaint term that her mother had used on occasion, as well. "I will bring my daughter out here and we shall sip a cup of hot tea. The water is still warm in the kettle." She smiled to herself again and added, "I reckon."

After helping Emmy Lu sit down on the wicker armchair, Nandria hurried to reset the kettle over the stove's low burning coals, and then made herself walk into the living room where the baby sat slumped over while Doris played with booties, mixing and matching blue and green, crocheted and knitted, even soft moccasin–like ones cut from brown felt and over stitched together along the bottom. Doris seemed oblivious to the baby's odd position, but Rose was puckering up to protest.

"Ah, so cleverly made, Mother Minnick. You have made little Rose very happy with all the attention, but I think I had better be getting her ready for bed now, if you do not mind." Nandria gathered her craft material and then gently lifted her daughter in her arms and started toward the kitchen.

"Who was at the door?" Minnick growled.

It was a direct question, and Nandria did not want to lie.

"Emmy," she said without to turning to face him.

"Emmy Lu, that dear girl?" Doris chirped. "Prob'ly looking for Winfred, but we haven't seen him tonight, have we, dear Mr. Minnick? Prob'ly out with his friends. He's got lots of friends, our Freddy has."

Nandria did turn then, but Minnick was staring at his wife with such speechless, electric aching pain that, unnerved, Nandria hurried to slip out of the room into the kitchen.

The kettle hummed as though clearing its throat to prepare to sing. Shifting Rose to her left shoulder, Nandria lifted it although she was unsure she was steady enough to pour the steaming water into the pot she had left prepared for the morning's tea.

"I kin do that, if'n you'll let me," a timid voice said at Nandria's side.

"Ah, Emmy Lu, thank you. I have about run out of hands." There were no hands to wipe her face of its tears, and no wish to let anyone see how deeply her father-in-law's anguished expression had affected her. "The baby," she whispered as though it were Rose rather than herself who needed mending. She hurried to the porch to check her little one's diaper.

Emmy gave her time. Nandria marveled at that. How could the girl know in the near dark how much Nandria had needed time to gather herself? To sit and hold and rock her infant and just work at pulling herself together? Something was so wrong. Nandria could feel it. She prayed it was not a feeling of doom that could in any way compromise Will, and then shook her head at herself for even thinking such superstitious nonsense.

"Oh, my darling," she whispered to the dark. The vapor struck between her body warmth and the cold air of the poorly heated porch materialized at her mouth and breathed its own silvery presence that she could see—briefly. She would need to stoke the fire in the stove once the Minnicks had gone to bed. This was too cold to be good for the baby.

She did not see, but only heard Emmy enter and set two cups of tea on the upended wooden crate Nandria used as a night stand.

"Is it Will Minnick worryin' ya?"

The voice was tender, nearly breaking Nandria's resolve. She shook her head, though unsure Emmy could see its movement in the dark.

"Will is fine," Nandria stated almost fiercely, then added low. "He must be fine."

"He in danger, is he?"

"Oh, Emmy Lu, you cannot imagine what is going on in Europe now. The cruelty. The unbridled, vicious use of power."

As Nandria's vision dark-adapted, she could tell that the girl's hand had stolen to her own face.

After a long pause in which Nandria began to wonder, Emmy spoke again, so softly it was like a biscuit rising in the oven, something you are and are not quite aware of.

"How did you meet our Will? He was so far away."

"I am from far away, Emmy. I was born in London. That is in England, across the Atlantic Ocean."

Emmy's "Oh," gave away her complete mystification.

"Do you remember in school where they had a big map hung showing the United States? Well, to the east, that is, to the right of your country on the map is a big expanse of blue water? That is the Atlantic Ocean. I live in the country that sticks out just a little into the blue across from Boston. The British Isles. In London. That is near the bottom of that island, closer to the big land mass that is Europe."

"I'm sorry." Emmy's voice told Nandria that she had needed to apologize many times in her life.

"Do not be. I had no idea where Missouri was in your United States, either. I needed to research in many books to look it up and to find out many other things about your country before I came. Sometime soon, I shall find us a map and show you where England is. And Ethiopia."

"Ee-thee-hope-ee-a." Emmy's tongue separated the syllables as though each had its own exotic, delightful taste.

"Ethiopia is in Africa. My father was there. He is—was—a diplomat for the British crown. A great deal of unrest had developed. The leader of the country of Ethiopia wanted my country England to help. He was afraid the Italians under Mussolini were going to invade and take over his country, a far smaller and less wealthy nation. He was correct, as it turned out. But England had sent my father to try to talk with him before they knew that. I suppose they hoped my father might find a way to deal with Mr. Mussolini without allowing the conflict to start a war."

Nandria paused to sigh. She looked down at the face of the girl sitting cross-legged on the floor at her feet, in the dark in so many more ways than one. Exhaling slowly to allow herself a moment to find simpler words to express herself, she leaned forward a trifle, speaking softly and patiently. "Daddy was trying to stop a war from starting. My mother and little brother Ned were with him, but the situation was becoming more and more dangerous. I was at college at the time, but my parents permitted me to come to Ethiopia to get my younger brother to take him home with me to safety in London."

What little Nandria could see of Emmy's expression showed her a child rapt in a bedtime story. Perhaps it would be all right to tell her everything. She might well think it was another fairy tale and lord knows Nandria needed to talk with someone who cared.

"But it weren't safe, was it?" Emmy Lu urged her to continue.

"No, it was not safe. We—Ned and I—were trying to get back from his school to our parents at the embassy . . ." She stopped, unable to go over this episode again, even in her thoughts. "He saved us. Will. Knocked us down and lay on top of us, though he did not know us at all. No idea who we w . . ." *But had he? Were we part of his assignment? Had he known who we were and been charged with protecting us? Would it make any difference if he had been? He still risked his own life. Unless it was a set-up? To get the English diplomat to take fond notice of an American? No, no, Will was himself, whether or not he had been assigned. And those machine gun bullets . . .*

"The bullets were kicking up the dry dirt in miniature dust fountains all around us," Nandria whispered finally.

"Was you scared?"

"Oh, yes, I was terrified—for all three of us."

"Will was like that. Being there to help when you're scared," she murmured, doing her own remembering from the look on her face in the dark. "Freddy . . ." she began softly and then shook her head and would not continue.

"Who is Freddy, Emmy Lu?"

"He ain't. No more," she managed, shaking her whole upper body. A moaning, keening sound escaped her, which she immediately bit back.

They were silent. Rose took that as her cue and squirmed in her mother's arms, opening her mouth to howl.

"Oh, dear," Nandria laughed. "Another country about to be heard from. I shall need to light the lantern, I fear. Otherwise I might stick the baby with a pin in the dark."

"Oh, no, please don't do that!"

She had said that as though she were afraid Nandria might. *What kind of life was this girl living?* Rather than ask anything, Nandria cuddled Rose and struck a fat wooden match to light the kerosene lantern.

Ashamed, Emmy Lu had already twisted away into shadow so Nandria could not see her face. But Nandria could see the edges, and she gasped.

"Emmy! I am so sorry. What happened? Who . . . ?"

"Don't let the little one see . . . Please!"

"Oh, Emmy!" Nandria's tears flowed down her cheeks, but, irrationally, she held the baby at an angle so she would be unable to see the bruises on Emmy Lu's cheek and jaw or the rich maroon and green colors under her left eye. Fresh violations on top of old beatings, from the looks of them. "This happens often, does it not?"

"It's not so bad this time. Please, Miz, don't tell."

"Tell?" Nandria was at a loss. Whom would she tell? Who could make a difference that would not bring more harm than good to this girl unless she could be rescued from whoever was repeatedly beating her? "I will not tell anyone, if that is what you wish, Emmy Lu. But I wish I could do something to help you. You came to see Bodie; is he a relative?"

"Somewhere back, Mama says. She keeps track of all of us, but I cain't no more."

"Too many?"

"Oh, I know everybody. There ain't too many for that."

"But not all the interrelationships? Who is cousin to whom? And to what degree? Is that it? I have heard the same thing from friends in Africa. Many times," Nandria laughed, and Emmy Lu gazed up at her with a near smile.

"I likes the way you talks sometimes, Miz."

"Nandria. Please call me Nandria. You are about my only friend here in America."

Unable to speak, Emmy rose to dim the light from the kerosene lamp. "There," she intoned. "Out of sight . . ."

"Out of mind? Hardly, Emmy Lu. I know now, and I shall do anything I can to protect you," Nandria promised as she lay the baby on the bed to change her diaper. Startled, Nandria stared at the fierce denial on Emmy's face and in her voice.

"You cain't, Miz—Nandria. Please, promise me you won't never try."

Nandria stared at her. Only Rose whimpering took her attention off that battered face. She twisted to take care of her daughter's needs.

Again there was silence between them, this time strained.

Emmy picked up the half-finished yarn angel Nandria had been working on. She fingered it tenderly.

"What's this be?"

"A yarn angel. I need to fashion wings from a wide bit of ribbon. See, you pinch the ribbon and slide it through the upper part, above the tie. It makes simple wings if you trim the ribbon just right. And all the yarn at the bottom makes a full skirt for her. I used to try to make arms, too, but just the wings let you know she is an angel. The Minnicks do not seem to do anything to celebrate this glorious holiday coming up so I thought I would make a few of these for Rose to see here on the porch, at least. After all, it is her very first Easter. Would you like me to show you how? You could make some for your family and your home."

Emmy peered at the angel with saucer eyes filled with tears.

Without speaking, Nandria laid Rose in the girl's lap for her to hold and love, and grieve.

CHAPTER SEVEN

As Nandria carried the wet clothes out to the yard, steam rose from the basket.

"A mite cold yet for hanging outside, ain't it, Miz? You'll hafta just take 'em back in and spread 'em to dry inside, won't ya?" Bodie was smiling, but he was also tucking his hands into his armpits. It was funny that Doris had crocheted and knitted dozens of booties for Rose, who had already outgrown most of them. Evidently Doris had only one pattern and did not occur to her to try to make the little footwear any larger for the growing child. But for all her needlework, Doris had not created mittens or gloves for Bodie, who was clearly in need of one or the other.

"I must learn to knit," Nandria told him. "You require mittens."

"Oh, no, Miz. The missus has rattled me up some, but pink and yellow just ain't my colors, don't you see."

"Pink? Really?" Nandria chuckled. "I shall be sure to secure more sedate colors, Mr. Bodie."

"Well, never you mind, Miz. I reckon it's gonna be spring one of these days soon. It comes like 'at sometimes. Way early. 'Course then we kin follow a month'a sunshine with weeks of deep snow, but that's the chance ya take, livin' here in Missouri."

Nandria set the basket of clothes toward the end of the clothesline and eased the prop pole down to lower the rope. She shook the first of the diapers and began the pinning them with the wooden pegs.

"How long have you lived here in Missouri, Bodie?"

"Near all my life, I reckon. Was borned in the hills of Kintuck, but my folks brung me and five brothers here when I was just about to walk, so I don't remember them hills much."

"A large family," Nandria commented. She was beginning to find shirts now to hang carefully by the shoulders. If they dried with few wrinkles, they were so much easier to sprinkle wet again and then iron.

"Large family? Not hardly. Not for them Kintucky hills. I guess most men worked toward a dozen or more, even if'n it took more'n one wife to do the deed."

Nandria lowered her arms and peered at him. Such a poor use of women. Such a waste of what a woman could do besides bear children. She nearly spoke of her concerns, but Minnick bellowing from the barn cut into whatever conversation they might have had.

"Bode!"

He jumped, twisted in the air and came down limp–running, scurrying toward the barn. "On the way!" he yelled, and he was.

Nandria lifted Doris's underdrawers and pinned them, and then lifted the basket to move it on down the line. She raised the first pole slightly to keep the long johns from scraping the frost–stiff grass. Wearily she shuffled toward the second pole to angle it lower. The squeak of the grass against her too–large borrowed boots caught her attention. She smiled.

It took the slightest thing to give Nandria delight, and that was a good thing, as there had been only those tiny distractions and reminders of the richness of life to keep her going.

Nearly three full months now without word. Eighty–six days since that morning in Liverpool when Will had had to tell her he would not be able to join them on their planned sail aboard the "Salty Healer." Three months since he had learned about her family on the *Athenia*, but had not been able to do anything to comfort her for that loss either. *Eighty–six days of loneliness . . .*

There had been Christmas, of course. Rose's first, and she was the focus of joy for so many of the wounded and of the doctors and nurses aboard ship. Sister Kerwitz's subdued and beautiful candlelight service in honor of Mary's laboring to bring a child into a hostile world. No room in the inn.

Room in the officer's small room, though. Nandria smiled, remembering. German bombs exploding along the coast. Villagers running to seek shelter in the military base. And the fledgling Air Force the British men were trying so desperately to raise. Oh, those brave boys. How many had come down, burned almost beyond recognition as having been men?

And in the midst of it all, Rose deciding it was her time to enter the world.

"Oh, my precious daughter, how like your mother you are, unmindful of the 'shoulds' and 'should nots' of a world you disagree with," Nandria whispered to a tiny slip of a dress she had not been able to get quite all of the food stains out of. She hung it close by the prop pole, hoping the sun might help bleach it clean.

Labor alone, but what else could she do, now, or then? Early stages, she really only needed privacy, and had found the major's room. So many frightened people. None of the personnel had time to spare for a young woman in early labor, even had they known. But then, when she had wanted—needed—help, there had been panic and chaos. No one heard her call. No one heard her "Help!" amid all the screams of fear. So Rose had been delivered by her mother.

The rush, then, of indescribable relief and joy.

And then the private who had entered, finding the most beautiful baby girl in the world. Nandria smiled, remembering the young man's excited announcement of a new life and the spontaneous applause of the entire ward, patients, staff and fearful visitors.

"It was worth it, Will," she whispered to the bibbed overalls she pinned next. "Rose was worth it, and so are you. Where are you, my darling? Please be well. Please let me know you are alive. Please . . ."

She wept into the tea towel she had just hung.

Sniffling, she turned at the sound of cursing, glad for a distraction from her grief but also mildly curious. Although both the men cursed when they thought they were alone, she had seldom heard cuss words loud enough when they would know that she would overhear. It was a singular courtesy, but one she appreciated, though she had no way to acknowledge it.

As she hung the last of the laundry in the weak sunlight and cold air, she picked up the basket and carried it toward the porch stairs, and then peered at the barn. Through the open door, she could make out what she guessed was Bodie standing, shoulders slumped, before that ancient threshing machine deep within the barn. Both the men of the farm spent an inordinate amount of time and effort trying to bring it back to useful life and service. Nandria was sure Bodie, for one, would gladly assign it to rusty retirement, had he been the one to make such a decision. She watched the occasional glitter as light from hanging lanterns gleamed off the tools at his belt and in his lowered hand.

The lanterns then back-lighted Grover Minnick as he stormed to the open door where the sun lit him in full frustration. He glared at her and at the partly open door to the porch. She startled at his bellowed, "Close that damn door! You think I can heat the whole out-a-doors?"

Nandria lifted her chin and swallowed. "The baby is on the porch," she answered, not defiantly, but definitely unyielding. "The door is open so I can hear her if she cries."

Minnick's broad shoulders squared, but Bodie hurried up behind him and touched the irate man's arm.

"Whyn't we work on thet spreader now?" he coaxed. "We ain't gonna need the thresher 'til near fall, no how."

With a look of murder, Minnick closed his mouth and stomped back into the barn. Bodie shrugged at her helplessly and turned to follow him.

Nandria side-stepped to her left and stooped to pick up a pebble made shiny by the wet. It was shinier and prettier for its damp coating than it would appear when dry and on its own.

Sadly, she pocketed the pebble she felt more akin to it than to anyone of this entire farm. Sighing, she was stepping up to the bottom of the porch stairs when something caught at her peripheral vision. She turned, balancing the basket against her hip and raising her other hand to shade her eyes.

Someone was coming across the west field.

"Will?"

But of course not. Whoever it was sat ungracefully on a beaten nag of a horse. The figure, far smaller than Will, was evidently having trouble staying on the animal.

Dread filled her as she realized who it must be. "Emmy?" she cried. "Emmy Lu!"

Nandria slid the basket onto the porch and ran in to check her infant, fast asleep in the bureau drawer, which she now filled three quarters of. Listening a moment for Doris and hearing nothing alarming, Nandria hurried back outside.

The on–comer was definitely a woman, though her age was not apparent. The only thing sure was that whoever she was, she was in need of help.

Running toward the figure, Nandria acknowledged finally what she had not wanted to know. It was Emmy Lu, and the girl was indeed in distress.

Disheveled, lurching as the gentle animal moved, head bowed over the hag's shoulder, Emmy looked about to fall off. Nandria raced to her at a dead run.

"Oh, Lord, Emmy, what happened?" she cried, but she already knew. She had only met Horace Bratton once—the brute of a man who had approached the Minnick truck when Bodie had first come to town in the Minnick pickup to fetch her from the railroad stop in Boonetown. But Nandria knew in her bones that that bully was fully capable of inflicting this kind of damage on a slip of a girl. Nandria wanted Will to kill him. But Will would probably never know about this. Will would probably never come home, and Nandria was as trapped in this house of twisted love and prejudice as Emmy Lu was trapped in her own hell.

"Emmy, can you hear me?" Nandria called low as she reached her. "Can you lean on me until I can get you into the house?"

Lifting her battered face, Emmy tried to shake her head. "No," she rasped. "Can't go in the house."

"What? Why not? I've got to clean you up and see just how badly you are hurt . . . Maybe call the doctor . . ."

"N–no, don't. If'n Horace comes, he'll blame Minnicks for takin' me in. Jus' lemme . . ."

But she slumped and it took all of Nandria's strength to hold the girl on the horse and lead it awkwardly into the back yard near the porch stairs.

"Bodie!" Nandria cried. "Bodie! Come quick!"

"N–no, Miz Minnick, please," the girl protested. "Jus' let me set a minute. Out here. You don't know what he'd do, and the poor Missus wouldn't be no match fer him. He'd come when the men is away . . ."

Nandria knew in her bones that the girl's prediction was probably truth that simply had not happened yet. "Just the porch, then. That way he can blame me." Nandria's tone told even Emmy Lu there was no point in arguing.

Lifting the slumping girl, Nandria helped her dismount and supported much of her weight as she guided her up the steps and into the rocker. Nandria dragged the comforter from her brass bed and, fighting back tears of frustration, anger and helplessness, wrapped Emmy tenderly in the blanket.

"I will get Bodie."

"Jus' leave 'im be, Miz. Please. I'll be all right in a minute. I didn't mean to cause you no harm."

"No harm. No bother. I just want what is best for you."

"Mebbe let Ole Gertie where she kin nibble grass? We don't have much for her at our place."

"Of course." Nandria went back out to lead the horse to the shelter of the elm where last year's grass stood bent by weather but probably edible. Most probably a feast for the starving animal.

When she hurried back onto the porch, she touched Emmy's shoulder, but drew back her hand quickly when the girl winced.

"Oh, sorry! I had not meant to hurt you. Listen, I shall make you some tea to warm you. And bring a cloth to wipe away some of that dirt and blood and see how badly you are hurt. You just sit here, then. I shall be right back. All right?"

"Don't go to no trouble . . ."

"I shall decide what is trouble and what is not, young lady. You just hush and stay put, do you hear?"

With a hint of twisted smile at the corner of her mouth, Emmy closed her eyes and sank into what comfort she had found.

"Yes'm," she murmured.

Nandria thought the girl was asleep when she got back to the porch from setting the kettle on, wringing out a towel at the sink and checking on Doris, who snored softly in the corner of the sofa.

"Here, let me wipe your face . . . Oh, sorry, dear Emmy Lu, but I need to be sure how badly hurt you are," she whispered.

"Feels good," Emmy assured her as though from her dream. "So good, Miz Minnick. So long since . . ."

"My name is Nandria, remember? We are friends, Emmy Lu. Please call me Nandria. It feels good for me to hear my own name spoken. You are doing me a favor."

It began with an 'N' but quickly drowned in a gasp withheld to the best of the girl's ability as Nandria wiped and dried carefully. She was hurt: abrasions, a few lacerations that Sister Kerwitz would have sewed up tidily and saved later scarring, but the greatest hurt was evidently from punches. Bruises, deep into soft tissue and probably into bone, especially on the side of Emmy's face and left cheekbone.

"Zygomatic arch," Nandria whispered and Emmy opened her right eye, which was not swelling shut as yet. The girl tilted her head to look at her questioningly. "Your cheek bone is called your zygomatic arch by the doctors, though who in the world knows why when cheekbone is simpler and describes it perfectly well." Nandria kept chattering as she dabbed and inspected. The more harm she found, the closer she came to deciding to kill Horace Bratton herself and not wait for Will to come and do it.

No bones broken that Nandria could find, except perhaps a rib or two on her left side that were made evident when Nandria could coax Emmy to stretch out on the brass bed, hopefully for an hour or so of sleep.

"He'll come . . ." Emmy whimpered, swollen eyes trying to widen in fear.

"Let him!" Nandria snapped. "You just sleep. I am here, and nothing is going to happen here. You just lie still while I get us some tea. Sounds like the kettle is ready."

"Thet preacher come," Emmy explained after a quiet while when they'd sipped their sweetened tea. Both eyes were swollen closed now. She lay unmoving but wanting Nandria to know it wasn't always like this.

"Kylie, is it not? The pastor? We have not been able to get out much with the snow and then the mud. I have not met him, but Mother Minnick speaks almost worshipfully of him."

"He preaches, even when he visits. Horace was purdy mad by the time he finally gived up and left."

"I imagine he had said something about Horace's drinking."

"Oh, yeah, and 'bout us not gettin' to church on Sundays—even on nice days. I'd go, if'n . . ."

"So Horace waited until after he'd left and then took out his frustration on you."

The girl was quiet for a long time, and then stirred. "Tell me 'bout Will. How he rescued you in Hee–thee–hope–ier."

"Were you sweet on Will growing up, Emmy?"

She tried to shake her head, but it hurt. "Not Will . . ."

Nandria had leaned forward a bit, hoping to hear something more about the brother Will had never mentioned to her. "Freddy?"

The anguish that crossed Emmy Lu's face was too painful for Nandria to see. She changed the subject quickly.

"Will and I were married in London," Nandria related softly to give the girl a quiet time of rest. "My parents were there, and my younger brother, Ned," she added low. "Will had an Army buddy stand up with him. It was a quiet ceremony in my parents' home. My father had a beautiful garden in the back yard. We had champagne out there, sitting under a bower Daddy had somehow conjured. A bower is a wooden arch he and my mother had decorated with every color of ribbon you can imagine. Mother arranged vases with bouquets of Daddy's roses on the table, and they had attached flowers tied with pink and yellow and blue bows to every surface in the yard. The sun shone the whole day, which does not always happen in London. We do get our share and then some of fog and mist."

Emmy was breathing through her mouth, which turned up in a smile. "Sounds purdy," she managed, and then she seemed to sleep.

The baby stirred, working one tight little fist free of her blankets and using it to threaten the air above the bureau drawer.

"Ah, wee one, I was hoping you would awaken soon," Nandria smiled, possibly more anxious to hold her infant to her than Rose was to nurse. She lifted her daughter into her arms.

When she looked up, she saw Emmy, right eye open as far it could, gazing longingly at Rose.

They both startled at the sound of Doris calling weakly from the living room.

"She is awake," Nandria stated the obvious. "Most times Mother Minnick is confused when she first wakes up. I will need to go to her." Nandria rose with the baby at her shoulder and hurried into the house.

Footsteps scraped on the porch stairs, and Emmy Lu cowered, trying to roll onto her side to get up. Bodie stopped in the doorway and stared. His agile face twisted in a series of rapid emotions while his gaping mouth muttered blue curses. Emmy listened and heard his love. A smile worked at the corners of her battered lips.

"Ah, Child! I seen your mare. Let me kill 'im. Just lemme kill the bastard."

"No, Uncabodie," Emmy Lu rasped. "He's got papers. Says them papers'd kick Pa and the kids right off'n their claim if'n we tries anything. I didn't mean for Will's Nan to see me. I just had to slip away. But I couldn't find you."

"Working in the barn," Bodie told her, clenching his fists and pressing them into his thighs to try to contain himself. "I am gonna kill 'im, Gal. Damn all the evil spirits in this world."

"Jus' help me up, Uncabodie. I got to get home. He'll come roarin' if'n he wakes up and finds me gone. You wanted to protect me, I knows it. Thet's comfort 'nuff." She sat a moment, with his help, at the edge of the bed. Her breath was shallow and she pressed at the ribs at her left side. "You – you ain't drinkin' no more, is you?"

"Nary a drop, Child. I swear it on my worthless life. Not after . . . Not after I promised ya. I'm so sorry, Em. Ta take you away from . . ." He lifted a hand to gesture out toward all areas of the Minnick farm, " . . .and leave ya with thet Horace."

"Hesh, now. Please, jus' gimme a hand up so I kin get back afore Will's lady comes. Wouldn't want nothin' to happen to her, or Will's mama."

They heard Nandria coming back through the house. Bodie fled, leaving Emmy fighting for balance on shaky legs as she clung to the brass rails at the head of the bed.

As she entered from the kitchen, Nandria saw the porch door pushed to, but unlatched and went to close it.

"That was Bodie, was it not? One of your many relatives here in southern Missouri." For that moment, Nandria envied the large family Emmy Lu had been born into.

"Horace says my kin breeds like rabbits." She gazed longingly at little Rose sleeping, and then added, low, "'Cept me."

"I am glad you can stand up, Emmy Lu, but there is no hurry. You are welcome to stay until you get your strength back. If it were my home, you would be welcome to stay until you are strong enough to leave him."

"Marriage is 'til death do us part,'" Em whispered.

"There are exceptions, and I would say that physical abuse is the basis for one of the major ones."

Nandria set a glass of water at the bedside stand and fumbled in her apron pocket for an aspirin. "Tale this, please. It will help with the aching, and with the stiffness you are going to feel."

"Are you a nurse?" Emmy wanted to know when she had dutifully downed the medicine and the water.

"No, but the Sisters on the hospital ship taught me a great deal, mostly by example. Will and I and Rose were to come across the Atlantic by ship carrying wounded Canadian soldiers back home. But then, at the last minute, Will was unable to come with us," Nandria explained, chin high but tears glistening. "I was helping with the record keeping, but by the time we had lived through submarine scares and a number of surgeries and lots of changes of dressings on gunshot wounds and burns, I was pretty much in the thick of things trying to help. I had to learn some things, at least."

Emmy Lu shook her head slowly in admiration.

"Wish I was strong as you, Miz Minnick, er, Nandria," she whispered. "I'll remember what ya said, but fer now, I gotta get back. If'n he does come to and finds me gone . . ."

"Stay here, Emmy Lu, please."

"Cain't. You jus' don't know. Please, you just take care of thet beautious baby girl. Do whatever ya has to do ta protect her."

Frowning at the seriousness with which Emmy Lu was telling her more even than her words said, Nandria nodded solemnly. "I will."

With a quick nod, Emmy hoisted herself away from the brass rails to stand on her own. She stood swaying a minute, and Nandria rushed to take her arm to steady her.

"Would ya kindly fetch Ole Gert?"

"Your mare? Of course."

Nandria propped the door open and kept glancing back over her shoulder as she went to the elm where the nag was chewing blissfully. Emmy Lu wanted her dignity, and Nandria, biting her lip, would give it to her.

Emmy did need help mounting. But she kneed the mare in the sides and spoke to her low, and the faithful animal started out toward the west field.

Bodie watched from the barn door, but said nothing, though his face was flushed with anxiety, or anger. Nandria could not tell which. Probably both. As he turned back into the cavernous barn, Nandria fingered the pebbles in her pocket and spoke to the sky above the elm tree to the east.

"We are experiencing war here in your home country, too, Will. There are casualties, but at least nobody is being killed, so far. Lord, I do not know how to do anything about this one, either."

Whimpering from little Rose made Nandria lift her chin to face whatever was to come next, but she whispered a prayer before hurrying to the house. "Please, Lord, let him come home. Safe and whole. We shall make our own home. Somewhere where there is peace."

CHAPTER EIGHT

The next morning dawned with bright streaks poking through multicolored layers of cloud slowly fading to chill gray. Nandria stepped from the doorway where she had been watching the progress of sun slants climbing painfully among the bare elm branches. She turned back to her little Rose just as she heard her mother-in-law entering the kitchen.

"Girl?" Doris called.

"Out here on the porch, Mother Minnick, changing the baby."

Shuffling from the kitchen, Doris stood at the doorway, rosy-cheeked and delighted, but still obviously weak.

"Now ain't he gettin' big?" she gushed. Her smile faded as she stared. "Oh, where's his weenie?"

"Uh," Nandria sat a moment looking between the generations from infant to grandmother. "Well, Rose does not have a, er, a weenie. Rose is a girl."

"I never had no girl."

Snugging the cloth close against the baby's hip, Nandria pinned one side and then the other and then lifted her daughter onto her shoulder.

"Just the two sons?" she questioned as though it was of no particular importance, though she was pursing her lips trying not to show her curiosity.

Doris merely stared at her, confused enough to sway a little into the door jamb.

"Please, Mother Minnick, will you come in and have a seat with us?" Nandria invited, shifting the baby's clothes so Doris had a place to sit on the corner of the bed near the brass head rails. "You just had the two sons? Just the two boys?" she prompted, and then went on trying to reorient the bewildered woman she had had so little luck befriending. "Two boys, Will and Fred, was it not? What was Fred like?"

"Oh, Winfred was such a good boy," the woman gushed. "Not as book smart as Willard, but good with his hands. He could settle a fussin' cow right out of her panic, and that is not easy, let me tell you. And he was the best milker." Twirling the bottom of a long strand of loose, graying honey–brown hair, Doris seemed to transport herself into a long–ago time. She sighed before adding, "Mr. Minnick was so lookin' forward to passin' this here farm onto his sons."

"Was Winfred in the Service?"

"Will was the strange one," Doris went on with her own train of thought, seeming not to have heard Nandria's question.

"Will? Strange?" Nandria blinked.

"Oh, yes. He could work wonders with numbers. Since he was a toddler. Mr. Minnick would set him up on the counter at the general store in town, you know? He'd stand there and add up sums men'd throw at him. Like 7 + 21. And he could do it, quick–like, sometimes before I could do 'em myself, standing off in the corner just swelling with pride at my boy. Mr. Minnick wouldn't say nothing, but he was as proud-feeling as me, I knew it."

"That is remarkable." Nandria managed as she settled into the rocker to nurse little Rose, but she was intrigued by this story she had never heard about her husband. Perhaps this trip to his boyhood farm would end up being worthwhile after all.

"Oh, yes. And when he got to school, he'd outshine near all his teachers." Smiling and self-satisfied, Doris tipped back against the brass rails and hummed, evidently lost in memories of her sons in their growing years.

"Was Winfred taken into the U.S. Army?" Nandria asked, afraid that Doris's mind would slip away completely into her memories.

"He might'a been, if'n he..." Doris mused, rocking her upper body and swinging forward to thump her feet hard onto the wood floor of the porch floor.

Rose startled, unlatching from the breast. Nandria held her close and rocked to comfort her. But there was no comfort in Doris Minnick's face as she stared at the porch floor. Fear for the woman's ability to return even to a semblance of reality rose slowly in Nandria. Supporting her daughter's back as much to give herself assurance as the child, Nandria exhaled through pursed lips. She leaned toward her mother-in-law to ask quietly.

"How did Winfred die, Mother Minnick?"

With a sly grin, Doris tried to straighten her twisted hair ends using her spread fingers as a comb.

"You calling me that—it makes me feel like we was in a nunnery. Superior, that's me. Mother Minnick."

She looked up almost guiltily when Bodie opened the porch door and peered in and then popped his head and shoulders back out so Minnick could toss his shoes onto the porch as he entered. His bellowing voice caught as he saw his wife sitting so close and evidently intimately talking with the colored girl.

"Lunch ready?" Minnick growled.

Doris half stood, confused and fearful, but she sank again onto the mattress as Nandria's hand on her arm calmed her.

"The stew is simmering. Whenever you like. Come in."

Nandria's apparent invitation to enter his own house deepened the man's scowl. He stormed into the kitchen, then leaned back to address this uppity slip of a woman.

"Kin you drive a tractor?" he demanded.

"Uh, I never have."

"This afternoon, so I don't need to take time from plantin' later. Come on, Mother. Time for vittles."

Nandria stared for a moment, then called plaintively to their backs, "What will I do with the baby?"

No one answered.

* *

With a worried look back at the porch stairs where Doris stood holding Rose, Nandria picked up and pocketed a pebble from the edge of the driveway. She gathered her shin-length full skirt and climbed awkwardly up onto the tractor.

With a grunt, Minnick heaved himself up and roughly past Nandria to seat himself on the fender over the huge, right, rear wheel. He pointed and growled, and Nandria did what she could with only his nonverbal directions. Adapting what she knew of driving a car and her few experiences driving truck, she turned the ignition key and found out by experimentation which was the clutch and which the brake pedal. The tractor lurched forward, and Minnick swore aloud.

Ignoring him except as she could gather in clues, Nandria did fairly well driving out to the west field beyond the farm lane. She clutched the steering wheel as ruts and clods of dirt jounced the tractor and flipped her bodily up from her seat. She had to deliberately ignore her mental image of his landing in a shallow puddle of mud, but she could not completely suppress the smile it brought to her lips. A small part of the back of her mind hoped Minnick would be thrown off completely, just as she had pictured, but he clung tightly to the fender and made it with her onto the edge of the field.

Using the volume of his grunts of disapproval and his swaying to right or left as clues, Nandria eventually determined what he wanted done in the plowing of rows, their direction, how far apart and how near the edge he wanted her to go.

At the end of one row closest to the house, he brushed past her and jumped to the ground at the turn, only to wince and grab at his left knee. His pain gave her pause, but only made him angrier with her for having seen it. Turning his back with only a growl, he lumbered away, leaving her to do—what? Finish plowing this field? Bring the tractor back in?

Deciding for herself, Nandria turned off the tractor, jumped down and hurried past his snarl of protest to the house to check on her infant.

On the porch, she had changed Rose's diaper and was nursing her with a shawl wrapped discreetly around both of them when Minnick stormed past them.

"You think you're done out there?" he roared from the kitchen.

"I shall go back out when the baby is satisfied," she answered calmly, though her heart was pounding in her chest.

"Hummmph," he answered as though he was master by having the last word.

* *

Rain fell, a relief from weeks of snow and sleet, but again drowning any hope of getting the head start on the plowing that Minnick had wished for. The Minnicks tiptoed around their master as he clumped through the house, muttering under his breath.

Dr. Ricartsen arrived, cold and drenched and grateful for hot coffee and a change of clothes Nandria found upstairs in Will's closet and drawers.

"I'll have Sadie wash these up and return them to you, thank you."

Surprised at the sound of his grateful words, Nandria waved a hand to tell him there was no hurry, and then she scowled. "Sadie? Are you married, Dr. Ricartsen?"

He laughed aloud, a strange, braying sound that might well have reduced any prospects he may have otherwise had.

"Me, married? No, but my elephant-sized nurse Sadie is, and to the smallest, most compact man in the region. They are caution to see together, but close. Devoted to each other. You can tell just by watching 'em. So much so that I find myself envying the guy at times, though as my nurse, she is stubborn, opinionated and incorrigible. I couldn't function without her. You two will have to meet," he added as though the description of one applied equally well to the other.

Nandria smiled, and the crinkling of her face felt strange. He peered at her, seeming to understand what she was feeling.

"News on the radio, if you're interested?" he offered as he tucked Will's shirt in at the waistband of his trousers.

"Oh, you have news from England? Please."

"Well, Europe, at any rate. I gather that running battle between Finland and Russia got decided. The Finns weren't too happy to lose territory. It doesn't look to me that they had all that much to begin with."

Nandria shook her head and fingered pebbles within her apron pocket. Her expression showed such devastation that the doctor yet again wished he could unsay something he'd blurted without realizing what its effect would be on his hearer. He leaned forward, reaching as though to pat her arm before he recollected himself and drew back his hand. But he did speak softly as though he hoped that might make amends.

"It won't be long now until the sun will make this the prettiest spring you've ever seen in your life. It's like that here."

Touched at this awkward man's attempt to console her, Nandria helped him turn the discussion to small talk. "You are not from this local area then, Dr. Ricartsen?"

"City boy," he said, straightening and shaking out long limbs to settle his borrowed clothes. "St. Louis. Actually across the river in East St. Louis, so rural life took some getting used to. And now here I am, a country doctor traipsing all over creation in all kinds of weather seeing to ingrown toenails and double pneumonia, with much of the time just my coming to the house doing as much good as any skill or medicine I can bring with me. But don't tell anyone I said that," he begged, suddenly contrite, if not guilt-stricken. "I am tired."

"Why don't you lie down for a spell? The brass bed . . ."

"Bodie says that bed is magical, the way it's served so many generations of family and hired hands. But it wouldn't be seemly. Anyway, with dry clothes and hot coffee to warm my insides, I guess I can make it back to town from here."

He started to gather up his wet things, but Nandria shook her head.

"I shall launder them and have them ready to exchange with your Sadie for Will's whenever it becomes convenient," she said. "I look forward to meeting her."

"And Mrs. Minnick—Doris—is doing well under your care. I think she's actually put on a little of the weight she'd lost, but we'll check that for sure at my office when you can get her to town." He had opened his black bag and was pawing through it, evidently going through a mental check list of what should be in there. He closed it, wearily satisfied and met her eyes. "And your infant is thriving, so I guess you Minnicks don't need me again for a while."

Praise. Praise from a white man. It felt good, however reluctantly it had been given.

She saw him to the door and then donned the yellow slickers Bodie had unearthed for her and headed for the tractor in the barn. The rain was no more than mist now, and Nandria wanted to get to work before the master could demand it of her.

The rain held off for nearly half a field's worth of plowing before it became too soupy. Parking the tractor in the barn, Nandria was so stiff when she climbed down that Bodie hurried over to steady her, but she recovered on her own and stiffened at his offer to help.

"The mister's just done with the coop," Bodie told her. "Best get supper started right off."

Snatching up a pebble from the ground at the barn door, Nandria stood for a time staring at the pounded dirt floor. With a sigh, she lifted her chin and headed for the coop to gather half a dozen eggs for tonight's meatloaf and tomorrow's breakfast. She cradled them as she plodded to the house, balancing them carefully to be able to reach to open the door to the porch.

"What?" she exclaimed, blinking, when she'd set the eggs in a blue bowl on the kitchen counter and hurried in to find Doris in the living room with Rose on the sofa. She'd been dressing her in old-fashioned baby boy outfits as though playing with a doll.

Doris looked up. "Gotta find just the right one to show him off at church."

Checking first that the baby was dry and content, Nandria sank into the living room rocker to watch. "Church?"

"Missed last Sunday, didn't we? That's near a sin. Lemme set in that rocker, girl. My boys always loved to rock when they was sleepy."

Little Rose seemed content. Rising with both hands pushing off from the rocking chair's arms, Nandria watched Doris settle comfortably. And then she hurried to the kitchen to mix the meatloaf and peel potatoes for mashing. With preparations underway, she sat at her end of the oak table, rested her elbows on the wood and buried her face in her hands.

"Will," she whispered. *I hope you are no more tired or frustrated than I am. Please be out of danger, Love. Please come safely home. Please.*

CHAPTER NINE

Bodie stepped to the porch door that Sunday morning. "I fed them chickens, fer ya." Bodie looked like a failed scarecrow in his ill-fitting hand-me-down suit. But he'd slicked back his hair and plastered it with some sort of thick, distinctly unaromatic goo of which Nandria could only imagine the color or the origin. She sighed as she glanced at him, aware even in her own frustration that he was trying his best to be helpful to her.

"Could you keep an eye on Mother Minnick, please?" Nandria asked, frazzled. "I have dressed her fully three times now, but she keeps slipping away and trying on new outfits, most of which do not go together at all well. And I must still ready the baby and myself."

"Well, by gum, that's one she hasn't tried on the mister, at least." He stepped up onto the porch and raised his arms in front of Doris as though asking her to dance with him.

Doris giggled. "Ah, now, Bodie, you know we don't dance on a Sunday," she chided, still smiling.

"And hardly any other time, for what thet's worth, but I declare, Missus, you look so ravishing, a feller kin hardly keep himself from wanting to see if'n there's any chance for him to get one go-round, at least."

He stepped toward her, palms up. Doris backed up a step, still giggling, and nearly fell into the rocker to keep away from his invitation. But it meant she was seated and probably unable to do much wardrobe changing in that position.

Smiling in gentle triumph, Bodie danced around and around her chair to keep her occupied—and got in Nandria's way again and again. Still, Mother Minnick was occupied, so Nandria did her own grateful dance with the good-natured handyman.

She had danced around both Bodie and her mother-in-law until little Rose was ready, and she merely needed to run a comb through her own hair to settle it around her face when Mr. Minnick looked in.

"Fussing like a woman! You'll make us late. Get a move on, will you?"

Nandria watched him stomp outside.

"I believe that would qualify as the nicest thing you have ever said to me," she whispered, smiling to herself. And hurried.

* *

Minnick sat behind the steering wheel of the farm pickup with Doris in the passenger seat beside him. "Come on, will ya?" he growled when Nandria hesitated. Bodie was already climbing up into the bed of the truck.

"Where?" she mouthed, but caught herself from saying. For herself, she knew where; she was also to climb into the bed of the truck. Her "where?" was what she was to do with the baby. Handing Rose to Doris to care for inside the truck where she would be out of the cold and wind seemed the smartest thing to do. But would Doris remain aware enough to protect the child from falling for the entire duration of the trip to town?

"Never mind," Nandria muttered to herself. She wrapped the baby closer to her own chest and clambered with her aboard up into the bed of the truck. Bodie, surprised, reached to help them to get up and in and to settle close up against the back windows of the cab where they would be best sheltered from the wind.

"Not much of a choice, I reckon, but mebbe for the best," he said, realizing her dilemma and approving with a shrug her decision. He scooched in his awkward suit to seat himself with his back against the sidewall of the truck bed. His one-size-too large across the shoulders but one-size too small across the belly coat rode up and twisted whenever he turned.

"Why do you not simply unbutton your coat, Bodie?" she suggested as they jounced along. "You will be much more comfortable."

"In front of a lady?" He looked almost as affronted as he was surprised.

She stared at him, eyes glistening.

"Even gentlemen should not be forced to suffer needlessly," she told him low.

Grateful in his turn, Bodie loosened the middle buttons and the coat rode more smoothly.

"That wind is cold," she muttered to excuse her tears.

"Aye," he agreed and looked away out over the fields as they passed.

New springs for the truck might have been on Grover Minnick's list, but the Great Depression had removed any chance of his being able to buy them. But for all the roughness of the road, it was perhaps the smoothest, most comfortable interval Nandria had enjoyed since her arrival in the United States. A compliment, and given with the sincerity of someone surprised she might think there was any other way to have something work.

Lady, she thought. *Strange how a single word can give you back your dignity. It should not be like that. When you know who you are, you should be able to withstand others' opinion of you. Daddy would have expected that of me. But day after day, week after week of the man's demands and humiliations?*

And yet I do not hate Will's father. I may be unable to love him, except for Will's sake, but there is something there in him. Something struggling as ingloriously as I am within myself.

Oh, Lord, Will, where are you, my darling? Are you safe? Please be safe . . .

* *

As they approached the north edge of town, Nandria could make out a worn, white steeple in need of fresh paint, and, under it as the once-blue truck swung around a corner and past several still leafless trees, she could see a worn, whitish, clapboard box of a church with broad, but steep stairs leading up to the front door. In front, a few straggling shrubs and a large open, rutted space before and beside it where trucks, carriages and wagons, and even a few sedans were already parked. Angular or sturdy but skinny horses were tied to hitching posts. A few munched on feedbags hanging from their necks.

Minnick pulled up just beyond a small pond of a puddle with bits of paper-thin, glistening ice clinging to its irregular edges.

He got out and came around to open the passenger door for his wife. He helped her out. He started to move away toward the half-flight of stairs up to the narrow church door, but Doris slowed and turned to be sure Nandria and the baby could get out of the truck bed without difficulty.

Bodie scrambled out first and reached back up to help. Amid a growing buzz of gossipy talk among late church-goers slowing to watch how gracefully Nandria could get down from the back of the pickup, there was a murmur of snatches of fiction delivered as Gospel.

"Minnick got her a maid."

"I didn't know he could afford hired help."

"Must'a been socking away two dollar bills under his mattress."

"Selling eggs knowing they'd been too long in the nest."

"How else a guy like thet gonna get 'im any nest egg for hisself?"

"You wouldn't catch me hirin' no nigger when we got good white gals ready and willing to help out and needin' the money, too."

"Brother Minnick," a sonorous voice spread out like oil on the sea of tittering speculation. The gossip went mute at the sound of the pastor's greeting. All eyes lifted to their spiritual leader standing at the doorway, his expressive hands touching his turned collar as though to remind them that they were entering a sacred place due their respect and quiet. "Welcome, Sir, to you and to the Minnick family. It's been some time since you've joined us for worship."

Blushing to the roots of his thinning sandy hair, Grover Minnick was forced to stop dead. Doris had gasped and gone as still and wide-eyed and pale as a chided child.

"Ah, Mrs. Minnick," Dr. Ricartsen exclaimed as he came up from behind the Minnicks and gallantly took Doris's other arm. "So good to see you out. It has been a while since the roads to your place have been passable for a lady of your delicacy, hasn't it? Do you think if we hurry on in, we can get a prime pew?" His gentle insistence got Doris moving again. "Good morning, Pastor Kylie," the doctor murmured as the trio reached the top of the stairs. "How nice of you to come out to greet us."

Kylie, silently blaming Sadie Bean for the doctor's gradual acquiring of skill in unspoken intimidation, glared at Ricartsen. Pursing his lips and jutting forward his ample chins, he then turned and left them to bestow his most gracious welcome on a faded farmer's wife, directing their seven children toward a seat well back among the congregation. As the pastor strolled on up to take his elevated seat at the front, Dr. Ricartsen and Minnick seated Doris in their accustomed pew mid-way down the center aisle.

The rest of the congregation hurried in with backward looks to see where the nigger Minnick had brought would sit. Surely not with the white folks.

"Choir loft," were a few whispered conjectures.

"Spiders up there. Ugh."

"Ever seen inside a nigger house? So dirty the gal'll probably never even notice no spiders' webs."

"True. True."

Under Pastor Kylie's dominating stare and frown, no one dared to crane his neck to see if indeed Nandria had climbed the narrow stairs up from the foyer.

She hadn't, though Bodie had urged her to. She remained standing near the hood of the Minnick truck, humming to her child.

"Come on in, Miz Minnick," Bodie insisted. "Thet there reverend don't take kindly to late–comers. You 'n' me 'n' the little one can slip up to the balcony and watch."

"No, thank you."

It had been said in that quiet tone, not of defiance, but rather of an unmovable insistence upon its own decision that Bodie had heard at times defeat even Mr. Minnick.

Bodie gaped at her. "Whaddaya mean? Ain't you goin' in?"

Gathering Rose close in her arms around the baby sling, Nandria strolled toward the scraggly wooded area at the northwest edge of the parking area. Dumbfounded, Bodie stared after her. He was so intent upon watching her that he jumped when a car rattled in and rocked to a halt at the foot of the church stairs. Bodie jumped away from the flying gravel and mud kicked up by the sheriff's patrol car's wheels.

Yakes, grunting with one hand on his protruding belly, clambered out brandishing a yellow envelope. Nandria halted in front of the small grove of trees that had beckoned her. Turning back to watch, she saw Bodie sidle close.

"Whatcha got, Sheriff?" Bodie asked as he bent and weaved, trying to get a look at the front of the envelope.

"News for Mrs. Minnick. War Department. Doris inside?" Sheriff Yakes huffed at the bottom of the stairs.

But Bodie had even reached to twist the telegram in Yakes' hand to be sure that what he'd thought he'd read was so.

"But this here says 'Mrs. Willard Minnick,'" he protested.

"Mrs. Willard . . . ? Here!" Nandria called, racing toward them. "Here I am!"

Glaring at Bodie, Yakes reluctantly let go when Nandria snatched at the yellow paper envelope. She tore it open. She stared. Seeing her face, Bodie stepped in even closer to read over her shoulder.

"But at least he ain't dead," Bodie murmured. "And, lookee here, it says he's in London so they kin take good care of 'im. It ain't like he's out in a field somewheres."

Nandria swayed. Bodie grabbed Rose from her arms. Without thinking, Sheriff Yakes caught her as she fell.

"There's a cot in the basement," Bodie said.

Repulsed at holding a Negro woman, Yakes grunted. "I guess we cain't just leave a nigger lying in the church yard." Scowling, Yakes carried Nandria as Bodie, with the baby, led the way around the corner to the cellar stairs at the side. They could hear the congregation's ragged but jubilant singing led always by the rich, full, but slightly off-key baritone voice of the pastor. Neither Pastor Kylie nor the congregation could have heard even if Bodie or Yakes had called for help, which neither did. Bodie was busy struggling around the baby to open the door to the low fellowship room. Yakes would have died of shame to be caught with a darky in his arms.

* *

The church basement was open about half the space of the nave above them. The other half, Bodie knew, had been left unfinished to house the coal-burning furnace and a tangle of pipes for heat and for water plus mops and brooms. With Nandria's slender figure draped in his arms, the sheriff headed toward to the utility area.

"Uh, no, Sheriff Yakes, the cot's in this here corner," Bodie ventured.

"For her?"

"She is Will's wife."

"You know thet fer sure, do you?"

"The mister got the letter saying Will'd married. Named her."

"Anybody could've forged that."

"Our Will's chicken scratch? I don't hardly think so. Anyway, here's the cot. Here, lemme help ya stretch out her legs. She's all catawampus. There, she looks better now. Here, you hold this babe . . . No, never you mind, I'll keep her and go get help. I seen Doc Ricartsen come in just afore you drove up."

Leaving the sheriff staring after him, Bodie hurried up the inside stairs. As luck and the usual practice would have it, the Bean family was just entering the foyer. Sadie bustled in, resplendent in shades of green, the dark ones of which helped contain her enormous chest.

"Ah, it's you, Sadie. Come, will ya? We gots a patient fer ya. Downstairs."

"Patient? Who? What's wrong?"

Sadie Bean, nearly six feet tall and close to being that wide as well, tight–lipped, skilled, gentle but fully able to take charge of any situation, stood stock still beside her jockey–sized husband and teen–aged daughter at the back of the congregation.

"We gonna need Doc?" Sadie asked as she touched the baby in Bodie's arms.

Bodie shrugged. "It's Will's Nandria." At the concerned expression on the wide face of the nurse, Bodie quickly assured her. "The babe's just fine," he said, holding Rose out for Sadie to judge for herself. "Miz Minnick fainted when she got the telegram."

Sighing in exasperation at the ragged way in which Bodie was giving needed information, Sadie demanded, "What telegram? Bad news? Was the woman all right before she read it? What?"

"You want me to fetch Doc, Mama?" Ronda, leaned back to ask in becomingly quiet tones.

"Is thet Grover Minnick he's sittin' next to? Best fetch him, too, if you can without setting the pastor off on a tirade. Thanks, Gal."

"Need any help, Sadie?" Ron Bean asked his wife.

"Can't think of why I would right off." Sadie was questioning Bodie with her eyes.

"I'll just sit in this back row so you know where I am if you need me."

Sadie gazed at this man who was, she felt, inside twice the size of any man in the community. She nodded, and he understood.

"Come on, then, Bodie. You got her on the cot downstairs?"

"Yes'm. Sheriff Yakes carried her."

Rolling her eyes at that revelation, Sadie followed Bodie to the stairwell. When they got to her, Nandria was already struggling to sit up. Yakes stood to one side, offering nothing.

"Where's Rose? Where's my baby?"

"It's all right, Miz Minnick," Bodie called, hurrying to her. "Here, I gots her right here in my own arms an' she's fit as any fiddle. Here, see?"

He settled the infant in her mother's outstretched arms.

"Oh, thank God," Nandria murmured as she inspected and then caressed her.

"You might thank Bodie, too, Gal," Sadie suggested, bustling up and looking Nandria over carefully. "He done everything needful. How are you feeling? Remember what happened to ya?"

Shuddering, Nandria closed her eyes and sat upright, rocking the baby back and forth. "Will," she whispered.

"War Department says Will's been wounded in action," Yakes ventured, still standing outside the circle of help.

"Wounded? How?" Dr. Ricartsen asked as he and Grover Minnick reached the bottom step. Ricartsen approached Nandria seated on the edge of the cot, but Minnick strode up to stand beside Yakes.

"My Will? Hurt? How bad?" he demanded of the sheriff.

Yakes shrugged and gestured at the telegram crumpled in Nandria's hand. Minnick marched over and tried to take it from her, but she clutched it. Startled, he backed off, scowling.

"It says he's in London, recovering. Don't say just what went wrong," Bodie hastened to inform the mister.

"Here, Gal, you cain't go anywheres just yet," Sadie soothed, but Nandria struggled to get up.

"Don't try to hurry things," Dr. Ricartsen commanded.

"I am going to Will."

Yakes bristled. "Like hell. They're not gonna let no darky just hop up and cross the Big Pond, no matter how pushy she gets."

Sadie shifted to cut the sheriff off from Nandria's view with her own broad torso. "Everything is being done for Will that can be done. You wouldn't be able to help even if you could get to him." The kindness in the large-hearted, large woman's voice nearly brought tears again to Nandria's eyes.

With officiousness, the kind-hearted but socially awkward doctor added his own obvious council, "Best to wait to hear from Will himself how things really are." He did bend to help steady Nandria's other arm as she stood shakily but refused to give Rose to anyone to hold. "There. How are you doing?" He held onto her until she was steady on her own feet, but Grover Minnick grew impatient with the fuss over her.

"Bodie," Minnick commanded, "get the missus. We're goin' home."

"This gal cain't ride in the back of your pickup," Sadie protested, looking at him as though he'd lost whatever sense she had previously given him credit for.

Minnick glared up at her implacable face.

"Neither can Doris," Minnick snapped.

The sheriff stepped between them. "I'll fetch Doris in my car, if'n you want, Minnick."

Although it was plain to everyone that he was not pleased with the proposed arrangement, Minnick nodded without looking at Nandria.

* *

Up in front of the congregation, Pastor Kylie had arms and eyes lifted toward the top of the cross, his voice soaring with emotion as he implored his Lord to save his people. But once more rustling movement at the rear of the church jagged at his peripheral vision and annoyance clawed down his lofty phrases. Shoulders raised to take in more air to expel slowly to regain control of himself and the situation, Kylie half turned to face the disturbance. Minnicks again. This time, Grover Minnick had come to fetch his wife, but she was too bewildered to go with him quietly. And the sheriff was with them, looking on, one hand on his protruding gut.

Breathing out, Kylie summoned the smile of a gracious host.

"Troubles, Brother Minnick?" he called from the pulpit.

It was Sheriff Yakes who answered. "Telegram. From the War Department."

The congregation erupted into murmurs, speculation, the buzz of frightened people adding details they had no way of knowing, but which allayed or increased their fears.

Pastor Kylie's face took on his expression of fortitude in the face of calamity. "Willard?"

"Will?" Doris asked, piteously confused.

"Wounded. Don't know how bad," Yakes declared.

"What, Mr. Minnick, dear?" Doris asked.

"It's nothing, Mother," Minnick tried to assure his flustered wife. "But we're going to go on home now. Come along, will you?"

"But we're in church, dear."

Gertrude Haynes leaned forward in her pew and patted Doris on the shoulder. "Poor dear, poor woman," she intoned. "No mother should have to endure the likes."

Instead of yielding to Minnick drawing her to end of the pew, Doris twisted to talk with this Quilting Circle friend from south of town. But she obediently faced forward and folded her hands at Pastor Kylie's command to gather their hearts and speak to the Lord.

"Fellow Saints," he intoned, "we need to pray for our fallen brother."

"Oh, yes, Pastor, we need always to pray," Doris agreed aloud.

Scowling, Minnick bowed over the arm rail of the pew and closed his eyes as Kylie launched into pleading with the Lord. He did not see Bodie and Sadie helping Nandria up the stairway into the foyer and out the front door. When the minister droned on in his petition, Minnick reached again to yank Doris to him, but she pulled back.

"Why, Mr. Minnick?" she protested in screechy tones of annoyance. "Why are we leaving? God is here."

Low murmurs of 'Amen,' 'Poor woman,' and 'Lord have mercy' skittered throughout the nave.

Minnick finally lifted his gaunt wife bodily, and Yakes leaned in to help him carry her out. Shrill intakes of breath and hisses of "For shame!" accompanied them to the rear doorway. But Pastor Kylie made no comment. He had heard Doris's assessment that God was in this place, and he realized that she had given her pastor his due. Kylie merely kept one eye slitted open to be able to follow them until they were out of sight down the entry stairs before winding up his prayer.

In the yard, at the open passenger door of the Minnick truck, Sadie bent her massive figure close over Nandria who held Rose tight as she huddled in the seat. Nandria wept silently. Sadie did not try to console her except to rest her own hand gently on Nandria's shoulder.

A few steps in front of the truck, Bodie drew quick breath as he saw the Minnicks and Yakes at the doorway.

Sadie straightened, watching their difficult progress with Doris still protesting. "The girl said she'd rather ride here than in the po–lice car."

When Minnick reacted, Bodie stepped up close. "I kin drive 'er, Mister Minnick."

Sparse eyebrows lifted in relief, Yakes nearly smiled. "Yeah, Minnick. Lemme take you and the missus in my car."

Without answering directly, Minnick turned toward the patrol car with his wife struggling on his arm.

Dr. Ricartsen emerged from the building with his battered medical bag in hand and clattered down the half–flight of stairs. "I'll follow in my car, in case there's another patient needs me afterwards."

It should have been settled then, but Doris dug in her heels.

Dumping her into the back seat of the patrol car, Minnick stalked to his truck and snatched the telegram from Nandria, waved it toward his wife and then threw it to the ground.

"Because Will is hurt!" he yelled. "There, Woman, since you had to know!"

Doris's scream diminished only as Minnick slammed her door closed. He climbed into the front seat beside Yakes, and the sheriff pulled away. Ricartsen followed, his nearly bald tires slupping in the mud.

Bodie stood immobile. "Ah, ah!" he chanted, fighting for breath. Sadie shuffled to him, for once unsure how to help.

Slipping from the truck, Nandria clutched little Rose to her chest and bent to pick up the crumpled telegram and a pebble. It was only at her movement that Bodie seemed to come back to himself.

"Ready, Miz Minnick?" he asked quietly, though his voice was strained.

She only looked at him.

"Time we was goin' home."

Home?

Nandria stared at him, saying nothing aloud, speaking only with her large, dark eyes.

CHAPTER TEN

The men carried Doris into the house, but Nandria, clutching her baby and humming lilting African songs of woe, wandered the back yard, fingering the clothesline and studying the peeling blue dog house and then staring at the chicken coop. How many times had she gagged at the way the hens peck at one of their own who'd had the misfortune to get hurt or sick?

Peck and peck, often enough, until the miserable one died.

Shaking her head and cooing to Rose, Nandria finally lowered herself and her infant onto the swing seat beneath the elm.

Buds were forming. Tiny green defiances of what looked dead. Refusing to be denied life, they grew. Every spring, the defiant miracle. And every winter, again death.

"What is man, that Thou art mindful of him?" Certainly not mindful enough to keep Will safe. *You broke our bargain! If I stayed and helped here, You would keep Will safe, but You did not! He has been wounded and I cannot get to him, or even know how badly he has been hurt...*

She choked. She sat with bowed head, not hearing Bodie approach until he cleared his throat.

"Uh, sorry, Miz Minnick. Nandria. But the Missus is in a bad way. Do ya think you could mebbe bring the wee one in? She loves thet babe, and mebbe sight of that little face would calm her?"

After several minutes, Bodie again cleared his throat.

"Did ya hear me, Miz? Could you? Please? Bring the baby?" He scuffed the toe of one boot with the other one before pleading again. "She is our Will's ma," he added quietly.

Staring at the chicken coop, Nandria rose quietly and followed him slowly toward the house.

The Minnick bedroom was not overly large, yet it might not have felt crowded perhaps if the furniture had been of normal dimensions. But the bureau, dresser, vanity table and dual night stands were out-sized and heavy with carved decorations of walnut filigree dark with years of polish and then neglect. It smelled musty.

As Nandria came to the door, Dr. Ricartsen squeezed out past her, fluttering her long skirt with his black bag. Minnick stood up, turned to stare into her face, but said nothing and gave way so she could enter. He left without comment. Yakes, in the far corner, muttered something like, "Good girl," and slipped behind her to also vacate the room.

Nandria drew the chair that Minnick had been sitting on closer to the double bed. She sat and lowered the baby so Doris could see her. Both women wept—Doris in sobs, Nandria with silent tears. The women touched little Rose, but not each other.

* *

That night, Nandria slept on the porch with the baby's crib pulled up close beside the brass bed. A squeaking of ancient floorboards brought Nandria instantly awake, listening.

The sounds came from within the house, Nandria was sure. All day folks had come to offer their condolences to Doris and Grover as though Will were already dead. Their assuring comments drained Nandria's reserves, and she took haven in Will's room upstairs. Eventually Minnick himself fled to the barn to work on the recalcitrant thresher. The farmers took pity on him and stayed by the barn door, talking low among themselves, but the women congregated in Doris's bedroom and milled in the kitchen where Bodie was left to brew coffee and serve out the noon meal that Nandria had prepared. It was devoured in bits and pieces by nibbling guests.

Pastor Kylie played host at the oaken table until even he left late in the afternoon when it became apparent no one would be making an evening meal for those gathered.

Doris slept. Minnick sat at the table, picking up crumbs with the tip of his wetted finger and sipping coffee until his belly ached. Bodie limped home.

Once Minnick blew out all the lamps and crept in the darkness to his place beside his grieving wife, Nandria carried her little Rose downstairs and out to the brass bed.

And now someone was moving about in the darkness within the house. Someone from the household. Still Nandria kept her hand on the rim of the crib and listened silently. Doris, Nandria determined. She could smell the faint lavender sachet on her nightdress that Doris kept in every drawer. The frail, bereaved woman crept onto the porch, tiptoeing directly to Rose's crib, where she stood and stared down.

"Ah," Doris whispered finally, "wee Willy. My baby Winfred." Swaying, she began a low, off–key moaning that resembled a lullaby. The sound and the movement of the crib were beginning to awaken Rose. The baby stirred in her sleep and whimpered. Doris bent low, reaching to pick her up, and Nandria braced herself to say something when Minnick's voice called from deep within the house.

"Mother? Doris? Where . . . ?"

As though guilty, Doris rocked back, letting go of Rose. Turning with a stifled groan, she scurried to the kitchen.

Rising on her elbow, Nandria reached to pick up her daughter and drew her onto the brass bed with her, turned onto her side and gave her infant suck. It calmed them both. Something to live for, although without Will Nandria was not at all sure she wanted to, except for Rose's sake. On her own she would have returned to England and been glad to live out the danger of increasing bombing raids with her countrymen.

But Will had wanted Rose safe. If safety was to be had, perhaps it was here. At least for the time being. Beyond that, Nandria made no promises to herself or anyone else.

When the house was dark and quiet again, Nandria set the baby back into her crib and got up to stand at the doorway. She stood a long time staring at the populous night sky, wishing, longing, but with little hope.

* *

On Wednesday morning, Nandria left the prescribed breakfast for the men to serve themselves and strapped Rose into her sling against her mother's chest. She marched outside to the barn and stood a moment beside the tractor with the plow just inside the barn door. Readjusting the sling so the baby was secure, Nandria climbed up onto the high tractor seat.

Bodie appeared at the doorway, bleary-eyed, straggly hair uncombed. He usually completed morning ablutions at the trough just inside the barn.

"Whatcha doin', Miz Minnick? Why you got thet baby up there with ya?"

Without looking at him, Nandria started the engine. Frightened by the sudden noise, Rose cried out but let herself be comforted by her mother.

"Didn't ya ask the Mister who's gonna look after the Missus?" Bodie half-yelled up at her.

She shifted into low gear and eased forward.

"Miz, this ain't reasonable, and you knows it!"

Nandria pulled out of the barn and turned toward the driveway.

Limp-running alongside, Bodie yelled full voice. Minnick came to the door of the porch and glared out.

"Thet babe's getting' too big now. What if'n she gets to fussin' whilst you're makin' a turn?"

Nandria turned toward the north field.

Bodie, beside himself, yelled after her. "What if'n thet tractor tips over? Can't ya at least talk about it?" Giving up running, Bodie called low, knowing Nandria could not hear and would not listen if she could hear him. "You're gonna 'splode if'n ya don't let loose of some'a what's eatin' ya."

* *

After Nandria had finished more than twenty rows on the sloping field, Rose began to fuss. She'd been so good up until then, but every woman, no matter how young or old, has her limits. Nandria had wanted so much to complete this one section. She dreaded Minnick's comments about 'quitting half finished.' She'd been so intent, that she hadn't noticed Horace Bratton sneaking onto the field until he stepped out from behind a fence post and walked deliberately into the path of the tractor. Reflexively, Nandria looked around for Emmy Lu, and then for the two siblings who were nearly always tagging along after their bully brother.

It seemed Horace the Horrendous was alone. He stopped in front of her, hands on hips, pelvis thrust forward, grinning.

Nandria kept going.

"Hey, Sugarlips," he called, "don't pretend ya don't see me."

Without change of expression or speed, Nandria kept plowing her row.

His grin remained fixed but paled around the lips. His eyebrows raised with each turn of the huge back tractor tires. His hips straightened and his knees bent. He scowled, cussing under his breath. Her face was unchanged as she approached. The ground trembled under the worn thickness of the soles of his boots. He could smell tractor fuel, the newly turned earth, his own fear. And still her face was unchanged.

He jumped to one side, stumbled on clods of loosened earth and fell headlong.

Rising, he glared at her back as she continued down the row.

"Stupid whore!" he screamed. Then he grinned, this time slyly. "Feisty. The way I like 'em. At least first–off."

* *

Nandria, sweaty, dusty and obviously tired, drove the tractor into the yard a little late to be starting lunch for the men and knowing they would not have started it for themselves.

Bodie burst from the barn, laughing and yelling and waving his arms for her to stop.

"Whoa, Miz! He's near home!"

"What?" She stopped, soothing Rose and staring at him, mouth open. "What?"

"Here, lemme take the babe. Climb down, will you?"

"I've got to park the tractor."

"Never mind that now. He's near here."

"What are you talking about? Who . . . ?" Nandria slid the baby from her sling and handed her into Bodie's outstretched hands. She clambered down, far too anxious to ask anything further until she was on her two feet and peering into his sparkling eyes. She glanced at the house where, with the porch door wide open, Minnick was struggling trying to help Doris put on and lace her shoes as she sat squirming on the top step. "Bodie, what . . . ?" she demanded as she took Rose from him.

"He's comin! He's almost home, Miz! Telegram come from Chicago and he's comin' home this very minute. Come on!" Bodie tugged at her elbow, and she stumbled after him toward the house.

Doris struggled to her feet, one shoe on and stepping out of the other. She stumble ran to Nandria, stopping short of touching her.

"My sons! Praise the Lord, my sons are comin' home!"

Pastor Kylie appeared at the doorway, genteelly wiping his lips with a newly soiled cotton napkin.

"'How beautiful are the feet of those who bring good tidings,'" he quoted, looking down at his own polished, sturdy black shoes, pleased. "And it is good news indeed."

"Not 'sons,' Mother," Minnick insisted, evidently not for the first time. "Just one."

Doris, ignoring him, begged with her hands to take Rose, but Bodie stepped between the two women to run interference.

"The gal is gonna need to get ready, Missus. Let's us get ourselves dressed to go, too, now."

"Oh, my babies. My sons!" Doris exclaimed, dancing one foot high and the other, bare inside the folded white sock, off balance.

Minnick led his wife back to the steps and helped her to sit down again. He looked at Nandria in frustration. She stooped quickly with the baby at her shoulder to help Doris into the second shoe and tied them both securely.

"Today's train." Minnick told her. "You ready yet?"

Rising unsteadily, Nandria stared at him. “Will?”

“I happened to be passing the telegraph office,” Kylie explained officiously. “So of course it was only my Christian duty to bring the news all the way out here. Doris did not think to open the telegram until just now when the men came in for a bite to eat.”

“Will?” Nandria demanded. “Now? Coming here, today?” She looked from one to the other for confirmation of what she could not let herself believe.

“Aye, Miz. Look, me and the Missus’ll freshen the babe. You don yousself a purdy dress. We’ll go ta meet him right off.”

Kylie pulled a gold–plated watch from his pocket and checked the time. “Train’s due at 12:41. Thet’s thirty–seven minutes from now.”

“Don’t keep us waiting, girl,” Minnick scolded. “Hurry!”

Relinquishing Rose to Bodie, Nandria stood a moment taking in the news.

“Thank God,” she whispered. At Bodie’s touch to her elbow, she seemed to come awake and alive as she had not been. She raced into the house, tears streaming.

CHAPTER ELEVEN

Ten–year–old Pauly Simon yelled and pointed. Laughing and murmuring among themselves, the townspeople who had gathered to greet the train turned to look up the tracks. The engine was minute in the distance, but most Boonetown folks could make out puffed clouds billowing above it.

"Only eight minutes late this time," Sheriff Yakes declared, checking his watch against Kylie's. The pastor had not waited for the family to ready themselves. He had made good time both in driving to town and in spreading the word of Will's expected arrival.

"Wonders never cease," Kylie intoned with a modest smile.

"Indeed they don't," Sadie Bean agreed. Ronda Bean stood beside her, short, buxom, and beaming. It wasn't often her small town offered this much excitement. Will Minnick was coming. She barely remembered him, but somehow associated him with a scandal her mother refused to elaborate on. Anyway, he was coming. And who knows who else might arrive? Just finished with her freshman year at the consolidated high school, Ronda was ripe for new young men and adventure in her life.

"Here come the Minnicks," sharp–eyed Pauly Simon yelled and pointed again. His scrawny chest swelled at being the first to sight both awaited events.

The Minnick's once–blue pickup rattled to a stop, and Bodie was already hopping out of the back and reaching for that pickaninny.

Minnick was all but lifting Doris from the passenger seat as the train loomed. Nandria stood a moment in the truck bed staring at the train until Bodie reached up with his left hand to help her down. Minnick, pulling Doris after him, bulled his way to the front of the crowd. Nandria, baby in arms, drifted to one side.

The train slowed and finally halted so the second passenger car steps were at the town's road and the forward car emptied into scraggly grass only a foot or so from patched pavement. A farmer in overalls stepped off the front car and trudged in the grass to the road. Others were seen moving backward to the second car to emerge onto the pavement where most were greeted by women in large-brimmed bonnets or sun hats.

And then no one.

Minnick craned forward, nearly letting go of Doris's hand. She stood, blinking.

Boonetown folk mumbled among themselves. Several women approached Pastor Kylie, their expressions questioning him, but he lifted his chins and looked down his nose. They said nothing.

Doris began a rocking, swaying movement, chanting a mournful "Willard, Willard," under her breath. And then she gasped, loudly enough that Minnick stopped his eyes searching each car window and turned to look at her. Her final "Willard" was pitched in awed delight.

A Negro porter in starched white jacket carrying an Army rucksack stepped down to set it at the edge of the road and then reached back to assist Will off the train.

"Willard!" "Will!" "Welcome home!"

But the cries diminished of themselves, he was so gaunt and pale. Until Will himself grinned and shuffled into his mother's arms. The townsfolk crowded close, enveloping their farm couple neighbors and their son returned from that hated repeat of a far-away war.

Beaming, Nandria waited unnoticed at the edge of the crowd. Only she realized the porter's salute of recognition before he waved to the engineer and stepped back up onto the train, or Will's nod of thanks to him. Or Will's wince at his father's bear-like greeting. Or Will's eyes lifting up and away from those around him, searching until he found her. His smile widened to embody the joy of love. With gentle insistence, he extracted himself from his parents and well-wishers and went to her.

She closed her eyes, her world complete with his arms around her and their Rose.

Both of them had seen, and decided not to see, the expressions on those around them.

Pastor Kylie stiffened as Doris tugged at his sleeve.

"My son's home! Pastor, will you pray for us, please?"

Automatically, Minnick and the other men reached to take off their hats. Only as he brought its flat underbrim to his chest, did Minnick realize—for the first time—how slowly Kylie took up an opportunity to pray in front of a crowd.

Patting Doris's hand, the pastor slid his arm to free it and lifted it as though in benediction to all.

"Fellow Saints, let us pray! Oh, Lord, give us strength to remain pure in Thy sight and in Thy truth. Help us to have the courage to guide those who stray from Thy will. Lead us not into the temptation of forgiving even those we love who have brought upon us the threat of Thy wrath. We humbly pray to stay pure in Thy sight. Amen."

The townspeople stirred. Puzzled frowns played across their faces. Dr. Ricartsen's murmur was heard by those closest, but its contents were soon spread throughout the crowd. Kylie nodded in satisfaction as the group dispersed then, muttering among themselves, with no further celebration.

"The word is 'miscegenation,' Pastor Kylie," Ricartsen had informed him.

"Indeed it is, Doctor," Kylie answered. "Oh, indeed it is."

Of his family, only Will seemed to have heard or understood the label. Disturbed, Nandria stepped back within Will's arms to peer up at him.

"What is it, Will? What is wrong? Was it something the pastor said? Or the doctor?" She glanced at Dr. Ricartsen, hoping it had not been betrayal by someone she had come to think of as a possible friend, if not an ally.

Shaking his head, Will enclosed her again quickly in his arms and kissed his daughter. He started them toward the truck, laughing. "Are we all gonna fit into that thing? Let's go home."

He did not seem to notice Nandria's startled reaction to the word 'home.' With a look of longing to be somewhere, anywhere, else, she allowed her husband to help her into the bed of the truck.

As Minnick started to pull away with his family, he patted his wife's knee, if only to catch some of her overwhelming joy.

"Our boys are home, Mr. Minnick. Is that not fine of the Lord?"

He patted once more and removed his hand.

"One," he told her quietly. "And he's been shot up." But he pressed his lips tight, realizing he did not even know how Will had been wounded or how badly he was hurt. He hadn't asked, and now he probably could not. In his rear-view mirror and then again in the wide side mirror, he caught glimpses of that blamed dark gal holding him against her with the pickaninny on his lap, both absorbed in a quiet joy that was as enclosed as though the world were theirs alone.

Minnick shook his head, surprised to find a tear spilling down, fortunately, his left cheek, away from his wife. He did not feel up to trying to explain it to her, but hunched his shoulder to wipe it away before she noticed.

Bodie was humming and studiously keeping his vision out the tailgate of the truck when Will leaned toward him. "And how are you, old man?"

"Fair to middlin', you young whipper-snapper," he replied jovially. "'N' yousself?"

"Not complaining," Will answered, grinning, though his face was pale and dark circles drooped under both green eyes. He looked around. "It hasn't changed as much as I thought it would." He stared at the beaten-down fences and sagging barns.

"'Round here? Nah, with money bein' so tight so long, thet sorta beat any 'daptions or 'provements out of a body. But we've worked, Will. Kept up, mostly, but thet in itself was no lead pipe cinch."

"I'm sure it wasn't, Bode," Will sighed, agreeing. "Just maintaining can be almost more'n a man can do." Will went quiet, and Nandria, studying his face, realized that this was the first time since she had known him—and how long before that?—that he was seeing the area where he had grown up. How many years? He stared up a dirt road. "How's your family doing, Bodie? New kids?"

"'Course!" Bodie snorted.

"Not Emmy," Nandria said quietly.

Bodie shook his head widely side to side, looking down at the dirt country road coursing out from under the back of the truck.

"You've met Emmy Lu, bunnyduck?" Will asked.

"Bun...?" Nandria grinned. "That should be the pipsqueak's handle," she chuckled, stroking the baby's cheek as Rose fingered the stubble and ridges of her father's poorly shaven face. Nandria snuggled closer. "I am so glad you are here for her, Will."

Nandria realized only after a while that she had not answered Will's question, but the thought of the girl's beating was simply too painful to bring up in these precious moments of having her husband finally here, in her arms, after such a long time of fear and longing. She would tell him; just not right now.

The closer they drove to the Minnick's lane, the more pensive Will grew. Looking out with fresh eyes, Nandria took in the sloping west field and its isolated hill to the north; the rows she had plowed, many right up to the edge of the lane for maximum yield; the neglected yard in front of the neglected wide, south porch at the unused front of the house. It must have been lawn at one point, probably with flowers in what looked like beds beside the sagging front stairs. She had not looked in so long, it was like seeing them for the first time, only with the addition of Will's memories now, if only she could have access to those. Memories, most likely, of having ducked under that porch to hide from his brother. Of running wide–eyed and carefree, trundling his mother's back–achingly planted flowers. Or perhaps of bending in the dirt of those beds to help his mother plant what would come up to him as miracles of colors, like a shattered rainbow.

It was home. His. Not hers. But, from the look on his face, only partly his. There was a story that she had not been told. And, from the expression in his eyes, she might never be told that tale.

Yet it did not matter. He was here now, alive, breathing, smiling at his wife and daughter, laughing, even, despite his obvious pain. They would leave soon, on their own. She would nurse him back to health. They would share so many glad moments, they would simply lose track of the ones they had lost.

At the house, Bodie would not allow anyone else to carry Will's rucksack. "My privilege," he insisted. Nodding, Minnick helped Doris into the house.

With Rose in her arms, Will bent to lift Nandria in his arms to carry her over the threshold. But she saw the pain in his eyes and demanded to be allowed to walk in on her own. "With a little dignity, please," she told him haughtily, and then laughed. He grinned.

She laid the baby on the brass bed to change her diaper. Will hovered behind her, scowling at the crib and bed.

"You sleep out here?"

Chuckling without looking back at him, Nandria answered, "It is comfortable enough, if not overly private, especially in the mornings."

"He put you out here?"

Lifting the baby, Nandria turned to look at him.

"At first Bodie had us up in your room. But then he had Bodie set up this brass bed piece of history for us. He must have been realizing how hot your room would be in the summer. It is fine, Will."

Lips pressed tight, Will shifted as though to storm into the house to confront his father. Nandria held a gentle hand on his arm.

"Please, darling, not now. There is so much to sort out, but we can do it later. Please?"

"Hired hands go out here."

She shook her head. "Never mind now. Let us just enjoy this moment alone together, Will. It has been so long." She laid their daughter in his arms and nodded for him to sit down in the rocker. "She has missed you." *She needs you.*

He sank into the gentle movement of the chair, and as he gazed at Rose, his frown gradually softened.

She tidied up after Rose, bent to kiss them both and turned toward the kitchen.

"Where are you going?" he asked.

"To start dinner. He will be hungry. There was no time to put anything on even to simmer and stew, we left so quickly for the station once we got the word."

"What about this morning?" he asked suspiciously.

"That already seems like a million years ago." She smiled. "I did not finish plowing half that field before Rose got antsy."

"You could hear her over the noise of the tractor?"

"She was with me," Nandria said, reluctantly showing him the baby's sling. "I keep her with me. Your mother . . ."

Bodie slipped out from the kitchen, explaining embarrassedly, "Jus' gonna check the stock. Sorry, Will."

"Yeah, okay, Bode," Will told him absent-mindedly. As they listened to Bodie's heavy steps down the couple stairs, Nandria reached to cradle Will's face in both hands. She kissed him fully, hungrily, on the mouth.

"Darling, please. Just let us be?" Without waiting for an answer, she hurried to the kitchen, but listened carefully to hear Will rocking, and then cooing. At any quick break in her meal preparations, she stepped to the door to peer at them. Will and the baby were both sleeping contently in the rocker. "Ah, Loves," she whispered as she gently lifted the infant and set her safely into the crib. "Oh, my darling," she whispered as she substituted a small pillow for Will to hold.

CHAPTER TWELVE

"I shall have the meal prepared as quickly as I can," Nandria stated unapologetically as Minnick came into the kitchen from settling his wife in their room.

He sat down at his place at the table, silent but radiating disapproval. Nandria worked around him, refusing to acknowledge that he had something he wanted to say unless he said it aloud. Finally, he grunted as she set a platter in front of him.

"My wife is asleep," he informed her. "You gonna call my son?"

"When he awakens."

There was another period of silence as she worked until she reached to pour him fresh coffee. Bodie entered so quietly across the porch that neither of them noticed him. When he heard the topic of conversation, he waited in the doorway.

"I seen Horace Bratton in the field this morning," Minnick said accusingly. "What truck you got with the likes of him?"

"I do not know what he wanted," she said over her shoulder as she filled a platter for herself from the stove. "I did not stop to talk to him."

Bodie's sharp laughter startled them both. Looking back onto the porch to be sure he hadn't awakened Will, Bodie, still chuckling, seated himself at his place against the wall.

"She didn't hardly slow down," Bodie said. "Thought for sure she was gonna plow 'im inta fertilizer."

Minnick stared at him for a moment, and then returned to eating. "Be somethin' useful, at any rate," he muttered to his fork.

Back at the stove, Nandria added to the portions on the plate and handed it to Bodie, then again served a portion for herself while the men talked. Rather than join them, she ate standing up at the doorway to the porch.

"Say, Mr. Minnick, what was 'at 'missodomation' they was talkin' 'bout?"

"Dunno," Minnick admitted as he sopped up the last of the gravy with his crust of bread. "Shameful, whatever it was."

"Sure got the Doc and thet pastor riled up. But then there's always somethin' ta git their tails aflutterin'"

Minnick got up, wiped his mouth and set his huge cloth napkin across the remains on his plate and walked on out to the porch to lean against the east wall to hike on his boots. With eyes seeming to be on his task, he took in more hungrily than for any meal, the sight of his son asleep in the rocker hugging a pillow.

Hurrying with his food, Bodie was close behind him as he stepped out into the yard and lumbered toward the barn.

Nandria gathered their dishes and set them in soapy water in the sink. She was wiping the oilcloth table covering when her curiosity simply got the best of her. Wiping her hands in the front of her apron, she stepped to the porch door to check husband now as well as baby, then moved into the living room to stoop at the side table and pull out the heavy dictionary. She carried it to set it on the driest spot on the kitchen table and began to work through the "M's."

That night, Minnick sprawled in his overstuffed easy chair with a three-day-old Indianapolis News raised in front of himself. Doris twittered and fidgeted, all thumbs for some reason as she tried to crochet while covertly watching Will and Nandria sitting together on the sofa. Will held little Rose on his lap and laughed as she swatted at his face and then lunged forward to take his chin in her mouth and give it suck.

"Ah, wee, hungry Miss, you'll need to ask your mother for anything good to eat," he chuckled as he lifted her away and waited to hand her over until Nandria could arrange a discreet nest for them with the baby's blankets. "Speaking of good to eat, that was a good supper tonight, Love. I haven't eaten that well in weeks and weeks." She smiled and reached to take Rose from him.

"I used to be a pretty good cook," Doris chirped.

"Indeed you were, as I remember," Will agreed, smiling with long-ago memories. "I never lacked friends if they thought there was a chance to come out here to the farm over a meal time, Mother."

"She calls me Mother Minnick," Doris leaned forward to tell him conspiratorially. "Like I was Superior at the convent school." She giggled, and leaned closer. "My mother was Papish, did you know that? Oh, dear," she cried, suddenly pleading in fear. "You mustn't tell. Promise me you won't tell."

"I won't tell anyone, mother."

"Especially not Pastor Kylie," Doris begged. "I don't think he likes Catholics much." She brightened unexpectedly. "I invited Pastor to a Sunday dinner, did you know?"

Minnick lowered the paper abruptly. "When'd you do a thing like that?"

"Today," she simpered. "He likes my cookin'. This here mornin' afore we rushed off to the train to fetch our boy here. He couldn't come this Sunday or the next'un or the next, but the fourth, he said he'd be proud."

"Why in thunder?"

"Why?" Doris looked blankly at her husband.

"Why'd you invite him fer a meal here?"

"Now, Mr. Minnick, you know the pastor speaks to God for us."

"Speaks for . . . ?" Grover Minnick was so outraged that the newspaper fluttered in his hands before he spread it on his lap, spilling a good portion onto the floor. Finally he regained control enough to merely mutter, "It don't seem like he's got all that much good to say to the Lord about us."

Rose giggled as though in appreciation of his quip, and that set them all to laughing and cooing at her.

Setting her yarn and needle into their cloth bag and spreading out her skirt over her lap, Doris picked up with dignity her own line of conversation.

"We'll wanna have everything just real nice. The good linen, and the silver."

"The silver's been sold, Mother," Minnick huffed. "Along with near all the stock. You know that. Taxes."

"Oh, dear. But, still, it'll be so nice, all the family. Will home. And Winfred, and maybe that nice little Emmy Lu he's so het up about."

As she went on blissfully dream–planning, the rest of the family froze in their places, gaping at her. Will leaned forward toward her, gently taking her hand to draw her full attention.

"Fred won't be coming on Sunday, Mama."

"Nor any other day," Minnick growled. "Winfred's dead. When you gonna get that straight, woman?"

Nandria covered her own mouth with her free hand. "Oh, no, please . . ."

Will echoed, "Pa, don't . . ."

Minnick scattered the rest of the newspaper as he rose up from his chair to tower over Will.

"You lose me my son, but I can't even state the fact that he's dead?"

"Pa, I . . ." Will scrambled to rise from the couch, but sudden pain nearly doubled him, although Minnick was too angry to notice why his son was slow to face him like a man.

Open–mouthed, Nandria stared between the two men.

It was Doris who got between them. "Now, now, my dears, no fussin', please. Let's just sit down and mebbe we can sing a few hymns. Music is so good for the soul, you know."

Grunting, Minnick slumped back into his chair.

Will, swaying a little on his feet, took a moment to compose his expression. "I… I think it's time for us to go up to bed. Long day, you understand, mother?"

"Hymns is always a comfort," Doris began, but Minnick interrupted.

"'Up' to bed, did you say?"

"Willy, do you remember where you put your accordion? I ain't seen it in such a long time," Doris asked, still trying to organize a family sing.

"You go 'up.' Her bed's out where she belongs."

"Now where could that clumsy big thing be?" Doris chirped.

Jaw set, Will said quietly. "Nandria is my wife."

"So she says," Minnick retorted. "Mebbe in her country, but it sure wouldn't'a been no marriage if'n you'd'a thought to get hitched nowhere 'round here!"

"Oh, dear, you wouldn't think a big lummox of a thing like an accordion could just get lost." Doris sighed, looking about in consternation.

"Well, we did not 'get hitched nowhere around here.' But we are married, and my wife and I sleep together," Will stated, fists clenching at his sides.

Gathering Rose close against her, Nandria stood up beside him and rested her free hand on his upper arm.

"Winfred?" Doris called. "Winfred, do you know where your brother's accordion got to?"

Minnick lunged to his feet again. "NOT IN MY HOUSE!"

Turning, Doris stared at her husband, bewildered, and then at Will as he stated low, “We’ll be gone in the morning.” Leading his wife and daughter, Will took his family to the porch.

Cocking her head to one side and frowning, Doris pleaded with her husband, “Mr. Minnick, where is Winfred? I can’t seem to find my son.”

CHAPTER THIRTEEN

As she sat comforting Rose on the gently roving swing under the elm, Nandria could hear Will installing his things from his upstairs room to the porch with hers. There wasn't much to move, but whatever his wound had been—and he had avoided telling her about his mission or its consequences, so far—he was tired out tonight. The move was painful, slow and lonely, because he insisted on doing it alone.

Finally Will came out into the night. He stopped mid-yard to stare at the banks and blankets of stars. A swallowed moan was the only sound as she waited, watching with him.

"There's beauty, always beauty, no matter how ugly things get," he murmured as he approached the swing. "Even here."

"Do not say it, Will. Please. Nothing we say will change anything with your father."

Sighing, Will sat on the grass beside her. He went silent, looking off at the distance.

"Thank God you are well," she whispered.

"'Well.' Yeah."

Nandria peered at him in the dim light seeping from the porch, but he changed the subject.

"I'll be working in D.C."

She looked at him quizzically. "Oh, Washington, D.C. Yes. Is that bad?" she asked when he seemed about to leave the subject where he'd dropped it.

"For you. For us."

"They don't like niggers there?" she muttered, smiling.

"You are no ni . . .!"

"That would be difficult to tell by looking at me," she said, her eyes pleading with him to grin. But Will was not yet ready to find the humor they had used so often between them to cope with the difficulties their races had caused them. She studied his face in the dim light. "You had planned to leave me and the baby here, had you not?" she guessed.

"Not to be his servant," Will spat. "I'm sorry. I shouldn't have sent you here in the first place."

"It is a minefield," she agreed, "but how could we know until we stepped in it? That's what my mother would have asked."

"I… I knew." He hung his head a moment before lifting his face to peer into hers. "I just didn't know how raw it still was."

"Will, that other issue, that is where the rawness lies, is it not? Your brother Winfred was killed. It was an accident. It had to be."

When Will nodded and lowered his head, tired and nearly defeated, she reached to stroke his cheek.

"Oh, God, my love, I am so sorry."

But he sat very still, almost stiff, looking away from her to the stars flirting with the top of the west hill.

"He blames you for your brother. He is not a man who would forget a wrong, from anyone." *Even his own son. Perhaps most especially not from his own son.*

Will turned then, to touch her knee. Slowly he allowed his clenched fist to open and caress it. He looked up at her face. He sighed.

"The Depression, that's what beat him. He almost had this farm a going concern when we two boys were little. He was strong. Incredibly strong. He worked so hard."

Nandria leaned forward into his hands, now reaching for her.

"You love him," she said quietly. "Then we cannot leave in the morning."

He rose to a squatting position and then half-standing, his hand pressed against his side. "The way he treats you!"

"He has no power to hurt us," she declared, shaking her head slowly.

He rose full height, looking down on her with an expression of wonder.

"How did you get to be both strong and beautiful?"

With a wry smile, she chuckled. "Parental insistence. You knew my parents." She went suddenly still and her eyes closed in grief.

"I . . . In Liverpool," he whispered. "I didn't know then that they were on the Athenia. I wouldn't have left you to come all the way here on your own. I thought you'd be meeting your parents and Ned in New York, as we'd planned."

"And I thought you would be coming with Rose and me on the 'Salty Healer.' There would have been time to tell you of their deaths."

His eyes narrowed as though in pain. It was moments before he asked, "'Salty Healer?'"

"Our pet name for the Canadian hospital ship. It was an amazing experience. Although I would not be anxious to volunteer to do it again, I must admit that those blessed sisters are incredibly giving of themselves in their nursing. And the men. So torn, and yet most were unbitter, accepting their wounds as their fortune in war. People . . ." She let her voice trail away, words being inadequate for what she had learned about people's reality.

"So you had to give birth alone and even had to face your parents' deaths without me. I'm so sorry, Nandria. So sorry."

"It is funny," she exhaled slowly remembering his jeep approaching across the shore end of the great pier. All her weeks of anger and hurt and humiliation and grief rising like a tsunami when she had thought she had already coped with those emotions and could simply be grateful to have her husband back. To look forward to days with him where even the Intelligence Service could not take him away.

She had been wrong, of course. In war, the little people are always wrong. The best it seems you can hope for is that the big people, the ones who can actually decide something, will be right at least once in a while.

"Is 'funny' the word, Nandria?" he asked gently when she had been still for such a long time. He bent down to study her face.

"We cannot leave in the morning, Will. We cannot leave them without help."

He sat again on the grass beside her, lips tight, much as his father's got when he was trying to control his anger.

"To save this farm? It was never mine, Nandria. He knew when I left that I wasn't coming back."

"But, Will, we are here. And your wound. Can you help?"

His anger melted into something containing a sadness she had not known he carried. Something about Winfred? Not guilt; that she would have recognized. But loss, almost of himself.

When his eyes met hers and he realized how much she was garnering, he lay back abruptly in the grass. Shifting Rose in her arms, she got up to kneel beside him. Making a nest of the baby's blankets, Nandria lay beside her husband and tucked her infant close at her side to have both hands free for Will.

CHAPTER FOURTEEN

Minnick stared. Will lay sound asleep holding Nandria in his arms on the brass bed in the enclosed porch. The baby slept just as soundly in her crib beside their bed.

A myriad of emotions played across Minnick's tired face. He'd steeled himself so long that he'd forgotten that his face was expressive. His skin and deeper–than–skin had tanned and leathered over so many years that he'd lost track of feelings. Foremost for him was the anger now at what should have been his son's revulsion over touching that dark skin.

"Nigger. She's a nigger, Will," he said so low his engine noise–damaged ears could not hear himself, though the girl stirred as though she had caught his words. Funny, he hadn't wanted her to, he realized. *What have you done to this family, Wee Willy? Oh, God, what have you done to us?*

Finally, hiking his shoulders to get himself moving at all, he reached to snatch up his boots and stumbled across the porch and outside. Leaning against the outside doorframe, he worked his aching feet into his boots and lumbered to the barn.

With both Will and Nandria gently snoring, Bodie appeared at the outside doorway several minutes later. He, too, stared at them, but his own emotions were warmer, seeing Will alive and obviously happy with his family. He was about to go on out to the barn without breakfast when little Rose stirred and fussed, quietly.

"Ah, wee tyke, don't ya go wakin' up your folks," he chided low, tiptoeing over to gather her things and pick her up gently. He was carrying her into the kitchen when Will lurched up. Both froze for an instant, until Bodie could hum a soothing, "Z'all right, Willy, z'all right now, it's only the old Bode here."

Will rubbed his eyes and eased away from Nandria to stare at the kitchen door.

"Bodie? That you?"

"Yeah, Will, and I've got your babe. Gonna take care of this here wet bottom. Thought I'd make 'er snug and let the Miz sleep in for a change. Don't think she's ever slept of a mornin' since she come."

Will eased out of bed. "Mother have breakfast ready for you men?"

"Your ma ain't been up'ta that since your miz come. Or for a long time afore that, truth be told."

"That bad?" Will stood and stretched, but stopped to consider the import of Bodie's revelation.

"Slow a'comin', but worser and worser," Bodie told him seriously. "Your miz's been a savin' grace to her, Will."

Hurriedly slipping on the plaid flannel robe of his youth to keep Bodie from seeing his flank and hip, Will gazed at his wife.

"All the meals and the plowing, too."

They walked into the kitchen, where Bodie laid little Rose in blankets on the table to change her. His eyebrows raised to ask Will if he wanted to handle the honors for his daughter, but Will's terrified, helpless expression brought a grin to Bodie's lips. He worked, and Will watched to see how it was done. Chuckling, Bodie handed him a warm, dry little girl and laughed quietly out loud.

"Talk about plowin', the Miz near caused havoc with thet tractor first off. Thought she was gonna tear down the fences, let alone the chicken coop. But it didn't take her long to get the hang of it, for all its orneriness. No, sirreeee, not long a'tall."

"Carrying the baby with her."

"The Missus took her fer a while, but after a bit, none of us could be sure. Your ma just not in 'er right mind 'nuff to be sure for the kiddo's sake. Say, I kin start them eggs, at least. Kin you still flip a mean griddle cake?"

Will's pancakes weren't as good as Nandria's. Even Minnick allowed that to be true when he returned to the house. Which Nandria took as a compliment, unacknowledged, of course. But the smell brought first Nandria and then Doris to the kitchen, and it was nearly a joyous breakfast. Doris, smiling and gracious, seemed more like what must have been herself than Nandria had ever seen. Having Will at the table with them was evidently good for the whole family. No mention was made of last night's incident in the living room. Minnick even gestured for an extra cup of coffee to sip at and talk over before rising to leave for the barn. He ducked to kiss the top of his wife's hair, and Doris blushed and giggled in a way that brought a near smile to the corners of his mouth until Will leaned over to kiss Nandria. Minnick scowled then and marched out to the porch, grunting and muttering under his breath.

The men went on out to the barn; Nandria stayed behind to help Doris finish dressing.

"Ain't he handsome, girl? Ain't my son a handsome man?"

"He is that, Mother Minnick. I thought so the very first time he knocked me down," Nandria laughed.

Doris turned on her. "My son would never knock down a woman, even a nigger!"

Nandria's world collapsed in the middle, leaving her gasping for long moments until she could right her breathing and then anger flared to the back of her throat. She had to work to swallow it down.

"Will saved my life, Mother Minnick," she said as quietly as she could manage. "Mine and my younger brother's. There was no time to explain the danger, so he tackled us both to the ground to save us from the gunfire that zinged over our heads in the next minute. Will Minnick is my hero."

She stood quivering, trying to contain her emotions as both her parents had taught her from tiny childhood. It was never easy. Not when the person you were dealing with had hit a nerve so raw it threatened to razor off the top of your head. Swallowing again, Nandria sat down again in her chair at the table to regain her equilibrium.

There was no apology for that hated word. Doris seemed not to realize she had insulted Nandria to the depth of her being. Instead the woman merely cocked her head to one side as though contemplating.

"I didn't know that. About my Will saving your life. Gunfire? Really? My goodness, we have plenty of guns around these parts, but almost never nobody shooting at nobody else."

For a moment, Nandria thought of trying to explain that the wars had been in Ethiopia and then Spain, but after a moment's thought she gave up and shrugged. There was just too much to try to make clear to a woman whose grasp of her own reality seemed tentative at best. Instead Nandria rose and merely nodded as Doris made herself comfortable in the living room. Nandria carried Rose to the porch to nurse her, leaving Doris to again spar with her crocheting.

When the baby slept, Nandria laid her in the crib and donned the boots Bodie had found for her. It was a bit nippy this early in the morning to carry Rose outside. Maybe later in the day.

At the barn door, Nandria smiled to see Will working with the two old horses, one gray and swaybacked, the other chestnut and still strong, but leery of this man he did not remember, if he had ever seen him before. Soft words were calming him. It would not take Will long to be able to win him over. Will was that way with most people, too.

"I thought you was gonna finish that northwest field," Minnick groused at her shoulder.

Startled by his having gotten so near before she realized his presence rather than at the gruff tone, Nandria answered as calmly as she could.

"Yes, of course."

But Will rubbed the gelding's face one last time and stepped toward them at the doorway.

"I'll do it."

"No, I do not mind . . .," Nandria started, but Will told her with his eyes to let this be between himself and his father. Reluctantly, Nandria nodded and turned to pick up the spade and carry it to her beginnings of a garden between the chicken coop and the mulberry tree, and spreading a little toward the elm.

"Tell him, Will," she whispered, though no one could hear her. "Tell him now that we are leaving." She reworked the ground she'd turned over a few days before, chopping at lumps and smoothing what she could before going for the rake. She stopped now and again to try to listen to the men's conversation. The voices from the barn were occasionally loud enough to be heard, but usually unintelligible. There was anger there, anger a long time simmering and finally given vent.

When Rose let out a wail; Nandria jammed the spade upright into the ground and hurried into the house. Later, when she carried the rocker out to set it in the grass near the elm tree, she saw Bodie, raising his hands toward Nandria in seeming surrender, limping beside the barn with a drawstring bag slung over his shoulder.

"Thet there thresher's gonna be the death, but Will seems determined to get it goin'," he called. "I been up in the north pasture. Had some sowin' to do by hand. The mister likes to get all the way inta the corners." With a wave he limp-trudged toward the house, though obviously the seed bag would need to go back to the barn some time. "I was gonna fill this here bag up again with seed, but…" He lifted his hands toward the barn. "Ain't no way them two want no interruptions."

Nandria went back in and brought out the baby and a large wool World War I blanket, which she spread out on the grass near the rocker. She laid Rose in the middle, knowing full well that the baby would squirm and roll and soon be off into the grass. She'd bear a close watch, but these days of warmth and air were good for her. For all of them.

Doris came out dressed in heavy boots and a faded housedress with a flowing scarf billowing at her neck. Instead of sitting in the rocker, she bent, grinning, to take up the rake lying at the edge of the garden patch.

"Ahh, how I love the feel of the good earth," Doris sang.

Nandria opened her mouth to suggest that Doris not overdo, but Bodie had limped up beside her.

"Now, Missus, you knows how sore and stiff you gets every spring with your working so hard in your garden. How about if'n you take it a bit easy this here year, for Will's sake."

"And Winfred's?" she laughed. "You always gimme oaths I wouldn't break for nothin' no how."

He looked as though she'd slapped him, but she was already humming over her regular lifting and smashing down of the rake, using it to batter stubborn clumps of Missouri ground.

Nandria lifted her eyebrows, asking if Bodie was all right. "You are limping a great deal more than usual this morning."

He shook his head and twisted to look sadly back at the barn. "Ain't no never mind."

"You could hear what they were saying?" Nandria asked. "When you passed the barn? Are they still going at it?"

"After the yellin' comes the 'tense part. The Mister kin carry only so much afore it seeps inside him and takes up his whole entire self. Thet's where he be with our Will now, I reckon. An' nothin' I kin do," he added, head down. He let the seed bag slump to the ground.

"Sit down, Bodie," Nandria commanded, and, at her tone, he did as he was told. She crouched to tickle Rose's tummy and scoot her back onto the center of the blanket and then return to her own work with the spade.

It was several minutes before Bodie hoisted himself to his feet. "Thet end of the ground is 'bout ready to sow. You got your seed?"

"In the barn," Nandria told him. They both looked over, unwilling to go there.

"So our Will's fixin' to leave, is he?"

"You could hear him tell his father that?"

"Nah, but I knowed it was comin'."

"Oh, Bodie, what can I do to help him?"

"The Mister?" He shrugged and shook his head. "Wouldn't know how, even if'n the mister'd let us. But help our Will? You best know that, Miz."

They both looked over as Minnick drove the recalcitrant tractor out the barn door, parked it and got down. As Will emerged, his father pointed north and east, then stalked back inside. Will climbed painfully up into the seat and fiddled with the gear shift, lips tight. Nandria ran to him. Seeing the determination on his face, she did not dare offer to do the plowing, but busied herself showing him the tricks she had learned the hard way.

"I've spent more hours of my life on this thing than I have walking," he sputtered.

"Been 'dapted some since you was here, Wee Willy," Bodie explained, coming up on them. "Wish I could do the plowing fer ya."

"Well, you can't with that dead foot. Can barely manage the truck," Will exhaled, nodding quickly at his wife and friend. His grimace eased. "Unless you've learned to plow in concentric circles."

Bodie chuckled. "Kin almost conjure up the image of thet purdy pi'ture."

The three laughed grimly. Bodie went for his seed sack and on into the barn. Will eased into low gear and lurched forward, almost as awkwardly as Nandria had, and a sliver within her felt vindicated, though she frowned to keep it from showing. And then she remembered what she had wanted to know. She hurried alongside the moving tractor.

"He did not let you tell him that we are leaving, did he?"

Will grimaced again and shook his head, but continued out to the drive and turned north beside the barn. Nandria watched him go.

"Girl!"

Nandria turned. Doris stood, leaning on her rake, in distress pointing to the baby crying on her blanket. Nandria hurried toward them. She hadn't heard Rose's cries above the noise of the tractor.

"Did that old tractor noise scare my little one?" she cooed, picking up the baby to comfort her. "Never you mind, little bud of a Rose. We will get Daddy safe out of here and join him soon. We will be just fine." She bent to pick up and pocket a pebble from the edge of the blanket that had been kicked there by the tractor wheel. "Too close," she whispered, looking out to where Will was turning east on the slope beyond the barn.

Doris was still leaning on her rake, her breathing uneven and her face pale. Nandria almost called to Bodie as he limped out toward the fields and then to Minnick as he emerged from the barn and headed past the chicken coop and away. But the expression on Minnick's face told her he was not to be disturbed with less than a true emergency. Nandria was pretty sure that Doris had merely overdone her labors in her enthusiasm.

"Come, Mother Minnick. Time we went inside to begin fixin' a picnic lunch for our menfolk," Nandria heard herself saying. How quickly she had 'dapted to the odd speech surrounding her. She was sure that only her language teacher at Oxford would appreciate how quickly her ear adapted to the colloquial.

With the baby changed and nursed and safely asleep in her crib on the porch, Nandria went into the kitchen and Doris followed.

"Best to get started on polishing the silver for thet Sunday treat for Pastor Kylie," Doris said as she gathered tea towels from the drawer. "We want to be at our Minnick best."

"We may need to use the flatware again before a Sunday weeks from now. Perhaps we had better start on the platters?"

Doris sat happily at the table, 'polishing' ceramic serving plates and pitchers that Nandria knew would need to be thoroughly washed again before use. But Doris was humming, and that was worth the extra work to Nandria. Besides, Doris was beginning to chatter, and Nandria had questions.

"Can't imagine where that accordion got to," Doris complained, shaking her head. "You ain't seen it, girl?"

Realizing she might glean information about Will's brother, Nandria asked casually over her shoulder, "Winfred's accordion?"

"Oh, dear, no. Winfred's never liked it none, though it was bought for him. At the flea market that rainy Saturday at the church, remember?"

"It was raining," Nandria said carefully when Doris went pensive.

"That day . . . and the other." She laid her towel on the table and smoothed and smoothed it out across the grain of the table top.

Nandria held her breath, afraid to turn and look at her or to say anything to prompt her silent mother-in-law. After several minutes more of rubbing and smoothing the narrow towel, Doris wiped silent tears from her cheeks and brightened. "Ah, but it won't even sprinkle on our special Sunday. It wouldn't dare. And the Reverend will see that the Minnicks can still put on a fine dinner."

Disappointed, Nandria packed the last of the meal in the wide–mouthed wicker basket. She went to the porch to change the baby and set Rose into her sling. When she came back for the basket, Doris was again smiling happily.

"You gonna go out to the field? I want to come."

Glancing at the clock, Nandria, too, brightened at the prospect. "There's time, if you truly feel up to it. The walk will do us both good."

In the delightful fresh air again, Rose cooed, and Doris giggled and touched her lightly and fondly on the head.

"Lemme help with that," Doris said, taking hold of the handle of the basket beside Nandria. They swung it between them, laughing.

In the northeast field, Bodie looked up first to see the women coming smiling and chatting together like school chums. He stood erect, stretching his back and motioned to Minnick.

"Your womenfolk must be plotting agin' us to be thet happy."

Frowning, Minnick stretched up and stared. But his expression softened as he watched his wife's joy. He lifted a hand to gesture to Will as he made a turn at the end of the row, but Will had already spotted them. They met near the lone oak at the southern corner of the field.

"Mother," Minnick nearly scolded his wife, but he was almost smiling as he greeted her, "you sure you're up to comin' all this way out here?"

"Dear Mr. Minnick," Doris laughed, "how many times I brung meals and new-baked treats out to my man? Remember, dear one?"

Surprised and overwhelmed, Minnick took the basket and led Doris off to sit in the shade of the tree. Bodie, knowing he was the third wheel to both couples, wandered off to tinker with the equipment. Will finished the row he'd been working. Wincing with his face away from his father, he climbed down from the tractor and went to sit with Nandria. Wiping his face on his cotton sleeve, he eyed his daughter as she played on her blanket at the edge of the grass. Finally he touched her gingerly.

"Our miracle," he whispered.

"You look so tired, Will. And in pain."

"Soft living," he shrugged. "I'll toughen up."

"Will you? How soon are you expected in D.C. ?"

"And when am I going to tell my father?" He drew his baby onto his lap and peered into her face before turning to look at Nandria. "The end of next month, and soon. I was going to tell him over lunch, but Ma's happier than I've seen her in such a long time and I hate to start another row. You're good for her, Nandria. Thank you."

She gazed over at the older Minnick couple. "She is plaster white and mine was rich mahogany. She is earth and hands; mine was ether, mind and brain. But she is the only 'Mother' I am likely to ever have again. She is good inside."

Will closed his eyes and then looked away.

"They both are," Nandria whispered.

He shook his head slowly. "We are leaving the end of next month. You and Rose with me."

"But we . . ."

"Nandria, we cannot save this farm for them. It can't be done. The best we can do is to fix up what we can so it sells for a good price. He should have done that ages ago when she first started failing."

"Oh, Will."

"Reality, Love. You haven't shrunk from that a lot before this. You do want a home of our own, don't you?"

"More than anything. Privacy! Oh, my."

"So there it is."

"But not today, Will, please. She is so thrilled about putting on fancy for the reverend coming one Sunday a few weeks from now."

"Reverend, bah! Did you know he is the man who hosts the local KKK meetings?"

"KKK?" Nandria questioned. Will lifted his hands.

Doris had set out the food on a spread blanket; she called for them to come over to the shade of the tree before Will could think of a way to explain. Bodie reached the shade first.

"Never mind, Love," Will said as they gathered the baby and their blanket. "I just hope you and Rose never do learn those three letters."

Will winced in pain as he reached to give Nandria a hand up.

"Oh, Will, you are hurt more than you are saying."

"Never mind," he muttered, telling her with his eyes not to make a fuss that would attract his father's attention. She set Rose in her sling, and slipped under his arm to help him walk to the tree.

* *

That evening, Nandria was busy with the leftovers of the meal she had prepared. Will kissed the back of her neck and went out onto the porch. The baby was asleep again in her crib, having giggled and played with her mother's food at the dinner table, much to the delight of Doris and Bodie as well as her parents.

"Sleep well, little angel," Will whispered. He went to the outer door and descended to sit wearily on the lower step, legs spread before him so he could maneuver his torso and relieve his aching side and hip. When his gnawing pain eased somewhat, he gazed up over the west field to the sunset streaking the horizon with oranges and tangerine colors more luscious than the fruits themselves. He exhaled, relaxing.

"Ah, there you are, Wee Willy." His mother stepped past him and leaned to pull up his hand. "Come on," she urged. "It's best when you get to see them come out one by one."

"What?"

"See that sunset? We ain't got a lot of time to get there."

"Ma, I . . ."

"Come, my wee mouse. Come. Mama wants to show you!"

Reluctantly, Will rose and allowed himself to be led across the yard.

He followed, stumbling now and again, to the knob of his mother's favorite hill. She was breathing a little hard, but her face was wrapped in a smile of child-like joy as she gazed back at their farmstead and then out at the few others scattered across the countryside. Starlight from an intense Milky Way was enough to silver the creek runs and now gray white-painted fences and homes.

"Ain't this the most beautiful place you ever been?" she whispered, clutching his hand.

He looked as much at his mother's ecstatic face as at the rural view before answering with a nod. Her animation was breathless now, and her eyes full of wonder. She looked to be a young woman. His eyes widened and he swallowed hard to see her thus transformed. No wonder his father continued to adore her. He remembered. And must ache to wish it could come again, this vision of delight and joy in this woman he loved.

"Young bride," she was confiding, "I'd steal away up here. Like I could skip up among them stars. Even roll in the grass and diamonds. See how the blades sparkle? And so many stars! I did try to teach you and Freddy the consummations. That there is the Big Ladle . . ."

"Big Dipper. Nandria's family in England called it the Big Plow, I think."

"That's the saddle or something on the huge bear."

"Ursa Major," he whispered so as not to interrupt the flow of her jumbled explanations, but she looked up at him and frowned.

“I don’t like bears much. Ain’t sure why anybody’d want to ride one.”

Her unhappiness made him wonder if there were a story. A fear. “Have you ever seen a bear in person, Mama?”

“Little girl. Woods, upper Minnesota. I was so scared,” she lowered her voice, her face distraught. “I peed my panties. Couldn’t tell Mother. Shame.”

“Surely she’d understand that you’d just met up with a . . .”

Shaking her head vigorously, Doris let him know there would be no excuse for a shameful act like that. None. Not even an encounter with a bear. After a moment she calmed.

“We was almost on the Canada border. Wouldn’t that’a been funny?” her mood switched again to gaiety. “Two countries mine. I could’a run from one t’other when I was scared.” She paused and stared up into his face. “Like you’re doin’, my Will. And ya don’t hafta. I forgive ya.”

He swallowed again and pressed his side. “Forgive?”

“For killin’ my sons.”

“Ahhhh, Mama. I didn’t know you thought that, too,” he cried. His knees gave way under him and he sat down hard on the damp grass. “That was an accident.”

“’Course it was. Had to be. You ain’t got a mean bone in your body, for all you’re bein’ in the Army. I think mebbe that’s why your father don’t know what you are.”

Will wept so quietly, she either didn’t hear, or chose not to, but gazed out for a long time at the array of stars.

"He… he was drunk," Will started.

"There's that."

Without looking at him, she started slowly, sadly, back down toward the house.

Will sat a long time on the knob before moving to rise and stumble down the slope.

CHAPTER FIFTEEN

Doris walked into the yard where Minnick stood drumming his fingers on the hood of the truck. “Was you alone, Mother?” he asked before he'd studied her face. “Ah,” he gasped and let her walk on into the house without answering. Nandria rose from her seat with the baby on the swing under the elm and hurried into the house after her.

Minnick watched them disappear onto the porch and then into the kitchen. He drummed louder, until he saw Will coming slowly across the field.

“Willard!” Minnick called.

Startled, Will looked up to see his father beckon impatiently. Concerned, he hurried to the yard.

“Get in. You're gonna make us late.”

“Late? To what?”

“It's second Tuesday, ain't it? Get in the truck. I'll drive.”

Nandria stepped to the doorway to watch the truck taillights slue down the Minnick lane.

* * * * * * * * * * * * * * * * * * * *

They drove in silence, Will trying desperately to compose himself before his father got a good look at him.

“Going to town?”

“They ain't changed the meetin' spot.”

Second Tuesday. Second Tuesday, oh, Lord!

Yakes' patrol car, mummied in mud spatter, had been left nose out at an angle near the base of the steps up to the church entry. Pickups, most with rifle racks behind the drivers' seats, were parked strewn across the open church lot. Minnick pulled to a stop at the edge where it was unlikely anyone would park him in.

"Guess there's a couple fellows not arrived yet," Minnick muttered under his breath. He hated to be late. And, as Minnick father and son strolled around the corner to the cellar steps, Horace Bratton did slip in behind them. They smelled his liquor breath curdling their shirt backs before they heard his footsteps. He hawked and spat, landing a wad beside Grover's left boot heel. Minnick's hesitation was momentary, but he did not turn except to enter the concrete stairwell through the open cellar doors. Will stepped to one side to let his drunken neighbor descend before him.

"Horace," he murmured.

But Bratton did not answer or acknowledge the newly home soldier as he clumped down the stairs and went to sprawl beside his brothers in the back of the room.

Pastor Kylie, heretofore congenial host, frowned with displeasure as Irwayne poured hooch from a small jug into Horace's coffee mug as he joined them. Grover Minnick strode up to help himself from the large coffee urn on the long table strewn with KKK tokens near the front of the room. A number of the older, weather–worn men greeted him with rough complaints about too much rain, or not enough, and too cold for this late in another farmer–defeating springtime.

"I seen ya got the road edge of thet west field of your'n pretty well prepared already, Minnick," drawled a slope–shouldered neighbor in what Grover at first took to be a compliment. But Will's father pressed his thin lips tight as the man continued. "Wassat a gal you had drivin' tractor? We didn't think your missus was up to doin' thet for ya no more."

Minnick mumbled without answering definitively and nodded toward Kylie, who was rounding up Sheriff Yakes and Dr. Ricartsen to get them to call the meeting to order. But the men had been talking and laughing among themselves and seemed reluctant to give up one of their few times of masculine conviviality.

"Here, Will," Greg Paisler called and tapped the seat beside him. Greg had been a class or two behind Fred in the regional high school. He'd been one of the few young men in the community who stood by Will through all the hatred and blame at his brother's death. "Good to see ya. We'd heard you was back. How's the wound? Where'd they getcha?"

Will might not have answered in any case, but did not get a chance as the sheriff, hand on his lower belly, piped up. "Gentlemen. Gentlemen, we got a meetin' to attend to."

The men meandered to their seats, but kept murmuring among themselves until Kylie raised a hand in irritated command. "Gentlemen!" he called in a sonorous voice that quieted them all.

"There, that's better. We ready to open?"

Paisler, younger than most of them, probably barely into his twenties, lean and hard, and possessed of an irrepressible grin, called, "Need jacks or better?" When Yakes stared at him, he added, "To open?"

Many of the men chuckled, but, at Yakes' frown of exasperation, settled quietly and looked forward toward the table with the banner and gavel for the opening ritual.

"Listen, men," Yakes began a bit loudly after the rote beginning, "there's a war on, which Will there could prob'ly tell ya about if ya don't know."

Several of the men twisted in their seats to turn to make low comments to Will, until Kylie rose.

"I think this meeting is serious enough that we need to ask the Almighty's blessing."

But the pastor's droning prayer sent Will's mind off into its own direction. He'd grown up with these men, most of them. He studied their faces down-turned, many with eyes closed. Leathered cheeks, unruly or thinning hair, lips thickened by drought and ice, deep creases with a lighter color—closer to their own—at the bases of crows' feet beside their squinting eyes. Chins dark with stubble or disguised by beards unkempt because there simply was no time for frills or personal luxuries. Men beaten down by politics, economics, and weather. Good men, he told himself. But men around whom he was uncomfortable now, especially in this setting. Was it these men, or the fact that this was a meeting of the Ku Klux Klan, no longer merely a social and help-each-other club like the Grange? Will had found out what other Klan members had done to 'niggers' in other areas. He wondered if these men knew about those atrocities. Or, if they knew, would they think it was wrong? Would they care?

The meeting progressed around him, but Will was no part of it. *How can I be here like this? What's happened? To me? To them? What?* "What?"

Will startled at Paisler's sharp punch into his thigh. Greg lifted his chin and tossed his head to motion toward the front table where Doc Ricartsen was peering at Will analytically.

"Will, you with us?"

"Yeah. Yes. Yes, sir. Right here."

"All right, then, I think we'd all be interested in hearing your opinion since you've had first-hand experience."

Paisler leaned close, whispering, "They're frettin' over this here Silver Shirt thing."

"What's Rousy-velt gettin' so het up about?" Yakes wanted to know. "Ain't this here still our free country? Ain't a man got a right to say whatever he's a mind to?"

Sighing, Kylie broke in with studied concern. "What I am against is that the FBI is calling people traitors when all they are doing is rallying to state their convictions."

Someone toward the back—Will could not see who particularly, but he knew it was the general sentiment—called, "We don't want this country hauled into another European war."

"Not our problem!" echoed around the room. "They got their troubles, let 'em settle 'em themselves." "Got 'nuff'a us killed and shot up in the last war." "We got our own troubles right here." "Don't see no Brits runnin' over here to take care of us."

Will took his lower lip between his teeth and waited.

"Seems to me, the president is pressing harder and harder for us to be getting geared up for makin' war stuff, if not for war itself," said an older man Will almost recognized as owning a large farm south of Fox Haven.

"If'n I had a wife as ugly as thet hell–in–whore he's got, I'd be working toward war myself, rather than face what I got at home!"

A few of the men guffawed. Fewer grimaced. Dr. Ricartsen's face twisted in annoyance that the meeting was getting out of hand instead of producing a meaningful discussion.

Yakes stepped toward Will. "How come they sent you across the Pond, Willy? Ain't they got 'nuff young men of their own to slaughter?"

Rising slowly, Will looked around at each man. Liking so many, if only from memories of childhood, he was reluctant to sound as though he was against them, though he thought they were wrong. Dead wrong.

"I'm with Army Intelligence, not the fighting units," he began.

Frowning, Greg Paisler looked up at Will's face. "You think they ain't expectin' us to send men over, Will?"

"They may need . . ."

"So you weren't supposed to get hurt?" Ricartsen, both concerned and curious, broke in without realizing Greg had asked a question.

"The chaos and terror are covering most of Europe, not just Germany. It's Finland now, and Poland just about swallowed whole. And it's not just Hitler. Italy's Mussolini is getting pretty big for his britches after his successful invasion of Ethiopia. That's in northern Africa," Will added when most of the men looked blank. They stared, obviously wondering why what happened in Africa had any claim on them in rural Missouri.

Will considered how to explain the background and the significance, but Horace Bratton in the back of the room wasn't interested in either.

"'Zat where you knocked up the nigger, Will? In some dark ditch one night? Prob'ly didn't even see how dark she was when ya jumped in for cover, did ya?"

Gall rising in his throat, Will spun on Horace, whose brothers were guffawing and pounding him on his back. Minnick slid around in his seat near the front table to stare at Will. His face showed concern and pride, then something else as he watched his son work to conquer his anger and ignore Bratton.

Yakes broke the impasse with a loud, disgusted, "Ethiope? I-talians? Whadda we care? It's our rights we gotta stand up for."

Watching Will's long, assessing look at Yakes, Ricartsen blurted, "Minnick, you have to admit that Europe, Africa, Asia—they've had centuries of wars. Nothing we can do to change their past, and maybe not their future, neither."

Will exhaled slowly, focusing on Ricartsen as the most reasoning of the men here now. "I think President Roosevelt is concerned about free speech because that is a foundation of everything we depend on to be free." Encouraged by the few men who nodded in agreement, Will continued. "But Mr. Roosevelt also understands how insidious propaganda can be. The Silver Shirts aren't just men expressing their own opinions. They are a group deliberately using charged words to stir up all sorts of hatreds and divisions within this country."

"And you're with 'telligence? How smart is that?" Horace Bratton cat-called.

Greg whipped back, "Sounds purdy smart to me."

Even Yakes seemed anxious to head off a fight. "I guess it don't hurt none to be on top of trouble afore it gets started. I keeps a loaded pistol close by near all the time," he admitted, shaking his head. "That don't mean I 'tend to use it, less'n somethin' God-awful was to happen. But there it is when I do want it at hand."

"Mebbe we should learn the best ways to produce guns and tanks here so we can make more, and the best, if we need come some time in the future," an old farmer from far south of Boonetown said thoughtfully, his squinting eyes nearly crossed as he thought through the implications of what had been said here tonight. "Be ready to defend ourselves if things do get out of hand." He looked up at Will's face, still cross-eyed but more now with wonder at his own conclusion.

Grover Minnick spoke up for the first time. He shook his head and muttered, "If you send guns, sooner or later you're gonna hafta to send boys to fire 'em."

"Well," Horace rose, disgusted, "No Demy-crat's gonna send me!"

"No, probably not," Will admitted low, but audibly, "we tend to send the best."

Greg Paisler guffawed outright; most of the other men grinned.

"Only the best suckers," Horace spat, coming forward. "They took you, didn't they, Wee Willy?" He glared at Will, but, getting, no reaction, stomped out and up the cellar stairs into the night. Jude, Irwayne and a few others scrambled out behind him. The rest of the men stared at each other.

Kylie took charge. "It's late," he intoned. I'm not sure we will be gettin' to what was to be our main agenda item."

"And that was?" Will inquired, pretty sure he already knew.

"Best put off for now," Yakes decided.

"At least until we got a better idea what we're dealing with," Dr. Ricartsen agreed.

Will stood with the others through the closing, then hurried to walk out without speaking to anyone. Greg sprinted to catch up with him.

"Never mind, Will," he said, falling into step beside him. "It's just that they wasn't expectin' what you brung. But I hear she's a beauty."

Will stopped and looked the young man up and down. Then, deciding to take him at face value, nodded. "More than you can know. It was good to see you, Greg. My best to your family. I'll try to get over to see your ma one of these days soon."

"She'll like that. We all will." Greg stuck out his hand to shake Will's but his eyes dark chocolate eyes were still troubled. "You was trying to tell us somethin' tonight, Will."

"This is going to get worse, Greg. A lot worse. Tell my pa I'm walking home, will you?"

"Worse?" Greg called after him. "Around here? Or their war?"

Without turning back, Will answered over his shoulder, "Both."

CHAPTER SIXTEEN

The days had droned into weeks. Will's hip and flank were healing despite the constant irritation of physical work. Nandria watched and nursed, but could not convince him to do what she knew the Sisters would have advised. It was all tied up with his standing in his father's eyes, and that he would not compromise despite his pain.

Nandria found that she'd expected things to be different once Will was with her, but the farm consumed them all. Spring was the busy time, the all–out effort time, and for each of the Minnicks the days were demanding and routine. The nights, fortunately, held their own joy, even if only as two aching, tired people lay at peace with the world in each other's arms.

It was a long time and a short time until the eve of Pastor Kylie's coming.

Rising from the sofa where he'd sat beside his mother, taking in her excitement at the pastor's visit scheduled for after church the next day, but none too soon for her, Will held her hands in his for a moment.

"You are a pretty lady, Mrs. Doris Minnick," he told her. He smiled to see even deeper blush come to her cheeks. She was a lovely woman. More handsome than pretty in her day, but with the green eyes and pert little mouth remaining among the deepening wrinkles, she was like the doll she had set in Winfred's crib until Minnick himself caught sight of it and banished it to the trash heap for next Saturday's burning.

But Will remembered how much she had wanted a baby girl. How much she had needed a woman companion. She'd had so little of that. No wonder she had loved the quilting bees, despite hating to sew.

"But I have a pretty lady, too, and I don't want to neglect her," he whispered too low for his mother to hear, knowing she probably wouldn't understand even if she had heard. She gave no indication that she had as he left her and walked to the kitchen to see what was keeping Nandria from joining the family in the front room.

The kitchen was tidy. No Nandria, but the tiny sponge marks on the floor caused him to lift one foot and study where she and his mother had spent Thursday evening and much of Thursday night and on into Friday morning on their knees, dipping small squares of cut sponge into paint and pressing the marks onto the plain dark linoleum. The pattern near the sink was random, decorative. As both women had tired, the pattern followed more nearly the arcs of their arms reaching to spread out rather than crawling forward on aching kneecaps. Still the overall effect was fancier than the plain, dark linoleum had been, and that was important to his mother. And a beautiful love gift of participation from his wife. Doris Minnick had wanted to show the pastor their "Minnick best."

"Nan?" he called softly, afraid that she had just set the baby down to sleep. Gingerly, he stepped across the crudely highlighted floor that no one had been allowed to trespass upon until Doris had been sure the floor was thorough dry. He slipped to the porch to check on his wife and infant.

Rose was there, sleeping in her crib, with a smile that wrenched his heart. She was growing so fast. He'd need to bring down Winfred's full sized crib from the attic soon, if they stayed. Maybe that was why he'd thought of that stupid doll.

No Nandria. With a kiss from his fingertips to his daughter's soft cheek, Will stepped to the outside door to peer into the yard.

And there she was, outlined by brilliant oranges and reds dramatized by roiling gray–black clouds. His beautiful, composed and competent wife Nandria with an ax raised over her head dashing in zigzag chase after panicked chickens. Hens flapped and fluttered. Feathers fanned and fell in spilled spirals. Clucking chaos. Frantic frenzy. Nandria, the lovely, the calmly dignified, the unflappable, reduced to Bedlam fodder, face glistening, eyes mad with focus on squawking, unmeetably fleeing goals.

Will stopped, his lips still formed in his unspoken praise of "Good supper, Honey." He stared at the riotous back yard, and had to duck as a terrified hen flew low and ricocheted off one wide window of the porch beside him with a thud that rattled the glass and raised the heavy bird's cries to screeching.

"Nandria," he called, and then again louder, but this time her name was distorted by the beginnings of his laughter. Carefully he entered the fray, finally intercepting her and holding her by the wrists, trying to bring her to him to stop and calm her without falling prey to the honed edge of that ax.

"Bunnyduck," he whispered into her hair. "Nandria, honey," he cooed, dancing with her frantic movements, trying to calm her, to slow her, to stop her in his arms. "Easy, love." And when he had her nearly still and looking at him as though she knew him, he took the weapon from her and let it drop at their feet. "You can't let them see the ax, silly lady."

"Oh, Will," she gasped, both shaken and chagrined. "I thought," she panted. "I thought that at sunset, they'd be ready to roost and easy to catch." She stared up at him, a failure and a disappointment to someone. She hated to disappoint anyone.

"And just why do you need a chicken so desperately?"

"It's Saturday night."

He shook his head still holding her, now for the joy of feeling her close against him.

"And?"

"That pastor's coming tomorrow and your mother says the chickens must be ssllllooooowww roasted."

"Ah, Kylie, yes," Will agreed, but not agreeing with his mother's assessment of the man. "Mama wants so much to impress him, and she did roast her chickens slowly, as I remember. No time to do that in the morning before we set off for church, I take it."

Nandria stood shaking her head.

"And no chance Mama will let you stay home to fix the meal. She'll want us all sitting up front posing in front of everyone as though it were no trick at all to put on a fancy feast." Will stroked his wife's cheek and kissed the tip of her nose. "Here, let me do the dastardly deed for you," he offered as they watched the frantic chickens slowly settle. Many were finding their way back toward the asylum of the coop. He gave her a small shove toward the swing dangling from the elm tree, nodding for her to go and sit down.

With a gentle, herding technique followed at the last moment by a dash and lunge, Will caught one hen and crossed the yard to pick up the ax in his other hand. He carried the flapping fowl upside down by the legs to a crude weathered and stained stand not much deeper than a sawhorse. With a flick of his wrist he laid the chicken so her neck was between two nails hammered only part way into the wood. They served to hold her from moving side to side, and, as she struggled, also served to help her elongate her neck. Before she could think to lift her head and neck up and away from the confining nails, Will had head and neck severed with a decisive blow of the ax. He hung her body by the legs from the clothesline and went in search of a second victim for Sunday dinner. And then, knowing the pastor's appetite, a third.

Nandria had slumped, exhausted, to sit on the swing to watch his sure movements and to recover her own equilibrium. While she concentrated on the dynamics of his stroke to accomplish the 'dastardly deed' with the least suffering for the poor chicken and least likely need for a second blow, the first hen, writhing, slipped out of her leg bindings and fell to the grass. Without its head, it ran in blind circles around Nandria. Shuddering and sucking air, Nandria raised her hands to cover her face but could not blot out the scene.

Will set the ax atop the chopping block and hurried to crouch beside his wife. "It's all right, love," he drew her into his arms to comfort her. She had seen too much war. Too much maiming of humans he had not been able to keep her from experiencing. He tried to remind her that these were farm animals, raised for slaughter. He appealed to her reason. "It's just nervous connections, brain to muscles that haven't died yet. It will be over soon."

When he was sure she had control of herself again, he rose and chased down the headless hen and tied it again to the clothesline. Wiping his hands along the thighs of his overalls, he went to sit beside Nandria.

"It's what happens on a farm. You'll get used to it. Or, then, no, you won't. We won't be here that long."

Nandria cuddled against him, tired from months of unshared frustration and grief.

"We'll be gone soon. Soon, my darling, our own space. Our own home," he assured her, lifting her face to look into her eyes. He smiled. "You can buy our chickens at the butcher's."

She nearly smiled. At least the panic and exhaustion lightened from her eyes. "You told him, then?" She slipped down to sit beside him on the grass.

"Tomorrow night, after His Reverendly Highness leaves. Pa'll be upset already, but Ma will be so happy he won't dare squawk and spoil her day." Grinning, he reached to kiss her forehead, the tip of her nose and then her mouth. They sat a long time in each other's arms as the stormy twilight darkened.

In the mulberry tree, birds were settling after the disturbance. So many hurrying to find shelter for the night, each one antagonized by just-arrived mates, setting the tree aflutter. As the evening darkened, Will and Nandria could no longer see individual birds or hear individual calls. But, in the near blackness, the tree itself appeared to shimmer and shake amid an angry, what should have been melodious cacophony. Nandria sighed and nearly laughed. She leaned into him in warmth and love that sent a rush throughout his body.

As they watched, the storm clouds seemed to close toward them until they could no longer distinguish even the mulberry tree. Will rose and reached to help her up. "I'll pluck these . . ."

Lightning flashed. Nandria startled, barely stifling a terrified scream.

"Rose! Get the baby to the bomb shelter!"

A low rumble in the distance to the northwest lumbered toward them. Nandria shuddered as though the sound had traveled through the ground and entered to possess her as well.

"Easy, love, easy," he whispered. "It's not bombs. Just lightning. Heat lightning. There may not even be any rain. Happens a lot out here."

He held her close, whispering, comforting. He'd have been amused if she hadn't been so obviously terrified.

"Oh, my darling warrior princess. You've survived onslaughts, gunfire, sieges, bombings, submarine attacks. And now afraid of a little lightning. But it isn't just that, is it, my darling? So much. Too much, eventually. Just a while yet, Nandria, and then I'll be able to protect you. Our own home. I promise."

CHAPTER SEVENTEEN

Early the next morning, Bodie bent to slip a wedge of firewood under the thresher's frame as Will heaved against it. "Better," Will breathed as he stepped back and scrutinized the arrangement.

"Still tippy some," Bodie observed, but he nodded, acknowledging that that wedge had indeed increased Will's safety as he worked on the ancient, many–times–'dapted machine in the back of the barn.

Will was already surveying it from all sides. "If we brace it here, it should be stable enough for me to be able to get to that connection. There, see? That's the source of the problem, I think. If I can fix that . . ."

"You always was the one ta figger out sources to problems 'stead of just 'daptions. Here, lemme help ya."

"What in tarnation?" Minnick bellowed at the wide barn doorway.

The sudden noise startled Bodie, whose stumble nearly caused the thresher to tip over onto Will. Minnick dashed forward to help secure the machine from falling.

"You damn fool!" Minnick growled.

"Oh, Will, I'm sorry."

"Could'a been sorrier," Will staggered up and away, laughing, but shaken. "Thanks, Pa."

"You two're a mess. Can't go to church lookin' like that."

"Church?" Bodie looked blank.

"My missus's been workin' her fingers to nubbins for weeks now."

"But, pa, we about figured out the problem here. Can't we stay and…?"

"We ain't gonna spoil your ma's day," Minnick thundered.

"I clean forgot," Bodie said. "Couldn't I jus' stay total out of the way?"

"Kylie's coming after. I'll be ready for that, Pa."

Minnick glared. "Your mother says it's a sin to miss."

"All right, sir. Let me reinforce the bracing, and I'll be right in."

"Just leave it for now. Nobody's allowed in this here barn without I say. And you, ya dern fool Bodie, my missus says, 'Come,' then you come."

Lifting his left hand in half salute, Bodie turned and limp–ran out of the barn toward his place.

"Hummmph," Minnick commented and twisted to go back to the house, but he turned back to see Will bracing what he could with a plank. "Willard!"

"Coming, Pa," Will called. "God, I don't like this," he added under his breath as he took a last look at the thresher.

* *

Will helped Nandria gather the blankets and paraphernalia from the wooden folding chair in the church balcony where he'd sat with his wife, as he said, to keep Rose from interrupting the long Sunday sermon.

"I should buy us a car, so you'll be able to ride inside out of the wind," he muttered. Nandria straightened to peer at him.

"So you are reconsidering taking us with you to D.C. ?"

He shook his head, then realized the inconsistency and stopped to look at her. "I guess maybe I had been thinking that way. Must have been, huh?" he laughed and drew her to him so they wouldn't be seen from the floor of the church. He kissed her. It was Nandria who pulled away finally.

"Your mother will be so anxious . . ."

He sighed and let her go. "I'll be glad when this day is over."

"You and me, both." She rolled her eyes.

"You're a good sport for doing so much for her, darling."

"All of which," she said with a tinge of emphasis, "will be lost if we do not get back to the farm in time for me to accomplish the final touches. She is so counting on this being a splendid affair." She stopped and lifted on tiptoes to kiss his cheek. "She is something special, Will. I cannot imagine what she must have been like before her illness. You are very lucky."

"Oh, yeah!" he breathed, reaching for her, but she eluded him and started down the uncarpeted stairs to the foyer.

Outside, families were climbing into wagons, pickups and sedans to start home for their own Sunday dinners. But knots of people were chatting and covertly watching Doris, breathless with excitement, cling to the pastor's arm. Will settled wife and baby in the back of their family truck with Bodie, again stiff and awkward in his mis-matched suit. Will strolled over to help his father with Doris.

"Come on, mother," Grover Minnick drawled when he could get a word in edgewise. "The reverend will join us in a bit. Ain't that right, Reverend?"

"Unless you'd like to ride with us?" Will proposed. Kylie peered at their truck with such disdain that Minnick stiffened.

"No, no, Minnick," Kylie declared. "You folks go on. I may need to make calls on the way home. A pastor's duty, don't you know?"

Doris looked crestfallen. "But you are comin' for dinner?"

"Oh, yes, Sister Doris. Soon as ever I can." He patted her hand as though it were a child's.

As the Minnicks loaded up and drove away, Sheriff Yakes and Dr. Ricartsen moseyed over to join Kylie on the church steps.

"You really gonna eat what them nigger hands has made?" Yakes asked, his hand resting lightly on his lower belly.

Kylie slid one finger between his neck and the reverse collar. "My mother employed a Negress as cook and housekeeper. The meals were delicious. Negro hands can be most valuable, in their place."

Grinning slyly, Yakes echoed, "In their place." The grin broadened to lewd. "Some valuable places—you just don't marry 'em."

Kylie, despite his dignity, grinned as well. Ricartsen, slower to catch salacious meanings, laughed as well, but his expression betrayed his bewilderment.

* *

"That chicken was tender as tissue paper," the pastor exclaimed around the large, off–white, linen napkin with which he dabbed his lips. "And savory! Ah, thank you Mrs. Minnick. Delicious!"

Ecstatic, Doris took Pastor Kylie's proffered arm and he led her, triumphant, from the slightly paler linen–covered kitchen table into the living room.

"So glad you come, Pastor," Doris burbled.

"Brilliant meal, Sister Doris. I've never had finer gravy."

Barely hiding his disgust at the pastor's prodigious appetite for food or for laudatory remarks, Will, carrying Rose, followed them into the front room. Bodie tried to wait to be last, but when Minnick remained a step behind and waited at the doorway, he scampered into the gap in the line and found a straight chair in the corner.

When the others were gone into the front room, Minnick gestured to Nandria to remain in the kitchen to clean up.

"Oh?" she questioned, nostrils flaring.

His lips tight, he leaned to her, saying low, "My home; my rules."

Nandria stepped back and let him disappear from her sight before turning on the ball of her left foot and striding to the porch. The outer door closed with a sharp retort.

As Will seated his mother, he heard what had to be the back door. He glanced around the room at the sitting men, Kylie in the most comfortable chair, which was Minnick's.

"Where's Nandria? Pa?"

Minnick let himself down onto the sofa beside his wife. He shrugged against the cushioned back.

"That girl must be tired after all her fine work," Kylie intoned, gracious to underlings.

Reading their faces, Will handed little Rose to his mother and turned to stride toward the kitchen.

"Your mother has a guest, Willard," Minnick called to his retreating back.

At the kitchen doorway, Will turned slowly to face him. "And I have a wife."

"Ahem," Kylie leaned forward in the easy chair. "I have been meaning to speak to you about that . . ." he started, but, seeing Will's face, hurried to continue, "but perhaps our talk can wait until a more suspicious moment."

Without bothering to correct the pastor's word usage, Will declared with a sarcastic bow, "Excuse me, all," and left the room.

"Oh," Doris cried. "Oh, dear." She turned to her husband, rigid beside her. "Oh, my," she chirped, fidgeting herself past bewilderment nearly into devastation. "Somethin's wrong, ain't it, Mr. Minnick?" As her husband kept his face turned away from her, her agitation increased and little Rose was handled with less and less attention. Bodie finally jumped up to take the baby from her arms.

"Eg–scuse me, if'n you please," the handyman apologized. "I think this little lady needs changin'."

Doris stared wide–eyed after him as he headed for the porch with the baby. Near tears, she trembled, her lower lip going slack.

Kylie leaned forward to pat her hand. "It has been a memorable meal, Sister Doris. You are in no way to blame. It is difficult when a man loses control of his household. We should pray." He closed his eyes and lifted his other hand as signal for prayer.

Furious with both shame and guilt, Minnick started to his feet, but Doris, tears streaming, clung to his arm, pulling him back onto the sofa. At last, he sat back and held her as the droning prayer unfolded around them.

"Oh, merciful Father, you who have ordained all creation in its rightful place and rank, forgive this unfortunate family their sons . . ."

With a grunt, Minnick did leap to his feet, eyes wide and staring at the head-bowed pastor. Doris peered up at her husband. Her eyes went vacant.

* * * * * * * * * * * * * * * * * * * *

In the west field, Will needed to sprint to catch up with Nandria stalking across rows she had plowed. She was nearly to the foot of Doris's favorite hillock by the time he could lay his hand on her shoulder and draw her to him.

"Bunnyduck, Nandria, darling," he called quietly.

They danced with her seething anger.

At last she quieted but was still trembling in his arms.

"I don't know what he said . . ."

"'Stay in the kitchen and clean up,'" she spat.

"God, Nan, he had no right . . ."

She shrugged. "His house, his rules."

"That's it. We'll pack right now and go."

Finally she exhaled, slumping toward him. "Oh, Will, I thought I could do it. I thought my father's discipline in diplomacy could give me strength to conquer anything, or anybody . . ."

"You shouldn't have to."

" . . .but this other . . .on top of everything else. So sick."

He held her away to study her face. "Sick? You're sick, Nan?"

Sighing heavily, she twisted to kick at a clod of plowed earth. Without looking at him, she said, "It is too soon to be sure, but it is just the way it was with Rose."

"Oh, Lord, Nandria, are you saying . . . ?" From incredulity, his expression blossomed into joy. "Praise the Lord! Oh, Angel!" He hugged her tightly, then tenderly. "Sorry. I didn't hurt you, did I?"

"Of course not, silly." She laughed, relieved and gladdened.

He picked her up and swung her around, then crumpled with a groan. She landed on top of him.

"Oh, Will, your side!" she cried, scrambling off of him.

"Nothing," he panted, grimacing. "Just the wind knocked out of me." He reached to caress her face, proud and joyous and awed, if a bit white around the lips.

She smiled, delighted with his reaction, knowing that whatever happened outside of them, they were still the universe that mattered, and they were intact. They cuddled against each other.

"It will be the perfect excuse. Your health," he said, stroking her hair. "We won't have to explain anything, even what your medical needs are. And there's nothing Pa or anyone can say."

They sat up, laughing quietly, and he drew her close again to kiss her tenderly. When she had looked deeply into his eyes and smiled, she turned to get up and that was when she saw it over his shoulder. She blinked and stared, scrambling up.

"Will? Will, that's Emmy Lu's horse."

He twisted to look where she pointed to see a half-starved nag grazing near the brow of a swell of ground to the northwest.

"No saddle," he commented as he rose to his feet. "Maybe she just got loose."

"He beats her, Will."

For a second he hoped that Nandria meant that Horace beat the animal. That certainly fit within Will's assessment of the Bratton brothers. But he knew almost instantly from the concern on Nandria's face that it was far worse even than that.

"Emmy refuses to allow me to say anything, but I have seen the welts and bruises on her arms and face."

"Damn," he swore softly, getting up. "Never ending. Never, never ending. Go back to the house, Nandria. I think I'll mosey over there."

"I shall go with you," she stated. He nodded, knowing from her tone that there would be no point in argument. They walked a little separated from each other quietly toward the mare, who eventually allowed Nandria to stand holding her mane.

Will needed to search a while, but eventually, in a small swale surrounded by tall grasses, he found Emmy Lu. Nandria hurried over at his grunt. She stopped to vomit into the grass. But as soon as she could, she gathered herself to do as the Canadians nurses had taught her.

"She's breathing," Will said as he lifted her gently to turn her face up.

"She has a pulse," Nandria declared, "but it is quite rapid, and not strong. The sisters would call it 'thready.'" Nandria quickly checked the girl with her hands. "I do not find any active gushing of blood, though there are dozens of open wounds oozing. Oh, Will…"

"We've got to get her to help. Run ahead, Nandria. I'll try to carry her down."

"Can we load her onto her horse? With your side still not completely healed…"

Nandria rose and approached the mare, which allowed herself to be brought up close to her injured mistress as though the smell of blood was so common to her that she no longer shied away. Nandria helped Will set the girl onto the mare's back.

"Fetch help, Nandria."

"Yes," she said, fairly sure he'd be able to keep Emmy Lu on the horse's back while she ran ahead to rouse the family.

* *

Nandria was yelling before she ran into the farmhouse yard. Bodie heard her and came to the porch door holding Rose. "Miz Minnick? What?"

"Go for the doctor! Oh, God, Bodie, I think she is dying."

At the top of the west field Will came into sight, leading the nag mare while holding a figure up on her back. The sagging figure of a woman. Bodie stumbled back. Nandria lunged to grab Rose from his arms.

"Emmy!" Bodie screamed.

"Go for the doctor, Bodie," Nandria insisted, but he didn't move. "No, wait, you can drive the truck. Drive up to them in the field. Perhaps we can take her to him in town faster than he could come out here."

Bodie remained rooted. She shoved him, forcing him to move to regain his balance. He ran, then, but on past the truck and up into the field.

"Beaver dam!" Nandria swore under her breath. Still carrying the baby, she dashed into the house and into the kitchen to search among the keys hanging on the board for the truck keys. She snatched them off the wall and turned to run to the porch, but Minnick intercepted. "Will found Emmy Lu beaten half to death. We must get her to the doctor."

"Keys?" Minnick demanded.

"Here. Here!"

Minnick grabbed them from her and rushed outside just as Doris stumbled into the kitchen. Kylie, behind her, eyes bright with curiosity, helped himself to one last sugar cookie from the platter on the table when he found himself blocked from further progress to the back yard.

"Girl, what's happened? What's wrong? Is it Freddy?" Doris begged.

Shifting Rose to her shoulder, Nandria guided her mother-in-law to the porch door. Together they looked out to see Minnick stopping the truck near where Bodie and Will could lift the girl's body from the back of the horse into Minnick's arms as he slid over to the passenger's end of the seat. Will got in and drove across the rough field to the gate and onto their lane. He stopped, cranking down his window to call.

"Nandria, she wants you."

Leaving Doris holding onto the door frame, Nandria ran to the truck. Minnick had propped Emmy Lu against Will in order to get out of the truck. He took the baby from Nandria and stood aside to allow her to climb in. It was one of the few times he had touched this infant, and his face registered his surprise that she felt like any other child he had held, even his own sons. But Nandria did not see that near pleasurable reaction. She was busy gathering Emmy Lu against herself so Will was free to drive.

And drive he did. Doris had stumbled out into the yard, and Minnick hurried toward her. They leaned together watching the truck slue out toward the country road. As the dust settled, they stood looking at Rose in his arms.

Bodie arrived with the mare at their lane. Minnick looked up and called roughly. "Bodie, get your hide over here and care for this here… bundle. I'll water and feed thet there horse."

Doris reached to pat the baby still in her husband's arms. "Ain't he sweet, Mr. Minnick?"

"It's a damn 'she'!"

* * * * * * * * * * * * * * * * * * * *

Will, intense, drove fast. Nandria, unable to look at Emmy after her first study of the girl to see what needed to be done for her, stared out at the fleeing rural landscape. At each bump and swerve, Emmy moaned in pain, but only at first. Before they were more than mile on patchily paved road, Emmy went limp and very quiet. Nandria found herself stroking the girl's matted, nut-brown hair and hum-chanting about silver bells and cockle shells and pretty maids all in a row.

Except for that first time when Bodie had picked her up at the railroad crossing in town, Nandria had nearly always ridden in the bed of the truck. From the front seat, Will seemed to be intent on committing suicide as he drove headlong on the wrong side of the road. Yet even that feeling of long disorientation was disappearing in the morass of Nandria's experience of Missouri in the United States of America.

The once-blue truck careened into town. Roused to righteous indignation by its speed and reckless disregard for the safety of his town, Yakes expelled blue phrases his mother had never let him use without the taste of soap and slipped his patrol car into gear to follow. Will slid the truck to a quivering halt in front of Dr. Ricartsen's house. Yakes slammed on his own brakes and leaped out, also leaving his door open as he scurried up to berate those Minnicks. But, seeing Will rush around to the passenger side to help Nandria scramble out and reach in for Emmy, Yakes instead clambered alongside.

"Wha'? Landigocean!" the sheriff swore, aware of the presence of a woman, even this uppity colored one. He elbowed past her. "Here, lemme…" Grunting, he bent over his own protruding gut to lift the girl's thin legs and help Will carry her up the walkway. Nandria ran ahead to open the front door and call for help.

Sadie Bean, large as a cottage in fresh, starched white, greeted them tight–lipped, skilled and gentle.

"In there," she directed and led them to the second examining room. She helped them lay Emmy Lu on the thin–padded table. "All right, then, you men get on out. They obeyed, with backward glances. "You," Sadie gestured to Nandria at the doorway, "come on in here and help me undress her so we can see what's needful."

As Nandria slipped around the retreating men, she heard Sadie's singsong. "Ahhhhh, child, we all knew that this was comin' but didn't one of us stop it. So sorry." The nurse then went tight–lipped and efficient. With Nandria's help, she stripped the girl, barely stifling a groan with each layer removed to show signs of new and old and older batterings.

Ricartsen arrived at the door to the small room. He pushed Nandria out of his way to get to Emmy Lu.

"We've got 'er now, gal," Sadie excused Nandria over his shoulder. "Best you wait with the others out'a the way."

"Yes, yes, of course." Dazed, Nandria stumbled into the hallway where her nausea overwhelmed her. She grabbed a basin from the shelf and vomited into it. Sadie looked over at her and gestured, "Never mind."

Ricartsen looked back for an instant, disgusted. “Shut that damned door!” he growled.

Nandria stood swaying until Will came up and took the basin from her to set it down. He closed the door on the doctor and led his wife into the waiting room to take a seat near the front door. “Here, this’ll help,” he crooned as he set the door slightly ajar to give her fresh air.

Yakes watched from his straight-backed chair on the other side of the room but did not offer any aid. Will sat close beside Nandria, and she leaned heavily into him. Yakes rocked forward, dangling his large hands between his knees. He picked up on a line of questioning he had evidently already begun with Will. Nodding his head toward Nandria, he demanded, “She was with ya?”

“I’ve said that,” Will answered with an edge of impatience.

“Don’t you use that tone with me, Will Minnick! Jus’ ‘cause the last sheriff let you off, don’t expect no favors from me.”

“Will,” Nandria cried softly, “what is going on?”

“Our master detective here is wondering what I was doing out in my family’s field with my wife in the middle of the night.”

“At night? It’s only barely mid-afternoon now,” Yakes protested, seemingly uncomprehending of the sarcasm.

“Night, or day, it is still my family’s property and I was on it with my wife,” Will answered sharply.

“Butcha gotta admit it’s suspicious when ya bring in another body just like before. If’n you ain’t in on the dee-struction, how come ya get to it so damn quick?”

Nandria twisted to peer up at her husband's face. He'd stared at the sheriff and then slowly closed his eyes.

CHAPTER EIGHTEEN

Nodding as though in triumph, Sheriff Yakes sat back in his chair in the doctor's waiting room and, grim–lipped, waited for Will Minnick to confess. He'd seen it before. Not often, as there were more accidents than actual crimes in his rural district. But he prided himself on knowing people, and he was sure Will had something to get off his chest, possibly something horrendous. He was ready.

But that nigger gal shifted from staring at her so–called husband to turn on him.

"Could it be that my husband is attuned to people and their needs and goes to help?" she demanded.

"Yeah," the sheriff admitted reluctantly, "but how'd he know so soon? That's my question. Both times," he added when he saw he'd caused the gal to pause to consider.

"Both? Are you referring to the death of Will's brother, Winfred?"

Will stirred. Though pale, he looked angry enough to be a handful, and Yakes sat up in his chair, wary.

"Let it be, Yakes," Will was saying quietly. He rose. "I'm taking my wife home now. As you could hear and see, she is not feeling well."

When Yakes literally backed away scraping the chair legs on the hard floor, Nandria piped up, "Sheriff Yakes, I assure you that what I have is neither contagious nor infectious."

Despite himself, Will grinned. "It ain't 'catchy,'" he interpreted, and then, soberly, weary again, he turned to his wife. "Do you feel up to coming on home? The sheriff knows where to find me."

Yakes, shaking his head, watched Will guide her lovingly to the door. He couldn't let it go. That ain't no way to treat a nigger. No way. As the door was closing behind them, he called, "You're right, Will Minnick. There is a difference this time. This body's got a head."

He was sure Will had heard him; couldn't help but. Yet the door movement hesitated only a fraction of a second—if at all—and then they were gone.

* *

"Oh, that man!" Nandria growled.

"The sheriff?" Will sighed, but at least he was now talking with her. "He's not so bad, I guess. He was a lot more prideful and stuck on his way being the only way when he first come to town, I remember. He'd pull you over for any and everything, some of which he must have imagined, but it was his way of telling the whole district that he was in charge and he'd brook no nonsense."

"Sounds like what they tell new teachers to do. Begin with strict discipline and only let up gradually on the students as long you were the one in charge."

"Well, it didn't turn out that way for Yakes, I'm afraid. It was only a matter of months that I'd graduated and left. Ma would write how awful it was when his tiny wife..." The area between Will's eyebrows scrunched together in vertical folds as he evidently tried to remember the woman's name. "Patsy Lynn, I believe." His forehead smoothed. He was nearing the section of the country road where you needed to start looking for the end of the Minnicks' lane. "Ma wrote that Patsy Lynn doubled over in pain one day at Owens' store. The doctors in St. Louis found she was filled with bowel cancer. She didn't have a chance. Took a while to die, horribly. Took quite a toll on Yakes. Rumor was that in the end he killed her out of mercy."

"Ah, me," Nandria whispered. "Poor, poor man."

"No one pushed hard enough to find out for sure whether he had killed her or not," Will continued as he pulled into the Minnick lane. "But evidently he did go around for a long time looking guilty. I guess maybe he felt guilty."

"Whether he had helped her die, or whether he had not," Nandria breathed as they slowed through the dip in the lane, now darkened by leaning, high trees. Her face was pale. "Please stop, Will," she added. Her tone made Will look over at her.

Will did stop. The sun was hanging more than halfway down the western sky casting dappled shadow patterns on this side of struggling early growth in the west Minnick field. Nandria had seemed to be watching it with the longing for beauty to refill her joy in life that he had learned was one source of her remarkable strength. He pulled over onto the berm just beyond the tree-lined dip in their long farm drive. He helped her get out, but the expression he saw on her face then was not quite the longing to appreciate what is good in life. Raising his eyebrows, he stepped back out of her way.

He heard her retching among the tall grasses at the edge of the field. "Ah, love," he whispered, but she'd gestured to him to leave her alone. It was several minutes before she came staggering back toward him, wiping her mouth. He hurried to help her.

"Was it this bad with Rose?" he asked as he handed her his huge cotton handkerchief. "So sorry, bunnyduck. I wish you'd told me. Here I thought you'd breezed through."

She gave him a doleful smile, but at least her lips were now unfouled.

"Rose was worth it. You had your work. If my father taught me anything, it was the importance, the near sacredness, of a man's work."

The sun helped reset a tinge of color to her cheeks. Will helped her sit at the edge of his driver's seat with the door hanging open to watch the open field and gathering sky. He eased his bottom onto the running board beside her slender legs and held her hand.

"I was in awe of your parents," he told her. He couldn't imagine what she'd gone through learning of their deaths on the *Athenia*, and without his being there to comfort her.

She shook her head slowly. He could feel the gesture; his guilt simply would not allow him to look at her just yet.

"Thank you. But they are gone." She sighed. "And so is my brother as well as yours. He was beheaded?"

It was Will's turn to sigh, almost laughingly, she was so direct when she wanted truth. "'Face an issue head on, then deal with it with compassion,'" he quoted. "Your father said that, how many times?"

She let out little breaths of painful amusement, remembering. "Hundreds more than you got to hear," she informed him with soft chuckle. "All through our childhoods, Ned's and mine."

"You come from great stock, Nandria Brown Minnick. Strong, caring, thoughtful. But you've got to be exhausted. Let's go on up to the house."

"Not yet, Will," she said, stepping forward and easing down to sit on the running board beside him. He settled his arm around her shoulders and drew her close. "Your parents have had so little time alone together in such a long while . . ."

"You mean like . . . ?" It startled him to think of his folks as having sexual needs or desires for one another. His eyes widened. He closed his mouth over his surprise. "They're too old," he said, trying to make light of the idea, but she would not let him.

"He loves her, Will," she said simply.

Anger rising again within him, Will stiffened. "He's got a funny way of showing it, working her like a mule to keep this . . ." He hesitated, knowing how much she abhorred profanity. ". . .farm," he ended lamely.

She stroked the veins along the length of his hand. "They've been through a lot together." There was something in the way she spoke that last word that gave it a subtle importance, as though whatever it had been they suffered was of lesser concern than the fact that they'd done it in concert. "I do not believe I would leave here if this is what you wanted." She looked up into his face.

"You're saying it was her choice. Her consequences."

"At least partly." She waited for him to digest some of that concept. Then she probed softly, "That must have been quite an accident that killed Winfred. Will, how did you get there so fast since I know you were not part of whatever caused it?" Her whole manner pleaded that she needed to know. She wanted to share.

He answered, choking. "I was chasing them on my bike."

"Ah, Will," she whispered and raised his hand to kiss the tips of his fingers. "I knew it had to be something like that. So he was drunk? Alone? No, you just said you were chasing 'them.'" She shifted to peer at his face. "Who was with him?"

He shook his head, breathing hard and irregularly.

"Nobody knows, do they? Oh, Will, you took the blame. Even with your father. Why?"

"You've seen my father's bull-headedness. What do you think he'd have done to whoever he thought had caused his son's death?"

"When you barely escaped with your life because you were his only other son. Is that it? To protect him as well as whoever was with Fred?" Sighing, she held him close. "Oh, darling. But it may matter now, Will. What will you do if the sheriff wants to blame you for Em . . . ?"

Shaking his head, Will struggled to his feet. She scrambled up beside him to hug him. They rocked in each other's arms until he saw dust clouds jouncing toward them along the farm lane.

"Uh, oh, company," he breathed and pulled her away with him to hide in the tall grasses.

"Whoever it is will see the truck," she whispered the obvious.

"Looks to me like it's Kylie's chariot of infernal mercy. He must have high–tailed it to town to spread the news about Emmy and is coming back to gather more fuel for his gossip. He'll see the truck, all right, but hopefully he won't see us. You want him to pray over you again?"

"Oh, Lord," she chuckled and shuddered, hiding in his arms.

Kylie's 1932 Chevrolet slowed, nearly stopping. The driver took a moment to survey the truck and surrounding grounds. The Minnicks huddled, barely suppressing their laughter. Finally the Chevy pulled on up the drive and stopped beside the farmhouse. A tallish silhouette tending to port crawled out and marched toward the back porch.

"Poor pa," Will laughed.

Nandria giggled. Will looked at her and leaned to kiss her.

* *

What seemed like hours later, the sun barely held sway in the sky. It seemed to be testing colors to advertise its spectacular, coming–soon exit. The Chevy was still parked beside the farmhouse. Nandria sat up, unable to suppress her shivering. Will rose beside her, hand on her arm, arranging his jacket around her and helping her into the passenger seat of the truck.

"Not so much cold as . . . My blood sugar must be low."

"Damn long–winded bastard. I've got to take you into the house, Kylie or no Kylie."

"C–could we go see Emmy Lu instead?"

"Think Ricartsen's gonna give us a warmer welcome?" As Nandria chuckled, Will realized what he'd said. He grinned and drew her close. "Why don't we just go on up to the porch, toss our things into a hamper and leave tonight?" He was almost serious.

"R–Rose, too? In the hamper?"

"If the stork can do it, what can't we? You've paid enough for the privilege."

"S–speaking of Rose, maybe we had better check on her."

"Bodie'll have made sure she is fine," he said.

"He is not all that well–equipped to feed her."

Grinning, Will slid in behind the wheel and reached for the ignition key. The engine sputtered, choked, and then caught.

"You like Bodie very much, do you not?" Nandria asked. "Why is he such a close member of the family?"

As Will parked the truck just inside the barn, he looked into her face. "It's a story I'll want to tell you, soon."

"But not quite yet."

He was shaking his head as he parked and got out to help her out the passenger side of the truck and walk with her up onto the porch. They could hear Kylie's preachy tone in the living room.

"I do not understand you, Brother Minnick. When you look out over this glorious farm you and the Lord have built, how can you not go down on your knees in gratitude to Him?"

"Pastor," Minnick growled, "you did not get to see this place when thet Lord had it all by Hisself."

"You are disrespectful, Grover Minnick. I tell you that to your face in your own home because you need to learn humility."

"As do some others I know," Minnick shot back, cold steel in his voice.

For a moment the pastor was silenced.

Will and Nandria stepped close to the brass bed as Kylie huffed through the kitchen. His huff became audible as he took them in standing there. Doris, pleading as she followed close behind him onto the porch, begged his pardon and wanted him to stay. Red–faced with anger, he refused to acknowledge her. It was Bodie's rising from the rocking chair with the baby in his arms that startled them into quiet. No one had observed him in the grayness of the corner of the porch.

"The royal princess's been wantin' you, Miz Minnick."

Nandria hurried to him and took Rose. She sat with the baby and quickly constructed a nest of privacy with her blankets.

Ignoring the others, Kylie zeroed in on Will. "I thought you must be in the field working with the stock when I saw your truck parked on the berm."

"Taking stock," Will murmured, nodding.

"I tell you, Will Minnick, I am about worn out begging the Lord's mercy for this family. Your actions . . ."

Doris wiggled her way under his arm with its pointing finger raised toward Will. She huddled at his side. "Reverend, Sir, it was good of you to come in our hour of need."

Minnick, in the doorway from the kitchen, nearly choked at her words. He drew Doris to him all but roughly by the arm. "Best let him go, woman. He'll be wantin' to pray over Emmy Lu."

Will's eyebrows raised as he watched Kylie's reaction to his father's words. "Of course you've been ministering to Emmy Lu, haven't you, Reverend Kylie?"

At the edge in Will's voice, Kylie brushed by him out the door and down the two steps. Doris hurried to follow, but Will caught her in his arms, soothing her as they listened to Kylie's Chevy start up and drive away.

"But, Willy, the reverend…"

"Never mind, Mama. The Lord sees us."

"How kin you be sure, Wee Willy?"

Minnick moved toward them and gathered his wife to himself. "How else could He keep His thumb on us like He does, if'n He didn't know right where we was?"

Bodie spoke up for the first time, uncharacteristically bitter. "It's Emmy Lu he oughta be prayin' over."

Will gently herded his family and Bodie into the kitchen. "Probably where he's headed now that we've pointed that out to him. The man cannot ignore congregational expectations, whether or not he could skip over any suggestion of ours."

Nandria listened to them talk low just beyond her line of sight into the kitchen. Doris must have been crying, but quietly now. She could picture Minnick holding his wife gently and Bodie and Will studiously looking the other way to keep from embarrassing them. These Missouri farmers had their ways, many of them more tender than she'd realized when she'd first stepped off that train in Boonetown.

"It's been some kinda day," Bodie muttered. He ducked out past Nandria into the yard with merely a wave. The sun had all but completed its glorious setting, leaving now only the western horizon remembering the paint it had put to canvas with fading tints and ghosts of colors to warm its way into night.

"Bed time for us, too, Mother," Minnick coaxed softly as he talked only to her.

Doris was giggling, and Nandria sighed, relieved.

"Mother Minnick. Superior. Makes me feel Papish, it does. Mebbe I oughta have them beads, Mister Minnick? For prayin'."

In the beat that followed, Nandria could picture Minnick looking blankly at his son for help.

"Whatever you want, Mama," Will assured her while nodding to his father that he understood what she was asking. "Prayer beads might just help if you want them."

"Might be they'd help lift thet thumb?" Minnick's voice was diminishing. Evidently they were moving off to their bedroom.

"Kin we have a hymn–sing then? The reverend don't seem to like them, neither."

Their door closed.

Will stepped out onto the porch where Rose was giving up on nursing and surrendering to sleep in her mother's arms. Will took her, checked that her bottom was dry and laid her tenderly in her crib, humming a few low bars of gentle "…in the tree top …cradle will rock…" until he was sure she was settled. He came then to sit on the floor beside Nandria in the rocker. He laid his head on her knees, and she stroked his hair.

"So sorry, love," he whispered. "Why did I ever get you mixed up in this?"

After a few moments Nandria asked softly, "Will, why was the sheriff so hard on you? Why isn't he arresting Horace Bratton?"

He twisted to look up at her. His smile held little warmth. "Have you ever seen Horace when he was drunk? Not many men have the balls to face him even sober." His smile changed. "Let alone threaten to run him over with a tractor, my little warrior wife."

"Oh! Do you think he bullied Emmy Lu instead of coming after me?"

"We won't let Rose out of our sight, but don't take this on as your fault, Nandria. It wasn't. Tomorrow I'll teach you how to handle a pistol. I should have done it a long time ago."

"I can handle a pistol, Will. It is the hate that I do not know what to do with."

CHAPTER NINETEEN

Nandria awoke to a sound she wasn't sure she'd heard. Quietly so as not to disturb Will, she slid out of their brass bed and into her robe to check Rose, who was just beginning to fuss.

"All right, little princess," she whispered, picking her up. "Let's make sure you are dry and warm and fed full to the top of that little tummy." Smiling, she tended to the baby's needs and sat to nurse her. *Ah, little one, how you are growing! Your daddy said you sat up on your own for more than a minute, but you know how prejudiced he is in your favor. Me, too, if you must know the truth. What a joy . . .*

A sound again. Faint again, but not distorted by sleep. With Rose in her arms, Nandria stepped to the kitchen to listen, but she could hear both Minnick and Doris snoring comfortably. She moved to the porch's outer door.

Something, like a child crying.

She stepped outside, listening carefully. The sound again, this time definitely from the bowels of the barn. Timidly Nandria crossed the lightless lawn and approached the dark barn. At the open door, she shifted Rose on her shoulder and peered inside. She waited as her eyes worked to adapt to the even deeper darkness. Listening, she heard only the scurryings, probably of night-feeding rodents. Their odor added pungency to the hay and oil, sweat and old cow droppings. She shuddered, but knew the presence of rats and mice was inevitable on a farm. Her only concern could be to be sure they had no toehold inside the house.

Again a scuffling sound, this time definitely accompanied by a child's whimpering cry.

"Hello?" she called tentatively. "Is someone in here? I thought I heard someone. Hello?"

For a moment she held her breath, wondering if it could be Horace Bratton or one of his brothers, but she shook her head. No, that was a child. She was sure of it. Clutching Rose to her, Nandria moved deeper into the barn. Rose whimpered protest.

"Hush, little rosebud. Mommy needs to listen. Someone is here," she whispered. Gathering her courage, she again called aloud. "I know you are here. I can feel you, even if I cannot see you. Please come out so we can talk. I shall not hurt you."

At the distinct sound of a struggle in the far back corner, Nandria startled, twisting to run away to the house. But a ragamuffin of a boy rushed to her and tugged at her robe.

"Please, Missus!" the child cried. "He's got a rope!"

"A rope? Why? Who?" Nandria stammered, but she was turning in the direction the child was pulling.

"Uncabodie. He's got it all 'round his neck!"

Confused for the moment, Nandria suddenly realized what the child was telling her. She dashed after him around the end of the thresher and into the back corner of the barn.

Bodie—it had to be his skinny silhouette darker on darkness—balanced tiptoe on a bale of hay. As she got near, she could see the noose around his neck dangling from the rope looped over a back beam far above them and tied securely above the empty horse stall. How had he managed to tie his hands behind him and still rig such a set–up? He was laughing and crying, but he groaned when he saw her holding her infant Rose. He needed only to lose his balance or to kick away the bale to be hung.

"Situs, Situs," Bodie stammered, "how could you bring the Miz into this?"

She had been hurtling toward him to save him, but at his accusation of the child, Nandria stopped abruptly and glared at Bodie, her eyes snapping even in the dim light.

"How dare you! Laying guilt on a child! Hurting two! Do you think that just because she is a baby, that my Rose will not be affected by what you are doing here?"

"Now, Miz, I never meant to hurt no kid," he wheezed, dancing a few desperate steps on the hay.

"Then get down from there! At once!" Nandria actually stamped her foot.

Struggling to regain his footing, Bodie nearly kicked the hay bale loose. With a cry, Situs dashed to prop it up.

Unimpressed, Nandria hollered, "Stop fooling around and get down."

"A… mebbe a little help, Miz?" he wheezed.

"Do you promise never to pull such a fool, crazy, cowardly stunt again?" she demanded. At his nod, she relented. "Well, all right, then."

Nandria laid the baby in a nest of hay to one side and stepped close to lift and steady Bodie as Situs climbed onto the bale and strained to loosen and push the noose from his neck. As Bodie fell free, the three tumbled together onto the barn floor, Nandria grunting as they fell on top of her. Bodie rasped for breath; Situs whimpered.

"Oh, Miz, the babe!" Bodie cried.

Struggling to a sitting position, Nandria stretched to one side to reach for Rose. She picked bits of straw from her baby, her own hair and robe. She giggled.

"Rose is fine, Bodie. We are all . . . Situs, are you sure you are all right?"

Snot–nosed, he raised his face to hers and nodded.

She giggled again, then, seeing their faces reflecting their horror, laughed, weakly at first and then more strongly as they, incredulous and then included, laughed with her. They rolled into each other and hugged, laughing in sheer relief and thanksgiving.

As they settled from their near hysteria, Situs, wide–eyed, clung to Bodie and wiped his nose on the upper sleeve of his tattered jacket. Bodie bent close against him.

"Thank you, Boy," he whispered, and then nudged his back to send him off. "You scurry on home now, Site. Your ma's got 'nuff grief with your sister. She don't need to be worryin' herself over you, too. Skeedaddle, now. Go!"

Looking back at them, Situs, no more than five or six, skinny and ragged, but fundamentally clean and mended, lifted a small hand toward them. His terrible pallor was pinking. Relieved, he turned again and scurried out the back of the barn into the night. Nandria hacked loose the odd rope knot tying Bodie's hands behind him.

"How…?"

"It's kinda like a slip knot. Easy to do, but the more you struggle agin it, the tighter it gets. Got purdy tight when I was stepping through my arms…" His weathered face distorted, and Nandria turned away to give him a moment to himself. With Rose in her lap, she rested finally sitting beside Bodie against the fateful bale. She stroked her baby's cheek and tears glistened in her eyes.

"Situs is Emmy Lu's little brother?" she asked.

"Yep. Their ma's my sister's gal."

"Hence the 'uncabodie.' You did not enlist the child's help with this, then."

"Lord forbid, Miz Minnick. But I wasn't in no position to keep him away once I was in it."

Nandria rocked the baby and stroked her back until Rose fell asleep on her mother's shoulder.

"My father," she started quietly, "neither of my parents, actually, would let my brother or me ask someone about something personal if we were merely curious. Whatever you tell me now, I will not say anything to anyone if you tell me not to. Not even Will."

Bodie glanced over at her, confused. With the onset of relief, he looked more and more dazed, pained and embarrassed. Nandria reached for his hand to lift it to Rose's back.

Snatching back his hand as though he did not deserve to touch the child, Bodie crumpled, shoulders shaking, sobs stifled as best as he could. Nandria waited there beside him until he regained a degree of control.

"I shouldn't hold thet wee princess Rose. Not even touch her. Every child . . . Every kid I'm supposed to protect . . ." His voice trailed off. Nandria waited, frowning. "Ev'ry child I'm supposed to protect," he began again after a time, "I end up hurtin." He turned away.

"Emmy Lu? You are not the one who beat her!?"

"Lord, no! I wouldn't!" He twisted to catch himself on all fours and stood up unsteadily. Swaying slightly on both feet, he peered down on Nandria. "It would'a been best." With tears spilling, he stared up the rope. "Would'a," he murmured to himself. Staggering back, he nearly tipped into the propped–up thresher. Bodie regained his balance and shuffled past her out the back door of the barn.

Nandria sat a long time humming to her sleeping Rose. At last she got up awkwardly and strode to the front of the barn seeing now what had been dark to her eyes when she'd entered. And yet seeing so little, even of what was immediately around her. Father would have understood. *Father would have intervened before it got to what had happened here tonight.*

She had not seen. She had not even guessed at the depth of Bodie's blaming himself. For what? For what had happened to Emmy Lu? Or was there more?

Still musing, Nandria stepped outside. The cool, dark air caressed her cheek, bringing her to gently back from horror to reality. Grateful, she stepped toward the house and sucked air to feel and almost see a dark figure hurtling toward her. She gasped and clutched little Rose, turning to flee back into the barn.

"Nandria?" It was Will's voice in the darkness of the night, racing to her. "Nandria, darling, what?" His hands checked the baby and then her.

"Fine, Will. We are fine," she exhaled, but her voice betrayed her.

He drew her close, supporting the baby in her arms but not trying to take Rose from her although she was shaking.

"It's all right, love," he whispered, looking around for any sign of danger. "I'm here. It's all right."

"Oh, Will!" She pressed into him. Gradually her trembling subsided and his eyes dark–adapted enough to know she was not afraid, only drained by whatever had happened.

"I thought I saw Bodie . . ." he prompted.

She shook her head and leaned away to look up at him. "Do not ask me, Will. Please. I promised."

"You're all right?" He searched her eyes, but in the darkness he could not be certain of what he saw. Yet he was sure she would tell him if she weren't well. "All right, then, bunnyduck," he agreed finally. "I won't ask what happened. But can you tell me what he said?"

"Nothing. Truly, nothing at all," she said, leaning her head against his shoulder and walking with him toward the house. "But, Will, he carries enormous guilt."

Will's expression would have told her, 'I know,' but, head down in her own grief, she did not see.

CHAPTER TWENTY

The sun rose, revealing everything that wise eyes will see, though Nandria was sleeping the unconsciousness of the exhausted. Will had fed his father, mother and Bodie and the three men had trudged to the fields. They'd let Nandria sleep in until Rose squawked her displeasure at not being the center of attention as soon as she'd let her wants be known. Rose gurgled a smile at her mother's face appearing above her crib, drawn and blurry. That haggard face dissolved into smiles of love as she picked up her cooing daughter.

"Hi, princess," Nandria laughed.

"We ready?" Doris asked brightly at the kitchen doorway.

"Uh, ready?"

"The menfolk told me not to hurry you, but you are taking me to town. Don't you remember?"

"Oh. Yes. Yes, of course. We do have quite the shopping list, do we not, Mother Minnick?"

"Mr. Minnick didn't give me no money, but Mr. Owens'll know to put it all on the Minnick tab, like always." Doris giggled and stepped closer to ask low, "You think Mr. Owens will have them beads?"

It took Nandria a moment to grope through her fog to remember the conversation of the evening before. "The Prayer Beads? We shall see. The men are gone?"

"Oh, yes. Will fixed breakfast, but the inside of the pancakes was doughy. Not like yours, girl. They've been out in the fields for a long time. Funny you didn't hear 'em clomping past you. The Mister never steps quiet. Never did." She grinned as though proud of her husband's firm step through life.

Nandria finished changing and dressing the baby. She carried her into the kitchen and set her into the wooden high chair that Will had brought down from the attic. Nandria stuffed small pillows around her fat little legs and hips to prop her up, though she hardly needed them any longer. Most of the time.

No one had tackled the dishes, of course. Doris cut a slice of cold pancake from Will's plate to set on the tray for Rose to stuff glob by glob into her mouth. The baby banged the tray and laughed.

"Will you look at this wee boy? He's settin' up near on his own already. So smart. So strong."

Rose was sitting up straight–backed, depending very little on the pillows. But that would last only for a while, and then she would sag, Nandria knew. So much of the world sagged when you weren't looking.

* *

Having successfully driven all that way on what still seemed the wrong side of the road, Nandria parked the farm truck just beyond the front of Owen's general store. She twisted to pick up Rose from the seat between herself and Mother Minnick, then went around the back of the truck to help Mother Minnick out on the passenger side.

"You're not comin' in?"

"Not for a little minute," Nandria said, taking a written note out of the pocket in Doris's jacket. She pressed it into her mother-in-law's hand. "Just give Mr. Owens your note, and he will know what we need. You will be fine, Mother Minnick. I shall return soon." She squeezed the woman's hand around the note. The fingers were so gnarled.

"You do think Mr. Owen's will have them, you know, them beads?"

Turning from having started away, Nandria nodded. "If he has not found them before I get back, I shall help him find them for you." It was funny which assurances got through to Doris, and which did not, no matter how often or patiently repeated.

Nandria stood with the baby in her arms, waiting to see that Doris had entered the store with its left front window frame repainted a delicious pale yellow. The far window frame had not yet merited or the Owens had not yet scraped together enough paint or money to replace its peeling gray. A little at a time. Everyone in Boonetown knew that, was constrained by that. It was the way things were. And had been for how many, many years.

When she heard Mrs. Owens hearty, "Why, hello, Doris Minnick! How are you?" Nandria resettled Rose into her carrier sling and started toward the doctor's home. But as she passed the sheriff's office, she veered abruptly to go in.

Yakes sat slouched in his tilted chair with his feet propped up across his desk. His hand rested lightly on his belly. He'd begun to rise at the sound of someone entering. But when he saw who it was, he settled back, sullen.

"I would like to see your prisoner," Nandria stated as she approached. When he looked blank, she spelled it out. "Your prisoner, Horace Bratton."

"Ain't got no prisoner by thet name."

"You mean you have not yet arrested him for beating Emmy Lu near to death?"

"No call to." He shrugged as Nandria flared. "Doc says she could'a got bruised up from bein' throwed offa thet horse."

"That worn-out mare could not have thrown a three-year-old."

"Nevertheless, we gotta wait 'til Emmy Lu wakes up 'nuff to tell us what happened."

"And if she never wakes up?" Nandria asked sharply, sickened that she was saying aloud the unthinkable.

He shrugged again. "Then I guess we never know."

"Sheriff, it has happened before. You know what happened. The whole town knows."

He drew back his feet and set them on the floor with a clump that startled little Rose. "You kin know whatever suits yer fancy, but the Law's gotta have proof." He glared at her.

She would not back down. "But you have talked with Bratton, surely. What does he say?"

"You think if'n I had, that I'd tell you what he said?"

"Meaning you have not even gone out to question him?"

He half-rose from his chair and leaned on his fists on his desk. "Time you was on yer way, girl. I don't answer to the likes of you. Go on, now, git!"

She could smell his sour breath. Her shoulders lifted as she determined to stand her ground in front of him. But, when Rose fussed in the sling, she frowned her disgust instead and left.

She marched toward Dr. Ricartsen's, each stride pounding out her fury with the incompetent coward of a sheriff. She was still fuming when she got to the doctor's door and knocked. It was long habit, even on a bedroom door at her parents' home if that door was closed. She glanced at the hand-printed sign hanging on the door just off kilter at the level of her eyes. 'Just come on in—welcome,' it said. Shaking her head at her loss of control of herself, Nandria opened the door and stepped into the waiting room that had once been foyer and parlor of the formal old home.

Sadie Bean ducked around the corner from the hall to the examining rooms. She was carrying a sloshing basin of who knew what liquid with two or three small blood-stained towels hanging from her ample forearm. Sadie's face lighted when she saw that it was Nandria.

"So you've come for her, then? Good."

"Come for? Who?" Nandria startled. And then hope seeped in. "Emmy? Then she's well enough to be cared for at home?"

"Well enough?" The woman stopped her progress across the room. The liquid slowed its sloshing and settled. It jiggled again when Sadie shook her head. "In my humble opinion, that gal will nev . . ." She bit her lip and started again her march toward what must have been the main kitchen of the old home. Over her shoulder she said the words that Nandria had hoped never to hear. "I reckon she can die better among them as loves her then she can here." She disappeared, but Dr. Ricartsen entered from his office.

"Who is it, Mrs. Bean? Oh, it's you. Taking Em to the Minnicks', are you? I guess that is better than to any of the Brattons."

"You will be tending her no longer, Doctor?" Nandria asked.

"I may drop by the farm if I'm out that way. I need to check on Mrs. Minnick now and again anyway." He sighed, his eyes dark with fatigue. "But I don't expect I can do much more than has been done."

"Too far gone," Sadie said as she came back without basin and wiping her hands and forearms with a clean towel. "Beaten too long and too often."

"We *surmise* that, Mrs. Bean. We don't *know* it," he admonished.

"You yourself've set her broke arm and fixed her halter slings for two collar bones, at least."

He shook his head, admitting that that had been so, but not admitting her argument won over his objection. She grimaced at him, presumably for stubbornness, then sighed heavily.

"She never woke up." Sadie's sausage–like fingers splayed. Her gray eyes held both pity and anger.

Ricartsen drew up his shoulders. "And undoubtedly never will," he added clinically. He turned to Nandria. "Are you ready to take her now? I have other patients . . . No?"

"I have only Will's mother with me now. But Will and I will come back."

"Today?" Ricartsen seemed impatient with the delay.

"As soon as Will comes in from the fields."

Appearing to make the best of an unpleasant situation, Ricartsen nodded and strode back to his office, closing the door behind him.

Sadie stepped closer to complain under her breath. "'Other patients' he has some hope of getting payment from. No, that's not fair. He ain't as like that as I am. He'd let folks go months and years not even giving him foodstuff on their bills." She took one last vicious swipe with the towel on her left forearm and tucked the damp cloth in her armpit so both hands were free to gesture angrily. "It's them Brattons. Horace especially. Them hangin' around is got us spooked. Never comes in. Never sees her. Just him or Jude or Irwayne, one or all of 'em hangin' 'round. Sometimes I turn and one of their ugly faces is staring in the window." She flung her hands outward in a quick, violent gesture as though scattering all three Brattons to distant places.

When she had calmed, Nandria asked quietly, "May I see her?"

Sadie studied her openly, nodded once as though in approval. "Come," she said and led the way into the back hall.

"She has never spoken about what happened?"

Sadie shook her head vigorously and opened a door into a tiny, dimly lit closet of a room in the back corner of the house. As Nandria entered, Sadie spat low, "What's to say? Don't them busted bones in her face tell it all?"

* *

Nandria was shuddering when she emerged from Dr. Ricartsen's. She stood a moment by the tall, ancient lilac clump to regain her composure before hurrying on to Owens' store to fetch Doris and the groceries.

"S–s–s–Sugarlips," a low voice hissed. Nandria jumped, clutching Rose to herself. When she'd regained control, she turned angrily on Horace Bratton, half hidden in the tall stalks beginning to bend under their weight of opening, scented flowers.

"What do you want?" Nandria snapped, peeved with herself for even conversing with this foul man.

He leered and opened his hole of a mouth above his unkempt beard when they both heard sharp heel strikes approaching on sidewalk. Horace puckered his lips and waved Nandria a smacking kiss before he slid away out of sight. Nandria stood trembling, angry with Bratton and with herself and, she had to admit, a trifle frightened.

"Crikey," she whispered.

The heel strikes approached, passed, and then stopped. Nandria looked up. A gray–haired lady was peering at her. The woman appeared surprisingly small for the heavy sound her footsteps had generated. Under her sagging–brimmed black fine straw hat, her broad dress collar poured out over the worn velvet collar of her cloth jacket. Stuck into that dress collar at odd angles was a myriad of straight pins and needles. Some had bits and lengths of colored thread dangling or wrapped about them.

The little woman turned and came back a few steps to approach Nandria and the baby.

"Are you all right, dear?" she ventured, her voice quavering but not quiet. "You're blanched white around the gills."

The description struck Nandria as funny and she giggled, then struggled to keep from crying.

"Ah, I understand. You've just been to see poor dear Emmy Lu. That is enough to take the starch out of anyone with an ounce of compassion. You all right? Would you like me to take you on back in to Doc's house to sit down for a minute? No? Then, be well, child. Life is no bed of roses despite what the fools on the radio sing about." Trilling what sounded like, "When the moon comes over the mountain..." off key under her breath, the woman turned and bustled away. Again her heel strikes proclaimed a woman far larger than she was, and again making Nandria wince that such positivity must jar the woman's spine. Whoever that kind-hearted lady was, she did not look back.

Grateful for the distraction and the thoughtfulness, Nandria took several deep breaths. Composed again now, Nandria stroked Rose's back as she hurried toward Owens' store.

* *

That evening, Nandria smoothed the quilt on the mattress she was sitting on in the bed of the Minnick truck and watched the faded pale reflected colors on the clouds opposite the sunset as they drove into town.

"Oh, Lord," she whispered, unable to formulate any coherent prayer, unable even to understand what exactly she was praying for.

The truck rattled to a stop in front of Ricartsen's, and Will came around to help her down. Minnick had started up the walkway, but his usual marching gait was slowed.

Ricartsen opened his front door. "Couldn't get here any earlier, I take it."

Minnick halted, peering at the physician. When he did answer, his lips barely moved. "Might'a, if'n you'd come to help in the fields."

His neck and jawline reddening, Ricartsen nodded. "Well, couldn't be helped, I guess. Come in."

The doctor led Minnick and Will, followed by Nandria, into the hall and back to Emmy Lu's tiny room. She lay wrapped in frayed blankets, her dark and swollen face centered on a shiny-smooth satin embroidered pillow. A pink thread 'L' peeked from beside her right temple. Three horizontal snippets of loops and a few tight stitches peeked from the left. When Will lifted Emmy in his arms, Nandria was to one side and was evidently the only one to notice his wince. But as he opened his closed eyes, his expression told her to say nothing. She bit her lip and looked down at the pillow where 'LOVE' had comforted Emmy Lu's battered head.

"Is this the doctor's?"

"No, gal, little Situs brought it days ago," Sadie answered.

"May I take it for Emmy then?"

Sadie nodded, her eyes glistening with tears, which she wiped hastily with the back of her hand. "That family ain't got much except that L O V E, but that they got in abundance. I think Emmy was the one who'd been workin' on that pillow. Situs tried to finish."

Remembering the child's devotion to Uncabodie in the Minnick barn, Nandria nodded, understanding. She gathered the rest of Emmy's few things from Sadie Bean and hurried to follow the nurse out after the men.

Will, his face pale but his eyes determined, waited impatiently near the front door. His father, standing in his way with its knob in his hand, argued low, "I seen ya wince, Willard. Why don't ya just give up bein' stubborn and lemme carry the girl?"

"Please, pa," Will growled, gesturing with his chin for him to open the door and step out of the way. "I've got her. You just drive slow and careful, all right?"

"Here, this gal needs to be settled in," Doc Ricartsen snapped, stepping behind Minnick to open it, forcing Minnick to move or get hit.

Gratefully, Will moved on outside. Ricartsen and Nandria hurried ahead of him to climb into the bed of the truck to receive her. They settled Emmy Lu as comfortably as they knew how to do for her. When he was at last satisfied, Ricartsen jumped down. Nandria bent toward him.

"Thank you for doing what you could, Doctor."

He whipped his head around to face her. "I do not appreciate sarcasm, especially from . . . you."

She rocked back, erect from the waist up. "Sir, you do not know sarcasm if you think . . ." She snapped her mouth closed and twisted to scoot back to comfort Emmy Lu as Will clambered up on the other side of the mattress. She looked at him, asking with her eyes if he was all right. He wiped sweat from his forehead, but shook his head and laid his head back against the truck's rear window and closed his eyes.

Sadie sidled up beside the doctor on the walkway from his house. "Ever since thet mammy in 'Gone With the Wind' . . ."

"Hattie McDaniel," Ricartsen supplied the name off–handedly.

"Yeah, McDaniel. Ever since she won thet Oscar, you been strugglin' with the idea mebbe Negroes are human, ain't ya?" Sadie questioned mildly.

Ricartsen looked over to stare at her a moment. As Minnick pulled away, Nandria glanced back at the doctor standing in the road in front of his office home. They locked eyes. Ricartsen appeared shaken.

CHAPTER TWENTY-ONE

Horace and Irwayne passed a jug between them as they sat in their battered truck on the berm of the country road near the turn-off for Minnick's lane. Irwayne bounced to a tune in his head while Horace smoldered in irritation, rising to anger with his brother's fourteenth shaking of his torso and elbows to the line-end, "Goody, goody!" Horace was near to explosion when Irwayne suddenly lunged upright, alert.

"Somebody's comin', Horey," Irwayne cried low.

"It's Jude. I kin smell him."

Chuckling, Irwayne pressed down the door handle and crowded over to let Jude in, but Horace roared at being pushed. Both brothers cowered.

"Sorry, Horace," Irwayne grimaced, but Horace ignored him to demand a report from Jude as he clambered in.

"So, stupid, who was at the house?"

"Just like you thought, Horey. Only Bode 'n' the old lady 'n' pickaninny," Jude gathered a grin to punctuate his report, but it was a smile dampened by the fear that that was not the news his oldest brother had been wanting to hear. He watched Horace's expression with growing apprehension.

"So they are fetchin' Em from Doc's," Horace growled.

Letting out his held breath, Jude blinked to realize that Horace's anger was directed toward the Minnicks rather than at himself.

Belching from the homebrew, Irwayne blurted the first thing that came to him mind. "But ya said she weren't no use to ya, Horey."

"She's still mine!" the man roared. Disgusted with his brothers and the world, Horace heaved upright in the driver's seat. "Come on." Without waiting for Jude to close the door behind him, Horace turned the key in the ignition and drove into the Minnicks' lane without turning on his headlights.

He parked off the drive near the bottom of the front lawn area, lights still off. He swallowed one more large swig from the jug and pushed at Irwayne close beside him. "Check the front," he growled. "Jude, be sure nobody ain't in the barn. I'm gonna have a look–see fer myself."

At the kitchen table, Doris chuckled at Rose as Bodie, seated in his place against the wall, helped the baby stay sitting up. Rose was laughing as his crooked finger threatened and threatened and occasionally tickled her belly.

"Ain't he just the cutest?" Doris laughed aloud every time the child giggled. Pale now, Doris was obviously tiring even faster than the baby. She turned in Nandria's seat and glanced at the window above the sink. "Agh!" she screamed and pointed. "A face! I seen a face!"

Scooting the baby on her bottom diagonally across the table toward Doris, Bodie leaped up and grabbed his shotgun where it leaned against the wall by the door to the porch.

"Shut them lights, Missus! Grab the babe and shut them lights!"

Barely waiting to be sure Mrs. Minnick would be able to handle little Rose and still pull the chain to turn off the dangling light, Bodie chased across the porch and outside. A figure loomed near the elm. Whoever had been at the kitchen window, he must have hurtled around the back corner of the house trying to escape. That shaggy, it had to be a Bratton who had scared the missus.

"Gotcha!" Bodie muttered and raised the shotgun. The figure stopped, large mouth open. And then long, gorilla arms flailed and it bolted back around the east side of the house. Limp-running, and struggling to keep the shotgun lifted in front of himself, Bodie gave chase. He reached the lawn near the front porch steps just in time to see two dark figures piling into a pickup at the bottom of the lawn. The truck groaned into life and clattered across the lawn to turn itself around, driving off without lights.

A cloud unshuttered the moon and Bodie could see yet a third dark figure. It clung onto the truck's bed wall, unable to climb inside with the truck's jouncing movement. Flailing first an arm which finally grabbed hold, than a leg flung out in its own desperate, solo dance alongside the fleeing truck, the figure howled its anguish, if not actual pain.

Chuckling, Bodie allowed the shotgun to lower and rest on its butt in a clump of wild grass in what had been the Minnicks' front lawn. "Good riddance to bad rubbish," Bodie called after what he knew must have been the Brattons. He bit his lip, knowing that, if pushed, he would have had to admit to Sheriff Yakes that he had not seen one face well enough to positively identify. He patted the shotgun's barrel. "Good ol' gal, Becky Sue. Good ol' gal."

* *

In the dip under the bending trees, Horace slowed the pickup just long enough for Jude to clamber into the truck bed. Irwayne cranked down his dusty window the remainder of its way, and gaped out into the night, west and south.

"Lights, Horey!" Irwayne warned. "Somebody's comin' from town!"

Gunning the engine, the eldest brother took off again, headlamps still unlighted, making for the county end of the Minnick drive. Jude was sent sprawling into the bed of the truck.

"Double damnation," Horace groused, but eased his swearing if not his foot on the gas pedal as they rocketed up out of the dip. He ducked his head to peer under the top rim of the steering wheel to his right to judge how slowly the approaching vehicle was going. "Should make it," he swore with accompanying colorful language.

At the intersection with the county road, he peeled to the left, sending Jude spread-eagle again amid empty jugs in the bed of the pickup. The Bratton truck disappeared just ahead of the none-too-bright headlight range of the on-coming truck.

Had Minnick not been concentrating on making the slow turn into their drive as smoothly as possible, he'd have seen the Brattons' dust settling. But Minnick's concern was with making this journey as painless as he could for Emmy Lu. He drove up and parked as near as he could on the drive by the back porch, and lurched out of the truck and to its tailgate to intercept his son.

"I got her, boy," he ordered. "I carry her this time."

Doris stood in the way as Minnick tried to carry Emmy in. Will helped Nandria down and took Rose so his wife was free to take care of Emmy Lu. He hurried forward to lead his mother out of the way as Nandria followed Minnick into the house and up the stairs to the second floor.

"I didn't know we was gonna have company," Doris told Will plaintively. "She gonna be with you out here on the porch?"

Will checked Rose and set her carefully into her crib and rocked it gently. "No, Mama. Nandria wanted her with us, but Pa wanted Emmy upstairs."

"Emmy Lu? Why, that's Fred's gal."

Will closed his eyes and stroked his daughter's back for a moment before being able to answer.

"That was a long while ago, Mama."

"She gonna stay long? Is she still so purdy?"

Will caught his breath and cleared his throat. "I'm not sure how long she'll be with us. And, no, she's not quite as pretty as she was. Not quite."

Doris leaned to brush her lips against the baby's cheek, then hustled off for the kitchen to fill the kettle and set it on the stove. Over her shoulder she gave Will information that made him catch his breath again.

"I'm sure glad them Bratton boys is gone. They was carryin' on so, she'd'a never slept."

Will smoothed his daughter's blanket over her as she lay sound asleep, in her crib. Pressing his hand into his aching side, he hurried into the kitchen. "Horace was here?" he asked, working to keep his voice quiet, though his free hand was clenching into a fist.

"I can't keep 'em straight, all of 'em lookin' nasty as their pa," Doris spat as she set a now–dry pan onto the shelf beside the stove. She looked up at Will as she straightened. "The old one, for sure. I remember how he used to pick on Winfred. Nasty," she snapped, wiping her palms down the front of her apron. She turned as she heard heavy footsteps coming down the staircase, smiling fondly as Minnick entered the kitchen.

"Come, Mother. It's been a long day," her husband said wearily merely acknowledging Will with a single nod.

"Of course, Mr. Minnick dear. Good night, Willy. Don't let the bedbugs bite," she added mischievously and followed her man to their room at the front of the house.

"Good night, ma," Will called softly. "Sleep well." He went to the stove to set the kettle away from the burner. At a sound at the back porch steps, he spun. "Rose!" he exhaled, and ran, crouching, ready to fight. "Bodie, it's you. I was ready to take your head off."

The old man stood there blinking before he could grin and lower the shotgun to point to the floor. "Just me, Will, though I do say you could'a got holes blowed in ya like a screen door. I got this loaded with buckshot," Bodie exclaimed, setting his shotgun against the kitchen wall again near the porch door. "It's only ol' me."

Gradually Will straightened to full height. He lifted his chin toward the shotgun. "The Brattons?"

"They paid a visit a while back, but they's allergic to shotguns, seems like. Just had to wave Becky Sue 'round a bit."

Will filled the top glass globe of the percolator he'd bought for his mother at Owens' store. He stood a moment drawing in the peace-at-home aroma of fresh coffee grounds. "Thanks, Bodie," he said quietly as he sat at the oak table.

Bodie sat down as well, his eyes squinting, his fingers testing and retesting the serrated edge of the knife at his place setting. "Yakes ain't goin' after him, is he?" he asked finally. "Never even questioned the S.O.B., did he?"

Will shook his head. They sat in tense silence until Will got up to check on Rose. As he returned from the porch, he stopped to pour out and carry over two mugs of strong coffee.

Bodie eyed his shotgun. His words were so low, Will might not have heard them if he hadn't been coming back to sit at the table.

"Guess it's our'n then."

Realizing that the small man was addressing the shotgun, Will passed him the mug and bent to stare into his weathered face. "No, Bodie. No."

"Ya gonna quote me thet 'The Lord giveth, and the Lord taketh away' stuff?" Bodie demanded. "Well, the Lord taketh, right 'nuff, but only after it's finally a mercy."

Will sat and wrapped his fingers around his too-warm mug. "Have you been drinking, Bode?" he asked quietly.

Bodie flared. "Am I drunk? Is that what yer sayin'? Listen, I ain't had a drop since . . . Not fer years, though a'times I retch with wantin'," he added low.

Will nodded. "Sorry to ask. I know it's been hard. But you've got to know that even if you get Horace, there's a ton of Brattons'll come after you.

"I gots lots'a shells," Bodie muttered, patting his bulging pocket.

"And no will to live?

"After what I . . ."

In the awkward silence between them then, Will raised the mug to his lips and sipped but tasted nothing. Finally Bodie's sloped shoulders relaxed forward, and he looked over to face this young man he had known since the boy was in diapers.

"Whyn't ya let me talk to yer pa?"

Will stared into the coffee long moments before speaking. "I couldn't at first. He'd have killed you, and then where would Ma be with him in jail? Now, it won't change anything. We're leaving soon." He raised his eyes to look at his friend. "Will you just let it be, Bode? And leave the shotgun with me?"

"This ain't yer fight, Will."

"If I need Becky Sue to protect Nandria and the baby?"

Bodie face betrayed a series of considerations and emotions. He rose to reach behind Will and hand him the shotgun. He shuffled around the table past Minnick's customary seat at the head and limped out through the porch without a word.

Will sat gazing again at his coffee, stirring only when he heard his father's tread across the living room. Minnick lumbered into the kitchen and sat heavily on his chair without straightening it from Bodie's exit past it. He banged his elbows on the oak surface and buried his face in his hands. Will watched quietly.

There was no obvious shaking of the heavy, sloping shoulders, no tears when he lifted his face to stare at his son. But Will had seen that look of devastation only once before, and the memory twisted his gut. He needed to swallow to be able to catch his breath before he could ask, "Would you like hot coffee, Pa?"

The answer was merely a slow blink that seemed to bring the man back to the reality of being here in his own kitchen.

He nodded.

Will poured for his father and warmed his own, moved the sugar bowl close to those gnarled hands and brought the tiny pitcher with fresh milk from the ice box. He checked the baby and then came back to sit down opposite this man who barely spoke, and refused discussions that might have led to understanding. As he stared at this man who had sired him, he no longer felt afraid, and it surprised him. Until that moment, he had not realized how much of his childhood he had spent in fear—of disappointing this man who was so hard to read. And how often he had done exactly what he feared to do. He coughed into his hand: *I tried harder; Freddy must have just given it up as a bad job. Oh, pa, I don't think that's what you intended. But it is what you did. Lord, please, help me with greater insight raising my own.*

He'd missed Grover Minnick gathering himself to speak. His father's voice startled him.

"I've seen men run over by a plow. Trampled by stampeding cattle. But them was accidents, not man–done. This…" He lifted his earth–stained hands to gesture helplessly at the ceiling. Will waited, looking down at the stress pattern of the grain in the oak table. When he looked up, his father was studying him. "I seen you pickin' up Emmy at Doc's. You're hurtin' more'n you're sayin', boy. Got hit by them Brit coast bombs Doc Ricartsen's been tellin' us about, did ya?"

Will almost told him the bombs had been few and far between before he and Nandria had left England, but he'd known they were coming. He shook his head, deciding he could not discuss his missions to central Europe. Better simply to let the man infer whatever would satisfy him. It was the first time he'd asked and he deserved an honest, if incomplete, answer.

"Shrapnel," he acknowledged. "It's healing. And then Nandria, Rose and I will leave," he added, but, as usual, his father talked over him.

"You helped put the crop in. Whyn't you say something?"

Will shrugged and again wrapped his fingers around his mug. "It wouldn't have changed what needed to be done."

Grover stared at him, his face scrunched in concentration. Will waited. Minnick narrowed his dark hazel eyes to peer at him, assessing. "That woman of yours. She a nurse?"

"No, she's simply had far more experience with wounds and death than either of us wanted for her."

"So the bombings over there was purdy bad, then. Is that why you wanted her 'n' her brother over here? But the brother didn't come."

"Killed."

Minnick stared. "A boy? What, ten?"

"Just fourteen. Sliced his cheeks with a straight razor the first time he tried shaving peach fuzz." Will sighed and tilted back his chair. "Nandria and I were to meet her family in New York in January before we came here. But at the last minute I got sent out on assignment again. We only had a few minutes together on the dock in Liverpool. She didn't tell me then, and I hadn't yet learned about her family being on the *Athenia* when that German sub torpedoed it."

Minnick lifted his hands.

"I guess that didn't get much publicity here in the States," Will continued. "German submarines have gotten more and more aggressive, not only with merchant vessels but now also passenger liners. Her parents were on the Athenia when it went down. They had her little brother Ned with them. She was devoted to the boy. Risked her own life to protect him several times that I know of, in Ethiopia and then again in Spain during their civil war. She lost her entire family to German torpedoes. And she'd had to face all that alone and pregnant. I wasn't there to help her. Any more than I was there for her when Rose was born."

"Why didn't ya send her to her own family?"

There it was, then. Will sank back in his chair and fiddled a moment with his cup before sitting straight and saying low, "There is no other family. Maybe that's why they were so close."

If Minnick took in the implications of that, he gave no sign. Had Will looked up he would have seen the uncertainty in his father's face. Instead Will took the tone of his voice as true expression of the man's feelings. All he heard was the rather lame, "You said something about that in one of your letters to your mother, but it didn't sink in."

Will shrugged and stared again at his coffee, now cold and undesirable. Steeled as he thought he was, still he startled when Minnick asked, "You don't want this farm, do you?"

Will looked at him. "Even if I did, pa, my work with Military Intelligence wouldn't let me stay. This war in Europe isn't going to stay 'over there.'"

"Thet's 'mongering', boy!"

"It's truth, pa."

Minnick half-rose in his chair, but Will took on the unintimidated expression he'd seen so often on his wife's face: not aggressive or defiant, but quietly assuming a respectful strength from which two sides could negotiate. Minnick sat back, breathing through flared nostrils that gave out little crinkling and then whistling sounds.

"We gave enough for their last war. Look what it did to us! We want no part of this one!"

"I'm sorry, pa, but I've been there. It's worse than you can imagine, and I know you would understand if you could see it. No matter how badly this country doesn't want it, we'll be damned lucky if this war doesn't set our own cities on fire."

"All a man here works his whole life to build . . ."

"And half the men in Europe. They don't want to see their work or their families torn down and trampled, either."

"It's their doin'! Why drag Americans into their doin's?"

Will lifted his hand, palms up. "Why do we have Emmy Lu upstairs in our home? Because sometimes you just need to protect what can't fight for itself."

"Because it's the right thing to do." Minnick's words might have been sarcastic, but his expression was not, leaving Will silent.

They faced each other and then looked away. Finally Will said low, sorrowfully, "It's going to get worse, pa."

Disgusted, scared, believing and disbelieving, Minnick rose angrily and stood swaying at the end of the table.

Rose whimpered and Will went to calm her. At the doorway from kitchen to porch, Minnick watched his son holding the cream-and-coffee colored little girl in loving arms. He shook his head. "Fureners!" he spat, and stomped back through the kitchen into the depths of the house.

Looking up from his daughter's innocent face, Will shook his head and murmured, "One doesn't need to be from Europe to be a foreigner to you, pa."

CHAPTER TWENTY-TWO

Long past daybreak, Bodie and Minnick lingered at the breakfast table watching Will help Rose 'stand' on fat, bowed legs, laughing and drooling. Doris, clapping her hands almost silently together and squealing with delight, reached out again and again to caress her husband's arm. Rose collapsed to a sudden sit again, still laughing. Will gathered her to himself to hold her tenderly. Nandria, standing at the sink, sighed, taking in this moment of joy for husband and daughter.

"Ah, wee Will, goosebunny," Doris stretched to touch her son's hand at Rose's back.

"Yeah," Minnick grimaced and stood up heavily. His hand strayed a moment to Doris's shoulder as he shuffled toward the porch and outdoors. Bodie hurried behind him, his face wrinkled in the broadest smile Nandria had ever seen.

Will, looking lovingly at Nandria, rose quickly with the baby on one shoulder to help his mother up.

"I'm gonna sit with Emmy Lu a bit," Doris sighed. "Just in case she wakes up. Sure does sleep in, thet gal."

"Thank you, mama," Will acknowledged, seeing her to the staircase. When he returned to the kitchen he saw Nandria, pale, seeming to be staring out the window over the sink. But, as he got closer, he saw that her eyes were closed.

"Nausea again?" he asked quietly. He stood on the section of the floor where his wife and mother had gotten tired enough to begin making distinct arcs of sponge marks on the linoleum. It was his favorite spot to stand. To anyone who could read it, the spot was like a document testifying to the love Nandria had shown to her unacknowledging mother–in–law.

After a few moments, Nandria's wave of nausea washed over, and she was able to relax her shoulders and open her eyes. Will came to her, drawing her toward the porch. "You take care of our Miss Popularity now. I'll get the kitchen straightened up."

She glanced at him, grateful, but still sporting tinges of green near the corners of her mouth. He traced them softly with the tip of his finger. "Sorry to seem to laugh, Angel."

"I guess I do look pretty funny."

"How long does the sickness last?"

"About as long as it decides to," she said, the corners of her mouth losing their green tint and lifting in weak smile.

"The folks are going to miss their wee 'boy.'"

"You've told your father about our going to Washington, D.C. then?"

"I've said the words to him. He wouldn't listen, but I think he heard me. Either way, we are set to take the train to St. Louis the second of next month."

"Oh, Will." They embraced, and Rose howled protest at being squished between them.

Laughing, Nandria carried her to the porch to sit to nurse her. Will cleared the table and set the dirty dishes in the soapy water

Nandria had run in the kitchen sink. When he left for the fields, his two loves were asleep in their nest together.

****

Will's arrival in the north field occasioned a mad scramble for Horace, Irwayne and Jude Bratton as they dived for whatever cover they could find. Will didn't see them, he was so intent on his own thoughts. Nor had Bodie or Minnick, sweating and irritated with the weeds.

"Damn things are the only things that really grow," Minnick groused. When Will stared at him, hands on hips, and laughed good-naturedly, Bodie burst into a muffled braying. At that, Minnick, glaring at the other two, broke his concentration on his bad mood and gave into a low chuckle that deepened until all three were bent over laughing at the world and ill fortune.

None saw the Bratton brothers worming closer, dragging handguns and a rifle.

****

Nandria pushed open the porch door with her back, and came out into the sunshine hauling a hamper of damp clothes. Setting down the hamper near the clothesline, she straightened to see Will and the menfolk as colored beads in the far field. She waved, knowing they probably had not spotted her, but it felt good to be in even one-sided contact with this man she loved. Such a lovely, bright morning. Spring-fresh, promising. Hope had such a delicious smell and texture.

At Rose's call—she was beginning to make demanding use of the consonants 'Mmmm' and 'D'—Nandria hurried back into the house to get her little daughter ready to spend outdoor time with her mother and the laundry. She didn't see the younger Brattons up in the field take instructions from Horace to slink forward with their pistol and rifle. Nor did she see Horace making his way down from the field toward the farmhouse.

Nandria had just settled Rose on the large wool Army blanket on the grass, when they were both startled by a shrieking scream from inside the house. Nandria snatched up Rose and deposited her, still surprised and on the verge of beginning angry, frightened tears, in her crib on the porch.

"You are all right, little one. Momma needs to help your grandmother," Nandria assured her breathlessly, then dashed through the kitchen and up the stairs to the second floor where wails continued the jarring sounds of deep grief.

Horace, just emerging from the barn, hastily ran to the corner nearest the lane and watched the Minnick men and Bodie stand to peer toward the farmhouse. The younger Bratton brothers hid deeper among the grasses. Will was first to throw down his hoe and start racing from the field. Minnick carried his, but he, too, lumbered toward his home. Bodie limped behind.

In the bedroom upstairs, Doris rocked and howled, hysterical. Emmy Lu lay inert, white, cold and still on the bed.

"Winfred! Freddy! My baby, my baby," Doris wailed.

Checking Emmy Lu, Nandria knew immediately that the girl was finally beyond all pain. "Mother Minnick," she comforted, coming toward the frantic woman to within reach of her fists.

"You killed him! You killed him!" Though she was frail and wasted, Doris's attack was furious enough to knock the surprised Nandria sprawling to the floor beside the girl's bed.

Leaping up the porch steps, Will grabbed the door frame to halt his forward progress and hurtle at a diagonal across the enclosed room at Horace, bent over the baby's crib.

"Damn you, Bratton!"

Horace backed away, hands up. "Wasn't gonna harm 'er none, Will. Was comin' to see Em. Them screams scared the kid, that's all."

Lifting Rose into his arms, Will glared. But as Doris shrieked again, he brushed past Bratton and raced with the baby up the stairs.

Horace, seeing Minnick and Bodie hurrying across the back yard, looked for a place to hide, and then decided to follow Will. After all, Emmy Lu was his wife, wasn't she? He had a right to be in this house. His lips clamped tight over jutting yellow teeth. He convinced himself he'd been wronged by the time he'd reached the second floor. He'd finally made out what the old lady was screaming about. He knew he deserved to wreak vengeance when he saw that nigger on the floor and Will reaching with his free hand to lift his mother away from whaling on that dark skin. Not that he wouldn't like to help the old woman beat on it. He could imagine feeling its smooth texture under his fingertips and under his fists. He lurched forward but felt Minnick and then Bodie crowding in behind him at the doorway.

And then his brothers crept behind the knot of men at the door, peering and peeping where they could. Both of their mouths hung open.

"Jude! Irwayne!" Horace called, startling everyone. "You hustle now and git the sheriff! Thet nigger done kilt my wife!"

CHAPTER TWENTY-THREE

Night seeped into the sky like sadness determined to suck away all light and joy.

On the Minnicks' back porch Bodie had scooted the rocker at an angle to be able to cuddle little Rose and still see into the kitchen. But he had not lighted the lantern.

In the kitchen, only the bulb dangling over the sink was lit. It illuminated the backs of the heads of Sheriff Yakes and Dr. Ricartsen, but cast their faces in angular shadows as they stared at Nandria, huddled at the foot of the table in the corner close beside Will. Her fingers worked restlessly among the stones in the pocket of her apron.

"Say what, Girl?" the sheriff demanded. "Whadda ya keep fiddlin' with them rocks fer?"

She breathed out slowly. "I have picked them up in difficult times. Feeling them reminds me that I made it through those and will, with my husband's help, survive these."

"Well, if'n you're gonna make it through this one, ya better tell us whatcha did."

Sighing, she sat a moment to compose herself to answer him civilly. "As I have said, I was hanging the wash when I heard Mother Minnick scream. I set my baby into her crib and ran upstairs to help Mother Minnick."

Yakes sat back, rolling his eyes and nodding as though to say, "Oh, sure."

Will leaned forward, partially blocking Yakes' view of his wife, deliberately deflecting the sheriff's unpleasantness to himself. "She's told you that before, sheriff. Again and again."

As though just remembering, Nandria eased up close to say quietly to Will, "She was screeching, 'Winfred, my Freddy. My baby. My baby.' It broke my heart."

"Did you hear that, sheriff? Emmy Lu must already have been dead and Mother slipped back to remember my brother Fred."

Startled by a thought that he had not considered, Yakes rocked forward again and looked over at Ricartsen, who was nodding thoughtfully. "One possibility, I guess. You think so, Doc?"

"Grief does strange things to people," Ricartsen acknowledged. "Probably especially so in Mrs. Minnick's unstable condition." The doctor and the others twisted toward the living room door when Pastor Kylie, in a huff so bloated he could barely contain himself, stormed into the kitchen from the front of the house.

"That man ordered me out," Kylie sputtered. "Can you believe such a thing?"

"My father?" Will turned to Nandria with a secret smile that worked to calm them both.

Yakes was too busy suppressing a grin of his own to notice, but Dr. Ricartsen watched the young couple share, and his frown deepened. He could not understand this Will who loved a colored woman. It wasn't merely infatuation or sex appeal, though those, too, were strong. Will Minnick truly loved his wife. It was evident.

He really loved her. Ricartsen shook his head. The whole concept was beyond anything the doctor had ever experienced.

Will sobered to address the seething minister. This was the Minnick home, after all, and his mother had raised him to be polite toward their guests. "My parents probably just needed a few minutes alone together. Sir," he added more from military training than from personal evaluation of the man before him trembling with indignant rage.

Yakes rocked back in his chair again. Will was afraid he was going to swing his legs up to put his feet on the table at which they ate their meals and was relieved when he didn't.

"Get the man some coffee, girl," the sheriff ordered.

"Never mind. I'm closer," Will said, setting his hand on his wife's arm. Tight–lipped, he got up to indicate his father's chair for Pastor Kylie. He stepped to the wood stove to fetch a mug from one of the hooks on the wall behind it. He brought the mug and the steaming glass globe pot to the table and poured for the irate man with the turned collar. He offered with a gesture of the coffee pot, but no one wanted a refill. He thought a moment about topping off his own cup, but he had not tasted the coffee for half an hour or more as it was and doubted adding more would make it any more palatable. He set the pot back on the stove.

Yakes rested his left hand across his rounded belly and turned to Kylie at the head of the table. "Will says Emmy could've already been dead when the missus started caterwaulin'. Whadda ya think, Pastor?"

Ricartsen, worrying his lower lip with his teeth, added, "Both Will and the girl say the deceased body was cold."

With all eyes finally properly on him, Pastor Kylie took a sip of his coffee, reached to add sugar from the bowl on the table, and sipped again, apparently mollified if not satisfied.

"I think the Lord's justice will only be served by a trial to get out all the facts," the pastor declared.

"What? No!" Will half–rose again, protesting. But, seeing the expressions on the faces of the men looking at him, sat again to try to explain. "My mother cannot possibly go through the trauma of another trial." He glanced at Nandria. "Or my wife."

It was Ricartsen who spoke with compassion. "Perhaps in the morning, after healing sleep, Doris will be able to give us a more coherent picture of what did happen." He pushed back his chair and stood up to brush with his hands down his front, wiping away crumbs of Nandria Minnick's delicious buttermilk scones. He swiped back a lock of limp, brown hair that fell across his eyes. "And I have one more call to make before I get any of that healing sleep. Good night, gentlemen."

Bodie got up with the baby sleeping on his arm to step into the back corner out of the way. Ricartsen's eyes caught Bodie's movement, but his gaze locked onto Nandria. He opened his mouth to say something, but then disappeared into the dark night. Kylie and Yakes rose to leave as well.

As he shuffled to the door, Yakes leaned close, his forefinger extended as though he would tap Will on the chest. "Mornin' then. You're responsible for her, Will," he intoned without actually touching this tall soldier.

Tight–lipped, Will nodded, then crouched and spun at the sound of angry voices in the yard. Motioning Nandria to stay behind him, he rushed across the porch and outdoors with Yakes following, hand on belly.

They saw Dr. Ricartsen push past Horace and Irwayne Bratton toward his car. Horace gestured obscenely after the doctor as he drove away.

"What's going on, Bratton?" Will demanded.

Horace's hate–filled eyes shifted from Will to Yakes and then Bodie coming up close behind and Nandria watching with that pickaninny in her arms from the doorway. Horace raised his fist toward her.

"Ain't you gonna take her to jail, sheriff?"

When Yakes hesitated, Will stepped purposefully in front of him.

"Not tonight, Mr. Bratton," he said with contained strength. "Now, if you will kindly leave this property where your welcome is tenuous at best?"

"Don't you try and bury me in them fancy words, Will Minnick. I know too much you wouldn't want bandied about. Jus' gimme Emmy." He glared at the sheriff.

"Well, I reckon a husband . . .," Yakes started, but Will interrupted.

"Then you are agreeing that nobody here killed Emmy Lu, except perhaps you."

"What?" Horace stared at him, furious, but wary.

Will explained as though to a backward child. "I mean, if you want the sheriff to investigate, then he is going to need to have her body as evidence. So if you take it, you cannot very well ask the sheriff to put anyone into custody."

"'Body as evidence'?" Jude's uncomprehending face screwed up as though he'd just tasted something rotten.

"Autopsy," Will explained quietly. "To see what actually killed her."

"Ought-op...?" Jude hawked phlegm.

Sheriff Yakes made slicing gestures across various places of his own body with his forefinger.

Irwayne snuck close to his brother. "He's gonna let thet doc cut 'er up like a cow?"

"Let him!" Horace spat. "The stupid cow never give me no kids anyhow."

Will looked between the two brothers and realized something he had not actually known until he saw the glances between them. "Emmy Lu was pregnant at one time, though, wasn't she?" he guessed, wondering if that baby might not have been Fred's. That would explain the surprisingly sudden marriage to Horace Bratton after Freddy's death. "What happened?"

"I told ya to slap her, not kick her in the belly, Horey," Irwayne wheedled.

"Shut up!" Horace's hate-filled eyes turned on his younger brother.

Kylie had maneuvered past Nandria and came to stand just outside the circle of men. His voice was grave. "Really, Will Minnick, we have no right to interfere between a man and his wife. As the Lord says, a husband is head of his household."

It took all Will's self-discipline not to turn on the man. Clenching his jaw, he spoke as reasonably as he could manage. "If Mr. Bratton wants his wife's body, let him take it. Just so he knows he is agreeing that her death was not caused in this house. Is that what you are saying, Bratton?"

The younger Bratton brothers cowered at this rare direct challenge to this sibling who had lorded over them all their lives. They held their breath, waiting to see Horace tear Will apart. But jerky twitching of the spittle-matted beard was their only clue to his suppressed anger, until Horace roared.

"Then the sheriff ain't gonna arrest thet nigger?"

Yakes raised his hands as though to placate, but, seeing Will's face, he said low but clearly. "If'n you take her, Horace, there's no trial."

"I'll fetch 'er, Horey," Irwayne volunteered, but Horace snarled.

"Leave 'er be! I want thet nigger."

CHAPTER TWENTY-FOUR

The constant sore ache in Yakes' belly made him want to double over. He was just about to slide his feet off his desk where he'd propped them, when a no-nonsense man beclouded by white wisps of what must once have been luxuriant hair rattled his door and opened it. With a look at those penetrating blue eyes, Yakes scrambled to a stand as the man entered on evidently painful feet.

"Yakes?" the man inquired while looking the sheriff up and down, assessing him with a dour frown. "I'm Judge Markus from the Southwest Circuit. Lucky for you I was already out on rounds. They said you had a near riot here in Boonetown."

"Your judgeship! I – I didn't know you was close at hand."

"May I sit down? My feet . . ."

"Ah, yeah, 'course. Sit."

Judge Markus seated himself heavily in the chair the sheriff offered. He rubbed his thighs, in obvious discomfort. "And the prisoner? Could you bring her out here for me to examine? I understand it is a Negro woman."

Yakes shook his head. "N-no prisoner," he stammered.

"No prisoner?"

"I mean, she's at Minnicks' place. She's got a little one and it didn't seem needful to slap her in jail."

"A woman commits murder and she's left at home?"

"Will's watching 'er," the sheriff explained.

"Will? Who is 'Will'?"

"Says he's her husband, but God knows why he'd go and marry some nigger."

Again the judge's eyes roved over Yakes from top to bottom. This time the frown turned from dour to sour. "And the near riot?" When Yakes looked blank, the judge all but spat, "The minister who called described civil unrest."

"Pastor, huh? Yeah, Kylie done got a queen bee in his britches, that's for sure."

"I've just talked with your physician . . . ?"

"Huh? Oh, you mean Doc Ricartsen."

"The most difficult part of riding the circuit is remembering the names for the same cast of characters in town after town."

"I'm Yakes," the sheriff said, leaning forward as though to offer his hand. He held himself in check as he saw the judge's expression.

"Yes, that I know. Your reputation precedes you."

Yakes' grin faded as the judge shook his head and sighed.

"Your Dr. Richardson seemed to believe that the murder of the unfortunate young woman took place some time ago."

It was Sheriff Yakes's turn to shake his head. Eyes wide and then squinting down, he finally asked, "Emmy Lu got murdered afore she got dead?"

"Here comes Dr. Richardson now. He's agreed to accompany us to the Monarch farm."

Thoroughly confused, Yakes followed the judge to the door where Ricartsen's car was parked. Ricartsen was motioning for Pastor Kylie either to slide over to sit in the middle or vacate the front bench seat for the judge.

"I'll drive us," Ricartsen said. "It'll be easier as I know the way."

Judge Markus nodded and gratefully lowered himself into the still-warm front passenger seat. As Kylie humphed his way to the far side and sat in back, Markus glared impatiently at Yakes. "Get in," he commanded. "The back," he added when Yakes still looked blank. It was plain that he was keeping himself from adding, 'You darned fool.'

Yakes clambered into the back seat, barely getting his door secured before the doctor took off.

* * * * * * * * * * * * * * * * * * * *

Will and Bodie looked up from working in the north field. Already this spring there was dust rising from behind Ricartsen's car as it turned into the long Minnick lane.

"Ricartsen?" Will asked.

Bodie nodded, pretty sure it was the doctor coming, probably to check on the missus. "Gonna be a tough summer if'n it's this dry already," he muttered, but Will wasn't paying attention. He raised his hand and waved to point out the car to his father tinkering with the tractor.

"This blanket-blank…" Minnick was muttering when he saw Will's signal and looked up, raising his toughened hand to shade his eyes. All three men watched, none expressing their common concern. Will took off walking toward the house.

* *

Shifting a squirmy Rose on her hip and wiping at the sweat threatening her eyebrows, Nandria stepped out into the yard as the car approached and parked. She counted automatically as Pastor Kylie and Sheriff Yakes struggled up from the back. Dr. Ricartsen emerged from the driver's seat, and with a little wave to Nandria, started around the front of his car. The judge waited until Ricartsen came around to give him a hand up.

"Almost prefer my pickup," he murmured to the doctor in apology. "Easier with these damn legs and feet of mine."

"I should take a look at them when we get back to town," Ricartsen offered, but the judge waved him off, for now.

Kylie and Yakes stood with ill grace near the back bumper of the car. As Will approached from beside the barn, the men could see Minnick driving the tractor to the edge of the field with Bodie perched on the high fender.

"Welcome, gentlemen," Nandria called to them. "Please come in," she added, gesturing for them to enter the house if they so desired.

"Girl, where's the missus?" Yakes demanded. "This here's the judge come to try you."

"Judge Markus, Southwest Circuit," Ricartsen added by way of explanation when no one else did. "I believe he merely would like to ask you a few questions." He had turned and raised his voice some so Will could hear as well.

"Thank you, doctor," Nandria acknowledged. "Good day, Judge Markus. Will you not please enter the house? We did not know to expect you, but you are most welcome. I shall rouse Mother Minnick."

"Looks like your menfolk have seen us and are coming in," Yakes observed.

"How is Mrs. Minnick this morning?" Ricartsen asked as they followed Judge Markus limping across the porch and through the kitchen to the living room. "Did she get a good night's sleep?" He nodded as Nandria told him quietly that she believed so, but that Mother Minnick was having one of her confused mornings, it seemed.

To the other guests, Nandria gestured toward the sofa and chairs. "If you gentlemen will be seated, I shall see if Mother Minnick is able to receive you."

"I'll get us settled," Ricartsen said, hauling an oak chair from the kitchen. "Or do you need help with Mrs. Minnick?"

Surprised by the doctor's civility, Nandria shook her head and went to set Rose in the makeshift playpen in the center of the room. "I believe I can manage, thank you."

Kylie sank into Minnick's easy chair. Yakes sat as far as he could manage from Judge Markus on the sofa. Minnick entered from the field, scowled at the minister in his chair and seated himself on the oak chair the doctor had brought in. Bodie brought in another for Ricartsen, and Will handed in two more from the table.

When neither Yakes nor Kylie rose to introduce the judge, Ricartsen did the honors. "Mr. Minnick, this is Judge Markus,

Southwest Circuit. Judge Markus, Grover Minnick and his son, Will. Bodie . . ."

"Just a hired hand, your honorship. Don't you mind 'bout me none." Bodie scooted to a far corner out of the way but where he could reach for the baby should need arise.

"Please don't bother to rise, sir," Will stepped in front of the sofa to take the judge's proffered hand. "Thank you for coming."

Minnick half–rose, but the judge waved away formalities. "My staff hunted me down after receiving a desperate call." Markus looked over at Kylie, whose color rose above his collar. "I had understood that Boonetown was near riot."

The men peered at each other, and then at Kylie as he pulled a large white handkerchief from his pocket to cover a sudden cough.

"Town was up in arms, you say?" Minnick asked.

"Perhaps it was too early in the day for the riot to show much when I came through," the judge said.

Will breathed more easily than he had since spying the doctor's car approaching. This was not a man to be easily hoodwinked. His relief for Nandria's welfare made him speak again when normally he would have merely kept to himself and watched in his father's house.

"We're grateful, sir, to have this burden dealt with so quickly. Thank you for coming."

Markus turned to study Will as he sat at the kitchen doorway near Grover.

"You are Willard Minnick, the young man who brought a Negro wife to downstate Missouri." His wise eyes glittered with curiosity.

Will swallowed and rose. "I sent her, and my child, actually. I was to have come with them, but was ordered out on assignment. So I sent them on."

"You are with the United States Army? Assigned at this time in England?"

"Army Intelligence, yes, sir."

"In the middle of the war they're stewing in Europe? I assume that was the reason for your last-minute 'assignment?"

"It was, sir."

"And you couldn't leave your wife in . . . ?"

"London, sir. She'd already been through more than one bombing raid on the English coast, as well as in Spain and Ethiopia, which is where I met her. Her own family members were drowned on the Athenia, by a German torpedo. I asked her to continue with our plans to come to America, at least temporarily. I would join her as soon as I could. I didn't know then that her parents and brother had been killed. I wanted Nandria and little Rose safe." Will let out a short, quiet exhalation as he finished his hurried explanation.

"You wanted your colored wife safe, so you sent her to downstate Missouri," the judge commented, then sat back, realizing the irony of such a choice and the sadness that it represented the best option available to this young man. For a long moment, he sat without speaking. "Ah," he exhaled finally, frowning. "I see."

Flushing with the unexpected recognition and understanding that he saw in the judge's expression, Will nodded and turned away to take his seat.

Kylie finished tucking away his handkerchief, oblivious to what had just transpired between the two men. He cleared his throat to declare, "We, of course, pray the Lord's mercy on all those in war, but we do not wish to be involved in what is no doings of ours."

Markus studied the pastor without comment until Kylie fidgeted.

Nandria's soft call was heard from the Minnicks' bedroom. Will rose. "Excuse me, please. I believe my wife needs help with my mother." He hurried between the sofa and easy chair and out the far side of the room. The men sat uncomfortably quiet. Kylie again snorted into his handkerchief.

"This house is in ungodly turmoil," the pastor noted, lifting his chins.

Under his breath, Minnick muttered, "Mostly when you are here." Aloud, he told the judge, "My wife may not be very helpful, judge. She's . . . she's been . . ." He stopped, lifting and dropping his hands again onto his thighs.

"Senile, your honor," Ricartsen explained. "Slipping these many months, although she is far younger than one would expect to be having such a problem."

"Mrs. Monarch, no—Minnick, isn't it? Mrs. Minnick is the chief witness?"

"And that girl," Kylie said. "But how can you expect her kind not to lie? What do niggers know about truth?"

Will, supporting his mother, with Nandria just behind him, entered the room just in time to hear the pastor's comment. Nandria laid her hand gently on Will's arm and shook her head. She shrugged just a little to tell him it had not hurt her; not to let it hurt him, either. But it was Ricartsen who spoke without realizing that Will had come in.

"Ever since the younger Mrs. Minnick came just after the first of the year, her help with Doris and the chores has kept this place functional. She seems to be a well-educated, unusually competent person."

Minnick half-rose to help Doris sit in the chair Ricartsen vacated for her near him. Nandria picked up the baby and went to sit beside Will at the kitchen doorway. Doris was dressed, her hair freshly combed out, her shoes tied, but she appeared disheveled, as though she'd been awakened from a deep sleep. She fussed with the pink and purple scarf at her neck.

"Hello, Mrs. Minnick. I am Judge Markus," the judge addressed her, but she looked at him blankly. "I see. All right then, to continue. Doctor, you treated the young woman who died?"

"Yes, but there was little I could do. Multiple fractured ribs and a broken collarbone, abdominal trauma. But the primary damage was from the vicious head wounds." He glanced into the corner at Bodie's soft moan, but knew to continue rather than make comment. "Brain trauma far beyond the help of human medicine." He chewed his lower lip and blinked his pale hazel eyes as though he could disguise the glistening tears.

"Head wounds?" the judge asked, weighing the doctor's testimony. "Sheriff, do we know what caused these head wounds?"

When Yakes fidgeted and the rest of the men sat silent, Nandria spoke up bitterly, "There has been evidence that her husband has beaten her. Numerous times."

The judge stared at her, then nodded to assure her. "You will get your turn, Mrs. Minnick," he said kindly.

"Yes, sir, I am sorry for interrupting," she apologized.

"Sheriff," Markus turned to address Yakes. "What evidence have you seen of these alleged beatings?"

Rose's fussing was a welcome distraction for the sheriff. Will took Rose from Nandria and, when she refused to settle, set her on the floor to scoot–roll–crawl to each set of feet and look up expectantly.

"Sheriff?" Markus snapped. "What evidence?"

"Of beatings?" Yakes swallowed and shuffled his feet. "Well, none. None I seen myself."

"What does the husband say? His family? His neighbors?" Markus pressed him.

Yakes shrugged and wiped his forehead with his own large handkerchief. "None I heerd."

"Did you question them?" From the corner of his eye, the judge caught Nandria mouthing those very words as he asked. It seemed the woman was not highly impressed with the sheriff's abilities or his courage, even if he was white.

Kylie sat forward, his expression fierce with suppressed anger. "It is not fitting for one man to interfere between another man and the household he heads."

The judge sat back, coughed, and, tight-lipped, surveyed each person in the room. He opened his mouth to speak when little Rose made her way to Minnick's feet and fussed to be picked up. Markus watched the tableau as Will started from his seat to fetch his daughter, but Nandria touched his arm to stop him. Doris seemed to come alive. She smiled down at the child and urged her husband to pick up the baby so they could hold her.

"Little goosebunny, ain't you just so cute? Can I hold him, Mr. Minnick, please?"

Hesitantly, almost reluctantly, Minnick leaned down to lift the child and set her in his lap for Doris to play with.

"Little Winfred. My Freddy baby."

"No, Mother . . ." Minnick started to correct her, but went quiet at a gesture from the judge. All sat, watching and listening as Doris pattered on.

"You come back, my wee Freddy boy. Your father says you lost your head, but we all do dumb sometimes. Sure enough, your mama does. Ain't right, you bein' kilt 'cause your mama couldn't give you enough smarts."

"Oh, no, Mother, no." Minnick's voice carried anguish it was painful for everyone in the room to listen to. In his grief, Minnick lifted one hand to his face, and Rose's play with Doris threatened her position on his lap. Will rose to go to her, but Nandria's hand on his arm again held him back to wait and see.

"Mrs. Minnick," the judge asked gently, "when did Freddy die?"

"Yesterday," she told him and then closed her eyes. "And so long ago."

"Yesterday? Where?" the judge inquired softly.

"Up in Will's room upstairs. He'd been sick so long. I set with him, in case he'd wake up, but he never did. I must'a fell asleep myself. When I woke up, I knowed he was gone. So cold. Never did say our good–byes."

"When you woke up, he was cold? Is that how you knew he was gone?" the judge pressed.

"Like ice. Like Mamma. Like Grammam. They was always so warm, until."

"Did this girl come into the room?" The Judge gestured toward Nandria.

"With Mamma? Don't reckon so."

"With Freddy. While he was still warm."

Doris shrank into Minnick looking confused and beginning to get uncomfortable with what is being asked of her. She shook her head, her eyes pleading with her husband.

"I was sleepin'."

Rose reached up to touch the old woman's face, and Doris collapsed so that Minnick was barely able to hold them both. Nandria, Will and Bodie rushed to the rescue.

Judge Markus watched, assessing, and then struggled painfully to his feet. "I think we can go now, Dr. Richardson. I would like next to hear from the grieving widower."

CHAPTER TWENTY-FIVE

Weeds abounded in the rutted yard surrounded by three shacks. As Dr. Ricartsen eased his car into the Bratton compound, scrawny chickens fluttered, squawking in raucous protest and flying in all directions. Spindly feathers splattered against his windshield, compelling the doctor to stop for fear of hitting a fleeing child.

Irwayne stepped out amid the garbage, shotgun in hand. Its muzzle was lowered to point at the earth, but its readiness to be lifted and aimed was a present warning.

"Doc?"

Pinched, dirty faces peeked and stared from multiple hiding places as the doctor, the sheriff and a strange, sour-pussed man sat rigid in the car. It was Will who emerged from the far back seat to stand beside the car and look over at the shack at Irwayne. Will smiled.

"Hello, Irwayne. Looks like your family is flourishing. How many young ones do you have now?"

"Z'at whatcha come to find out, Will Minnick?" Irwayne maneuvered a wad of tobacco in his mouth and spat, not missing the hubcap of Doc's front wheel.

"Well, no, actually," Will admitted, resting his elbows on the roof of Ricartsen's car to show that his hands were free of weapons. "We came to talk with Horace, if your brother is available."

"Whaddabout?" Irwayne demanded, but he had rested the end of the barrel of his shotgun on the toe of his own boot.

It occurred to Will that he remembered something about Irwayne missing some toes and wondered if he could be so nonchalant now because there were none of his own digits there now to be threatened.

"Who's the old geezer in the front with the doc?" Irwayne wanted to know.

Will hesitated as he saw Jude saunter to the door of the far shack, pistol in hand, wiping it carelessly with an oily rag. Now and then the youngest of the three brothers sighted down its barrel pointed at Will's side of the car.

Will's jaw tightened, but he kept his voice steady and his hands in view. "Well, seeing as it is really Horace's business and we should be talking with him, I can tell you that the older gentleman in the front with Doc Ricartsen is a judge from the Southwest Circuit come to talk with your brother about Emmy Lu. Is Horace around?"

"Whatcha want, nigger–lover?" Horace appeared, swaying in the doorway of the center house. He held no weapon, but Will and all the men in the car knew that at a word or even a gesture from him, his brothers would gladly open fire.

Will swallowed. "I was just telling Irwayne that we've brought Judge Markus from the Southwest Circuit. He'd like to talk with you. And, Horace, I believe he'd be more inclined to listen to you if you were to treat him civilly."

"Ain't no lack of civiliary here," Horace exclaimed, spreading his hands to take in the compound. "Only us Brattons don't take real kindly to rats or war mongers."

"Or nigger-lovers," Irwayne added, laughing.

"Yeah, that, too. But come on in. Bring 'em all, if they don't mind intrudin'."

Both Jude and Irwayne guffawed, Irwayne finally lifting the shotgun away from his foot. Horace motioned, and Jude aimed away from Ricartsen's car but both brothers held onto their guns.

Will walked slowly forward to open the judge's door and help him out. Sheriff Yakes climbed out reluctantly, and then Dr. Ricartsen. Judge Markus and Will moved up between the car and Horace still swaying in the doorway of his home.

"Don't do nothin' foolish, now, boys," Yakes called, his hands halfway raised to show he was not going for his own gun.

Judge Markus stood facing the middle shack. "Mr. Horace Bratton?" he asked in a voice that brooked no nonsense. When Horace nodded, he continued loud enough for all three Brattons to hear him clearly. "I am Judge Markus of the Southwest Circuit Court."

"Oh, yeah? How do I know you ain't one of Minnick's buddies trying to fool me into somethin'?"

"I have identification papers, naturally," Markus said, reaching into the breast pocket of his suit coat.

Horace spat. "You know I cain't read. Sheriff's bound t'ave told ya that."

"Is there somewhere, sir, where we can sit down and discuss the issue of your wife's death?"

Horace closed his heavy eyelids as though considering it, but opened them with such a negative expression on the leer of his thick lips, that the judge took half a step backwards before speaking again. It was surprise on his countenance, not fear. His voice, when he raised it, went intense and unforgiving. "No? Not here? Well, then I will tell you that I will remain at the sheriff's office in Boonetown for the next two hours, if you care to join us there. Otherwise, I will again be on my regular circuit route by this afternoon. Good day, sir."

Without waiting for Will's help, Judge Markus shuffled painfully back and got into the car. Will closed his door for him, and sat in the back. Ricartsen hurried into the driver's seat and started his car. Yakes stood a moment hanging on his door.

"Listen, you damn fool, there'll be no trial unless you can confess this judge it was the nigger."

As soon as Yakes had slid back into the car and before he had even closed his door, Ricartsen began backing up the car to turn around in a wet area that splattered mud in all directions. But the doctor seemed to think washing his car was a small price to pay to get away from there as quickly as he could.

It took a while for the chickens to settle again to peck among the weeds. A bit longer for the children to show themselves as they scurried away. Even longer before Jude raised enough courage to ask, "Whatcha gonna do, Horey?"

Horace glared at them with glassy red eyes and stumbled back into the darkness of the bowels of his dwelling.

"Too drunk to do much besides whup our asses," Irwayne assessed the situation. "Come on, Jude. I got half a jug in my place." The brothers had reached the threshold of the first shack when Doc's car eased back to the edge of the yard and back again into the mud. The chickens fled again in chaos.

Hearing the renewed racket, Horace stepped back to his doorway. "Wha'?"

"I'm not sure you are sober enough to understand, Bratton." Will had opened his door and was half–standing so he could call out across the car roof. "But our family and Bodie will be burying Emmy Lu on our place. Dawn tomorrow. If you want to come, we won't stop you."

Horace's face reflected many emotions, mostly anger. The brothers gaped at Horace and then quickly ducked inside Irwayne's shack out of the way.

Doc Ricartsen was in better position to exit the compound quickly this time, and he did so. The car was mere taillights driving away when Horace heaved up and screamed after them.

"Near your stupid brother, Will? At least I left her head on! Kin you say thet?"

* *

In the pale orange air of that evening's subdued sunset, Will helped Bodie and his extended family dig with spade and shovel a short, deep grave beside Winfred's in the family plot that extended from beyond the elm to a few grave sites north and east of the mulberry tree.

Clayton, Emmy's gaunt, silent father, repeatedly got down on his knees to measure the hole with a stick he'd marked and brought with him.

Will questioned him with his eyes, but there was no verbal answer. "He and the boys made the coffin themselves," Bodie finally took Will aside to explain. "He brung the stick he sized up so they'd know the hole was right."

"Ah," Will said, nodding. "That would work, but I doubt I would have thought of it."

"Wisdom of experience," Bodie murmured, turning away.

When they were finished to Clayton's satisfaction, they stood a moment leaning on their shovels. Clayton spoke for the first time.

"Family planed it good. No splinters. This'll do. She'll feel safe here, with the boy."

He began packing up the tools and started away, saying nothing more. The others followed suit, but Situs lingered behind to look up at Will.

"How can I help you, boy?" Will asked, leaning down.

"Was just wonderin'. Goodwin double-snot dared me to ask ya. I say you found yer brother's head to bury. Some say you couldn't. Did ya?"

Bodie stepped close and swatted the child on his rump. "Now, never you mind, boy! Ain't no business of your'n, no how." Red-faced, Situs ducked away, and Bodie shook his head, apologizing. "Sorry, Will."

But Will, opening fists he'd closed instinctively, called the boy back and crouched eye level with the child to talk with him. "We did, Situs," he said kindly. "You were right; my brother is all there in his grave."

"Run along, Site." Bodie ordered. "Sweet Jesus Lord. So sorry, Will. What a thing ta ask ya."

Will shook his head and returned to the graveside. He lowered himself in to dig to square out the corners. Bodie left him to himself.

* *

In Will's room upstairs, Nandria crooned British and African lullabies over Emmy Lu as she washed her body. "…and pretty maids all in a row…" she lilted as she dressed Em in one of her own loveliest dresses. Quietly she dug among the stones in the pocket of her apron to find the one Emmy had given her in welcome to Missouri.

"For you, angel friend, with my deep thanks," she whispered as she tucked the stone into the right side pocket of the skirt. "Lord, could I have kept you safe? Could I?" Quietly, Nandria wept, for Emmy Lu. For her parents. For her own precious brother. She had not kept them safe, either. So much was beyond any control she might have thought she had.

* *

With both the light bulbs dangling above the sink and the kitchen table aglow the next morning before dawn, Nandria, in a shin–length dark dress, worked to suppress her nausea as she finished making breakfast. Minnick, in clean overalls, led Doris to the table in a fresh, dark house dress that Nandria had ironed the night before. Bodie, moving awkwardly in his mismatched suit, stepped beside her and picked up the coffee pot to serve the Minnicks. "I gots it, Miz. And, there, I hear the babe, too. I'll get her. Don't you fret none. I kin help."

Will, in uniform trousers, entered from the barn as Bodie finished changing Rose's diaper. Will washed his hands at the kitchen sink and took his daughter from Bodie as he sat at the table. Bodie had been helping her feed herself scalloped potatoes and her mouth and chin drooled sauce. Will's laugh sounded strange within the solemn near–silence that had hovered around the table.

Bodie chuckled. "The kid likes yer sloppy 'taters, Will's Miz."

Minnick looked over and then at his wife, whose face was bright with amusement at the baby, and at Will's efforts to wipe her face while she was still within range of grabbing at the potatoes on his plate.

"Funny way to fix a breakfast," Minnick muttered, but there was a hint of upturn at the corners of his mouth.

"Special request from Mother," Will said. "It makes sense, I guess. For a special day. Nandria made plenty of food for your folks when they get here, Bodie. Be sure to tell them."

"Yes, if you will, please," urged Nandria as she finally sat down beside Will. "Please let them know they are most welcome." But she couldn't eat. Instead, she took Rose from him so he could eat hands-free.

"They won't come in," Bodie told them as he scooped another helping for himself of the sloppy potatoes.

Nandria opened her mouth to ask why not when Minnick unexpectedly laughed aloud.

"You should have seen his face, Mother."

Doris nodded and smiled, but her bewilderment showed that she had not followed what Minnick had been telling her. Will had heard enough to ask, "You mean Kylie, pa?"

"Thet judge says, 'I told them to bury the poor girl,' and Kylie just about connipsed right there on the pew where we'd gone to tell him the town was in no further danger of chaos and riot." Minnick paused to take the serving spoon from Bodie to shovel in a large spoonful of potatoes onto his own plate.

"So Bratton didn't show up at all to talk with the judge?" Will asked.

Minnick shrugged and lifted another spoonful without acknowledging that he liked them. "Thet judge didn't have to stop at the church to let the pastor know of his decision."

"It was nice," Doris intoned.

Minnick grinned. "More like he was rubbing it in thet there had been no real need for the judge to have made a special trip out of his regular circuit. Getting' back at the man for makin' a fuss over nothin' and he wanted Kylie to know he knew it was him who'd called."

"But we're glad he did," Will breathed, patting Nandria's knee. "So good to have that black shadow lifted from over us this soon."

Nandria nodded, pushing back her chair so Rose could not reach the potatoes. She gave the little one a crust of toast to gnaw on instead. She seemed to want to hold the child in her arms rather than set her in the high chair.

"I was so relieved at the judge's expression when we were driving away from the Bratton place," Will added. "Doc seemed to expect the decision he was obviously coming to, but Yakes sure didn't."

Minnick mopped up the last of the potato sauce with his toast. He turned to Bodie. "Your family still okay with the gal being buried here at our place?"

Bodie nodded. "They knowed how much she believed in Winfred. Would'a been good for him."

"And he would have been good for her, I gather," Nandria said.

Minnick lifted his eyes from his plate to stare at her. Again, she was saying and doing things he had never expected from any darky, let alone colored woman. But his consternation was cut into by Doris chirping, "Freddy? My Freddy's comin' home?"

As the others looked down or away, Minnick pushed back his chair, an anguished scowl distorting his face. He was stopped short by Bodie's laugh.

"Boarder–house, reach, Miz," he chuckled and pointed. "Will you look at that?"

Rose had lunged across her mother's lap, her pudgy hands grabbing up fistfuls of the scalloped potatoes. Sauce oozed down her arms.

The laughter was swallowed as the family startled at a knock at the back door. Nandria started to rise, but Will pressed her shoulder and got up to go to answer it.

They listened to his warm welcome as he greeted the guests. "Hello. Please come in. Bodie," he called back into the Minnick kitchen, "it's family."

"Company?" Doris cried in distress. "Oh, my apron. My hair."

Minnick patted her arm. "You're fine, Mother. Always have been."

When Emmy's family would not come in, the Minnicks pushed back their chairs and went out to them, Nandria stopping at the sink to quick-wash her daughter's face and arms.

In near silence, the two groups made their way past the elm and swing to the small family plot. Emmy's grave site was next to a plot with a wooden plaque reading, 'Winfred Minnick 1915-1933.' Bodie stood to one side of the hand-carved pine casket, between the gathered groups: Minnicks, in couples, nearest the elm tree. Emmy's family, of various ages, all obviously poor, but clean and patched, on the far side but scattered a few steps back from the hole as though they felt unworthy even to be there. Dr. Ricartsen and Sadie came to stand behind Will, now holding Rose, and Nandria. Greg Paisler and two of his brothers and their parents remained to the house side of the swing. Kylie, just arrived, processed, chins high, from his car to stand at the head of the casket.

"Dearly beloved," he began, then flushing, launched into a long, droning prayer. But even the youngest of Emmy's clan remained respectfully quiet. Throughout the prayer, one or another mourner would open his or her eyes and look around fearfully and then in relief close them again. No sign of the Brattons. At the 'Amen' every one of Bodie's extended family looked around furtively. A few of the smaller children exhaled audibly, then giggled low at having been heard.

A slender young woman, probably not yet twenty years of age but carrying a toddler in her arms and another in her swollen front, began to sing in clear, bell-like soprano. "Amazing Grace," she sang soulfully. She might well have been Emmy's younger sister. Her family joined her on the chorus, and Nandria listened in awe at the intricacy of their harmony. During the final verse, Bodie, Clayton and the man who had held Situs against his legs came forward, and, beckoning Will to help them, lowered the small casket into the grave.

The family filed slowly past. Each member from the oldest to the youngest dropped a flower or a clod of earth onto the coffin and walked on, heads bowed, tears flowing silently. The women and children melted away. The men took turns shoveling dirt until the grave was nearly filled. Will gestured for Nandria to come forward and pick up a handful to lay in where he was shoveling. He held her and their daughter in his arms a moment as they peered at the mound of earth that was now the remains of Emmy Lu, gone far before her time. Stepping back out of the way,

Nandria bent again to pick up a pebble and set it into her pocket. She started back toward the house to set out the meal.

Situs scurried up beside her. "Why do ya do thet? Pocket them stones?"

"Perhaps to keep part of what happens to us," she told him. "Will you please ask Uncabodie to tell your family that we have food at the house? Thank you, Situs. For so much."

The child stood beside her, looking confused. Bodie walked over.

"They know about the food, Will's Miz. They 'preciates it, but can't come. I didn't know for sure they'd come here, what with Horace and them Brattons holding papers on their homesteads . . ."

"So that is the hold Horace Bratton had on Emmy Lu," Nandria sighed. "She must have been afraid to leave him for fear her family would lose their homes."

"Yes'm, feared so."

Leaving Clayton and Emmy's male kin to finish mounding the dirt, Will lifted his hands in supplication. "Please, everyone. Come to the house for refreshments. Please."

But the crowd, including Dr. Ricartsen and Sadie Bean expressed their regrets and hurried to their cars and pickups and drove away. Pastor Kylie huffed. "I fear, dearly bereaved, that I, too, will be unable to stay." He waddled to his car and drove off.

At the porch steps, Doris waved forlornly to the last of the departing vehicles. Minnick sighed.

"Afraid, and I don't blame them. Them Brattons," he spat, then rolled his shoulders. "Well, work to be done. But may as well keep these duds clean for Sunday." With a quick look over his shoulder at Nandria, he escorted Doris into the house.

"Bodie," Nandria said, "please go to your family. They will need you now."

"Grievin's somethin' they's good at by now, Miz. I'll just change this here suit and meet ya in the north field, Will."

"I wish you'd take the day, Bode, but I know how much chance there is of you doing what I say."

As Bodie limped off west toward his place, Will hugged his wife and child. Then he too walked to the house to change out of his uniform.

"Ah, my baby girl," Nandria cried low as she settled with Rose on her lap on the elm tree swing. She sat a minute, moving gently forward and back and even sideways as much as the interwoven limbs above her would allow. "Precious wee Rose, how I wish—oh, how I wish we could give you the home surrounded by the love and security that you deserve."

CHAPTER TWENTY-SIX

Will and Bodie had reconstructed the playpen in the back yard before they left for the fields. Little Rose was delighted when her mother finished in the kitchen and carried her outside. A butterfly flapped near enough to catch the child's attention with its huge black and orange wings that lifted together in approval and glee, even without the sound of clapping. Giggling and lunging forward with such sudden force that Nandria needed both arms to keep her from falling, Rose tried to reach the enticing creature. Nandria sent up a silent prayer of thanksgiving that, for once, she hadn't tried to carry Rose and the laundry, too.

Laughing, Nandria wrapped her arms around her daughter and danced with her. Rose's squealing made the hens stop their pecking in the grass and lift their heads in wonder if not fear. Nandria carried Rose closer to see them. The baby lunged again, trying to get at those fascinating, strutting, feathery critters, but this time Nandria was half-expecting it and was holding tight with both arms. The few minutes of her child's wonder smoothed such healing balm over Nandria's soul, that for those few moments the London orphan felt at peace, even here. She found it hard to wait to tell Will all about his daughter's delight.

But then, of course as on any farm, there was work to be done. Kissing her repeatedly on the fat, pinked cheeks, Nandria set the baby into the playpen. She touched the baby's arms with the back of her hand as she lined up the stuffed bear and Raggedy Ann doll for Rose to reach for. "I think I shall get you a sweater, little gem of a cherub. There is more of a breeze out here than I realized. Have fun, my darling," she whispered and hurried back into the house.

Horace Bratton stood erect behind the chicken coop.

"That was close," he murmured, but Rose was engrossed in picking at the red embroidered smile of the Raggedy doll. He had not made any noise. Since her back was toward him, she didn't look up to see the man's relief or fear. Or his look of determination as he moved to get closer, still unseen. Checking and rechecking for anyone, Bratton gathered his shotgun close against his side and scurried from the coop toward the east back corner of the house, but dove to flatten himself in the grass just beyond the mulberry tree when Nandria returned to the porch door.

That annoying–intriguing colored gal was so intent on the heaving her weighty hamper of wet clothes through the doorway that Horace dared to worm his way to the elm tree. The trunk might or might not conceal him, depending how thet woman moved around in the yard. If only thet dratted female stopped to play with the pickaninny, he'd have time to get to the far side of the house. Sure enough, Nandria let the basket down with a thump just short of the clothesline, and unknowingly turned her back on him to lean over the playpen to talk with her youngster.

Not a bad backside, he thought. Especially for one who'd already carried a kid. Most women let their rump widen and get ugly . . . but he was wasting valuable seconds. Looking around again, he lifted on straightened arms, and, seeing no one else, crouch–dashed around the corner of the house out of sight.

Just in time. Horace hadn't seen Will come from the north to enter the barn through the back. He appeared now at the yard door and stopped to watch his wife and baby laughing and cooing together. His smile widened as he heard Nandria coaxing the little one with 'da' sounds repeated again and again. And then their delight when a Monarch butterfly fluttered near made him want to sing out to the sky or kneel in thanksgiving.

Nandria caught sight of Will as she lifted her head. Her surprised smile gladdened his heart. His father was wrong. There are far more important facets to a wife than the color of her skin. Striding to her, he set the errant tools he'd come to retrieve on the ground and reached for Nandria to plant a wet, possessive kiss on her luscious mouth. "Hi, beautiful," he whispered. Then, pulling himself away after hugging both his girls, Will hurried, loping with his bag of tools back through the barn toward the north field.

With the nigger holding thet babe in her arms and helping her wave good-bye, Horace took his chance to sneak along the back side of the house, but something alerted her. She set the baby quickly into the playpen and spun to face him. She showed no fear, even when he raised the shotgun and pointed it at her.

He stopped twenty feet from her, nonplussed. His brothers had tried to tell him some crazy story about her knowing strange magic, but of course he hadn't believed them—until this minute. And then Horace smiled and shifted the barrel of his gun to aim at the baby and was gratified at the terror that crept into the darky's eyes.

He closed the distance between them and reached to pat one pocket of her apron. She cringed but set her jaw and stiffened, glaring at him as he lifted out the pistol Will had put there for her before breakfast. Growling low, he slid it inside his own waistband and reached to pat her again. He frowned, feeling the pebbles in her other pocket.

"I've heerd of 'rocks in your head.' Why d'ya keep these, anyway?" But when she merely stared at him in answer, he shrugged and gave her front more intimate pats. "Well, you keep 'em then, Miss Uppity, and I'll keep your little toy gun. Say, why don'tcha call Will back here?"

"Because you would shoot him."

Bratton found it disconcerting to have her answer simply and directly. Women weren't supposed to meet him eye to eye, even though she had to look up to do it as he towered over her. But he knew he had the upper hand as long as he held the gun and had that little one for a target.

"Shoot Will?" he drawled. "Sugarlips, I plans to do thet anyhoo. Just thought ya might wanna watch. Or him watch me take you down a peg or two fer tryin' to run me over with thet tractor."

She stood her ground, answering without emotion. "You slithered out of the way without harm."

He grinned; she made this fun. "You got spine. Makes doin' ya a good battle won. No smart backtalk now?" he taunted as he slowly shifted the barrel of his weapon again toward the playpen. She'd gone pale; he hadn't known a nigger could go pale. "Don'tcha want the kid to watch? Learn 'er place early?"

He aimed at Rose, and Nandria went from intrepid to pleading.

"Do nothing to hurt her! I will do anything you say!"

"Always knowed ya would," he leered.

Laughing, Horace quickly raised his shotgun over his head in signal to his brothers concealed in the tall grass on the slope beyond the barn. They waved back with their own weapons and began to slink following Will north to where Minnick and Bodie labored unknowing.

"No!" Nandria cried.

"Scream, Sugarlips. Go on, scream. Warn 'em. It'll just bring 'em to be shot thet much quicker. M'boys was gonna wait 'til I was done with you so I could watch, but, except for your Will, it makes no never mind to me."

Nandria cowered, glaring. But as she hugged her arms around her upper body with her head bowed, her breathing slowed. Her own weapon reared within her, bringing a faint smile as she remembered the head nurse on the "Salty Healer" asking seriously before allowing her to disembark at Halifax: "That Voo-Doo priestess ploy you use on the sailors, and even some of the soldiers when they get out of line. Do you, are you really . . . ?"

"I have never traveled to New Orleans, Major Kerwitz," Nandria had answered. "I have been in Africa, but I have never seen a Voo-Doo ceremony or even met—to my knowledge—a Voo-Doo priest. But I do know that many bullies are at heart afraid and often superstitious."

"Then those incantations?"

Nandria'd shrugged. "Something I read about in a book when I was a girl in elementary school."

They'd laughed, Nandria chuckling within the hug and throaty laughter of the finest healer and one of the most courageous women she had ever known. Even as Nandria had carried her infant down the Salty Healer's gangplank onto Canadian soil, she had heard the deep, rich tone of Major Kerwitz's laughter. Its echo remained with her now. Would what had worked on those lusty sailors and on Horace Bratton's brothers work now on him as well?

Nandria lifted her chin, peering at him until she had his full, surprised attention. She began a quiet, slow, rhythmic chanting.

"You black witch," he muttered, "whatcha sayin'? Whatcha doin'?" He couldn't take his eyes off her.

Still mumbling, but now refusing to look at him, Nandria swayed and sang, gravelly low. Her dance moved her all but imperceptibly away from the playpen.

Open–mouthed, and with fear seeping into his eyes like a mist gradually consuming an overcast afternoon, Horace stared at her. Frightened now, but growing angry, he moved after her as though on a tether, keeping his distance. Suddenly, the anger—his most practiced and therefore best weapon—conquered his fear, and he shook his head and body in negation. His filthy beard trembled.

"Witch!" he spat. "But you ain't got me! Not yet, you ain't!"

He stalked back toward Rose in the playpen. As he stormed toward her, the baby, sitting erect with eyes and mouth wide, screeched and kept on screeching.

In the moments it took Horace to stride toward Rose, Doris Minnick appeared at the porch doorway, her paring knife in one hand and a broom in the other.

"You, Bratton! Get away from thet baby! You hear?" the woman screamed.

Nandria darted behind him to snatch up Rose in her arms and ran toward the barn as Doris Minnick dropped the knife to come at the man, swatting her broom, tackling the attacker.

Lifting his arms to ward off the blows, Horace closed in and ducked and reached to rip the broom from the frail woman's hands. With a string of obscenities, he flung it across the yard. Seeing Nandria running away, Horace back-handed Doris, knocking her to the ground.

"Damn you, nigger!" he cried, and dashed after Nandria. Slowing a moment to shoot one round from the shotgun, he took off again after her.

Nandria stumbled and, for a moment, seemed about to go down. But she righted herself and disappeared with her baby inside the barn.

CHAPTER TWENTY-SEVEN

In the north field, the Minnicks and Bodie looked up at the sound of gunfire.

"Sweet Jesus Lord," Bodie murmured, shaking.

"That's at the house!" Will cried, his feet already moving him toward his wife and baby daughter.

Minnick waved for his son to go; he'd catch up, but Will stopped abruptly. Near the edge of the field, Irwayne had stepped out, his shotgun aimed at Will's gut.

"You, there, Bratton . . .!" Grover Minnick cried, enraged at this ambush on his own property.

"Easy, old man," Jude scrambled up from where he'd been lying in the dirt. With one hand he wiped at the clots and dusting of fine earth clinging to his flannel shirt front, but not the spittle on his beard. With the other he pointed vaguely at the older Minnick. His handgun was old, but appeared to be still functional. Minnick swallowed his audible protest, but glared.

Still panicked by the implications of gunshots at their home, the Minnicks looked as though they might not stay frozen even by the threat of two weapons.

"Horey said you was to wait here," Irwayne informed them.

"'Til he's done," Jude giggled.

All three captives stared at him.

* *

Inside the barn, Nandria snatched up a pitchfork and, cradling Rose against her shoulder, ran to hide in the back corner beyond the thresher. She crouched, frantic to control her breathing and remain still. "Oh, Precious," she breathed to Rose, "you must stay quiet. Please, my darling, make no sound."

She could see glimpses of Horace entering the barn warily, moving in with his back up against the far door–jamb. He must have feared she had a rifle hidden somewhere, and she wondered if Will had left one to use as defense just in case. But where? Probably near that front door, but she had not even looked as she ran in.

Horace moved out of her line of sight. She could hear him poking around, lunging now and again in triumph, then cursing in frustration when he didn't find her where he'd expected to.

Rose began to stir, and Nandria rocked her, huddling protectively over her and cooing breathlessly.

"Hey, sugarlips, I got somethin' fer ya," Horace called. "Come on out, now; you'll like it. Come out, come out, wherever you are," he sang. "All–ee, all–ee, in free!"

It was not an expression Nandria had heard, but the singsong reminded her of the universal jungle luring call of sneak predators. As Nandria crouched she felt her left calf cramping, the pain demanding that she move to ease her position, but she held still.

As though giving up finally, Horace turned back toward the yard, but a whimper from Rose made him spin on his heel and stalk toward them.

Stifling her own scream, Nandria comforted the baby as best she could while reaching to soundlessly prop the pitchfork against the rough wall. She reached into her apron pocket for a pebble. Rising only a little to have a clear shot, Nandria tossed it to the far back corner.

Immediately, Horace crouched and hurried, gun raised, toward the noise of its landing.

Easing back, Nandria studied the open distance between herself and the back door of the barn. From where he was, he would see them. And he had that shotgun. He'd have a clear shot.

She tossed another pebble, trying to lure him toward the house side of the thresher, so she might have a chance at escaping out the back. But, with each frustration, he grew louder and angrier. Frowning, she calculated, realizing she might just be able to lure . . .

"Go on, you walking pile of manure," she whispered under her breath, "That way. Closer. That is the way to dusty death. Easy, now, closer..."

Distant gunshots startled all three.

Rose wailed.

Nandria cried, "Oh, God, Will!"

"Nobody messes with the Brattons for long," Horace sneered and leaped toward the sound of her voice.

* *

"Bodie!" Will cried as the handyman, bleeding, staggered and fell at Irwayne's feet where he'd tried to storm him to grab the shotgun from his hands.

Minnick hurled his spade. Its handle caught Jude in the shin. He shrieked and crumpled to the ground, clutching his leg. Minnick lumbered toward Jude rolling in the dirt as Will launched himself at Irwayne. With Army training, Will twisted the middle Bratton son until he dropped his weapon, but Minnick was no match for the younger Jude.

"Ease off, Will!" Jude yelled, jamming his pistol into the side of Minnick's face. "Your pa here don't need no lead shave."

Will stood, quivering with tension, but giving up his advantage.

With a final vicious poke at Will's side, Irwayne struggled up, wiping the blood from his nose. "Son of a bitch!"

The Bratton brothers stared at each other, panting.

"What're we gonna do with 'em, Ir?"

"I'd like to kill 'em, especially High and Mighty Will, here."

Seeing their indecision, Will moved quietly to check on his father and then crouched beside Bodie, bleeding into the earth.

"We ain't heerd nothin' from Horey," Jude whined.

"Yeah," Irwayne spat. His face slowly lighted. "He'll prob'ly wanna be in on finishin' this."

With guttural commands, the Brattons motioned for Will to carry Bodie toward the farmhouse. Grover Minnick stumbled behind them down the slope.

* *

"Almost," Nandria breathed. "Yesssss, now!"

Nandria broke cover and ran. But she had not counted on the cramp in her left calf. She stumbled, sprawling. She twisted in the air to land on her side to protect her little Rose.

Horace was lunging at her, but she scrambled up despite the pain and forced herself to run. With quick sidesteps she was barely able to evade his grasping hands.

Just outside beyond the barn door, Will gently laid Bodie on the grass near the empty playpen. At Irwayne's direction, Minnick sat heavily beside him all but glassy-eyed from blows to the face and head. Irwayne guarded them with his shotgun while Jude hurried into the barn.

"Horey?" the youngest Bratton brother hollered. "We brung . . ."

Horace slowed, glancing back over his shoulder, and Nandria ducked, crouched and spun on the ball of her foot to reverse direction. She whipped around to face him, hurtling forward to shove him with her one free hand.

He stumbled, grunting in surprise. For what seemed like long moments, he pirouetted, eyes wide in growing realization and terror.

Nandria, stunned despite her plotting, held her breath and remained bent forward, frozen.

With a guttural cry of "Noooo!" Horace clutched air as he lost his balance and was taken by inexorable gravity and momentum into the thresher. Before he could scramble up, it shuddered, swayed, and toppled over on top of him.

At Horace's scream, Will tackled Irwayne, ripping the shotgun from his hands and knocking him to the grass in the yard. "Jude," he cried, aiming the cumbersome gun at Jude's back, "toss that gun! You heard me, drop it!"

Whether or not he had heard Will's command, Jude, white faced, let the shotgun slide from his hands. It clattered against the wood of the barn and fell to the packed earth. Without looking back at Will, he bent double and vomited onto the door–jamb.

Irwayne, pale and shaking, stumbled toward the barn. He looked so shaken that Will, shotgun still in hand, did nothing to hinder him.

"I gotta see him."

"It can't be pretty," Will warned him.

Irwayne halted just beyond his retching brother. "Oh, pukingodsaglory," he moaned, transfixed.

Closing his eyes only for a moment, Will gathered himself for what must come next. "Pa, see about ma!"

Stumbling in his turn, Minnick made his unsure way to his own back door. "Blood," he cried as he saw a trail of darkening red on the steps and up onto the floor of the porch. Groaning, he disappeared into the house, for once not stopping to take off his boots.

Will gathered the abandoned guns and entered the darkness of the barn.

"Nandria? Nandria!"

Her distorted cry told him where to find her, retching.

Gently Will took the baby from her clutching arms, and checked Rose over quickly, but carefully.

"Nandria, darling, are you . . . ?" He reached to hold her.

Green and pale, she pushed back on his chest to look up into his face. "Mother Minnick . . ."

"Pa is checking on my mother. In the house, evidently. Are you all right? Did he hurt . . . ?"

She wept then, folding into his embrace. "Oh, my God, Will! Oh, my God."

CHAPTER TWENTY-EIGHT

Time had lost all proportion. Nandria huddled, cradling her baby, in her nest of blankets in the rocking chair in their corner of the living room. She looked up as Will came quietly to sit on the floor beside her and lay his head on her thigh.

"I did not hear him, Will," she explained, pleading that he forgive her. "The laundry. I had carried it outside a-a-and was just-and p-playing with the baby. She s-saw a-a butterfly . . ."

He stood up then and drew a straight-backed chair near so he could sit on its edge to hold her, murmuring into her luxuriant black hair. "We didn't hear his brothers, either. And I should have known they'd pull a sneak attack. I should have known."

"It was not your fault."

"I'm supposed to protect . . ."

"N-no, no, no, darling," she murmured. When he seemed to regain himself, she sat up some and, shaking her head, lifted his chin. "It was not your fault, Will." She could see in his eyes that he would protest no further, but might well never forgive himself. Shuddering, she began to pull away from this man she loved. "I-I should be helping Mother Minnick. She flew out that door with a broom, did you know that? A broom against a shotgun. To protect little Rose. You s-sure she is well?"

"The Paislers are with her, and with Bodie. Cynthia Paisler—Greg's ma—is as good a nurse as this community has ever had, bar only Sadie Bean. And Doc Ricartsen is on his way. He'd been way up country, almost to Fox Haven."

"They heard the gunshots, then? Funny, I would not have thought the sound would have carried all that way to the Paisleys'."

"Dinner bell." Will all but smiled. "They heard the infernal clamor of the dinner bell you kept ringing and ringing, till half the county . . ."

"Oh," Nandria said, managing a quavering smile at Will's expression.

"You know, Doc Ricartsen once asked me why you and I never seem to snap and dig at each other the way real married couples do."

"Oh? Does he think we do not qualify as a 'real' couple then?"

"That was just it. He knows we are real, and he simply cannot understand it. So I told him that our color combination helped us to see each other in very tight spots quite early on. It helped us iron out our different expectations of each other and our marriage instead of over surprise stumbling blocks little by little over time."

Will took her face in his hands and shook his head gently as he peered into her eyes. "I love you," he declared softly.

She twisted to lay her head on his shoulder. As Rose squirmed and gurgled in her sleep, Nandria sat up to reposition and soothe her. She looked up at her husband.

"Why did they shoot him, Will? Why in the name of the sweetness of heaven would those Bratton brothers shoot Bodie?"

"He tried to rush 'em."

"That is suicide!"

Will merely nodded. "It nearly was."

"Ah," she breathed. After a moment she turned to look at him with haunted eyes. "Check him, Will. Please."

He knew exactly who she meant. He shook his head.

"No, please, Will. I do not believe even his brothers . . . You just let them slip away."

"I know where they'll be," he said with lips nearly closed.

"But no one has gone near him. I cannot bear to think that he might be lying there, s-still a-alive, still a-alive." She started to pull away as though she would check for herself if he did not. It had taken all his coaxing to get her into the house. He held her now to keep her from staggering to the barn and that finally fatal threshing machine.

"No, love. Mr. Paisley looked, and Greg. He's dead, and good riddance, I say. Horace Bratton beat and killed and threatened. He got what he deserved. You have nothing to feel guilty about for having protected our daughter from a bitter, cowardly bully."

She sat up and held out—almost thrust—their daughter into Will's arms as though she could not stand the idea of her guilty hands touching their baby.

"I k-killed a h-human being."

"You shoved a murderer and he fell into his death." He set Rose against his shoulder and reached to hold his wife with his free hand. But this time she didn't melt against him. She only shuddered.

"This t–time I d–deserve a trial. M–make sure he is dead, Will? Please?"

CHAPTER TWENTY-NINE

Bodie lay listening to the sound of heavy rain. Not on his roof, he knew before he opened his eyes. Strange to be coming awake at all. He'd expected to have accomplished what he'd tried to do earlier. Evidently he failed again, only this time he hurt a lot more than merely a stiff neck and a sore throat. His gut ached fiercely. He wanted to double up, but any movement brought more pain than it was worth it to try.

"Bodie?" a sweet voice questioned. A voice, if not an angel's, was almost worth coming back to the land of the living for.

"M-miz?" he croaked. He had the sore throat this time, too, all right, but he hadn't noticed amid all the other pain.

"Right here, Bodie." Nandria came to sit beside him. He could hear her skirt rustling and smell the fresh lilac soap Will had gotten for her as a special treat. He tried to open his eyes, though he couldn't turn to look at her.

"Ya got me on your bed?"

"We have moved into a corner of the living room so we can be near to tend . . ."

"Fittin' for me to die here. Brass bed." He was surprised at his own deep satisfaction that this was so. "Thank you. Oh, the Missus? The babe?"

"Easy, Bodie, everyone will be well in time. On the mend. Mrs. Paisler and the doctor and Sadie Bean did such a good job. Mother Minnick was bruised and she had cut her lip . . ." Nandria paused to draw a breath and exhale slowly, " . . .when she f–fell. Bloody nose. Lots of blood on the step and the porch floor. It s–scared Mr. Minnick something f–fierce when he s–s–saw it." She nearly smiled at how quickly she was picking up the Missouri–American idioms. She had always been a quick study with languages.

"The babe?"

"Never touched."

"Thanks to you." His voice cracked.

"Let me help you take some water," she urged, drawing the pitcher close to half–fill a glass. "You have slept three days, now. Dr. Ricartsen said it was the best thing for you. How are you feeling?"

"Still alive, cause in Heaven there ain't gonna be no more pain. If'n I ever gets to Heaven, that'll feel some good."

"You will get to Heaven if bravery counts, and caring about and for other people," she whispered and wiped his brow. "There, now how are you feeling?"

"Cat's pajamas, Miz."

"American cats wear pajamas?" she questioned, eyes wide. "How odd. Why?"

"Cause I'm gonna get somethin' off'n my chest I should'a spoke up about years ago." It was painful to keep up this much effort, but he was grateful for the relief within his decision. He did turn enough to look into her lovely, understanding face.

"Not to me, Bodie. It is Will's father who needs to hear, if it is what I think it might be," she told him, low.

"Him, too. But would ya jus' lemme practice with you first off? You oughta know, too."

She drew her chair closer to the edge of the bed and folded her hands over the pocket of pebbles in her apron. "You were there when my husband's brother died."

"Will telled ya already?"

Nandria shook her head, and he extended his gnarled hand to rest atop hers.

"Ya gots uncommon sight deep into people, you do."

Nandria and Bodie both startled as Minnick clumped to the porch door. Both withdrew their hands quickly. Grover Minnick stared at the gesture with a frown. Nandria rose.

"Lunch is not quite ready as yet," she apologized, and started for the kitchen.

Minnick shook his head. "No, stay," he ordered. Nandria stood unmoving while he worked off his muddy boots and sat heavily in the chair Nandria had just vacated.

"Glad you come, Mister Minnick. Gots somethin' to tell ya."

"Fetch another chair, girl. I think you want to hear this," Minnick told Nandria gently. "Been wonderin', Bodie. You sure?"

Bodie winced as he nodded, but he twisted a little to ask another favor of Will's wife. "And fetch the Missus, too, will ya, Miz?"

"You want her to know?"

"If you think she's up to it," Bodie asked of Grover Minnick.

"Don't know how much she'll take in." Minnick said, nodding. "But mebbe some. Next week, who knows?" He shook his head; whatever was bringing down his Doris, it was getting worse and there was nothing he could find to do about it. "And Willard," he added, looking up. 'Never mind, he's comin' up now from the barn."

Once more Nandria searched Bodie's face to satisfy herself that he was sure of what he was about to do. "Excuse me, then. I shall fetch Mother Minnick."

"No excuses," Minnick muttered.

Nandria startled, until she saw the tiny lift to the corners of his mouth: a sly smile she'd never seen directed at herself before.

She left the porch with a flicker of warm hope she had begun to believe she would never feel in this house.

Doris Minnick sat in her corner of the sofa with her needles and hooks and yarn on her lap, but her hands idle. She looked up at Nandria approaching and smiled. The flicker of hope within Nandria fluttered to a warmth that touched all her insides. And then Doris frowned, concerned.

"Men are in already? I thought I heard Mr. Minnick's voice. I don't have their supper made."

"It is early; please do not worry. They came in because it is too wet and rainy to be able to get much done, they tell me. And because Bodie is awake," she added gently.

"Dear Bodie," Doris said, allowing Nandria to gather up and stow her craft materials and help her to rise. "I don't know what we'd'a done without him when Freddy . . ."

Sighing, Nandria helped her mother-in-law out through the kitchen and into the rocker beside Minnick. When Rose stirred and fussed, Nandria picked her up and held her on a chair back toward a corner, but Minnick reached for the child. He held her on his knee close enough for Doris to play with her, to the delight of both of them.

Will entered, shedding wet clothes. Nandria jumped up to help him as he stared wide-eyed at the gathering around the brass bed.

"You must be cold. I have coffee . . ."

"Sit, girl, for once. Sit and listen. All here now, Bode," Minnick told him and the aged handy man opened his eyes.

"Pa, what's going on?"

"Bodie's close enough to his Maker he wants to talk now he's got one last chance."

"Bodie, no," Will warned, his face contorted with concern. "Just let it be."

"Your pa's right, Will. This is fer me. I knows thet now."

"Sit, boy," Minnick told him. Will sat close beside Nandria and shut his mouth, but still he frowned and shook his head even as he took the hand Nandria extended to him after she had held the glass for Bodie to take another sip of water.

"There weren't no malice, Mr. Minnick."

"No evil in ya, Bodie," Doris assured him. "You was so good to us when my Freddy-boy . . . And all the years since."

Tears glistening, Bodie peered at her. "Plumb had to be, Missus. To make up. I'm the one who . . ."

"Why, Bodie?" Will demanded. "It isn't gonna change that he's dead. And Nandria and Rose and I are leaving in a matter of weeks . . ."

Bodie coughed, and then choked, blood at his nose and lips. Nandria went to help him. It was a few minutes before he could speak.

"Irwayne done me a favor," he rasped.

"And you charging that shotgun was nearly a breaking of your promise," Nandria scolded.

"Ya gotta forgive me, Miz. My Emmy Lu should'a been helpin' you cook these meals and hangin' out this family's clothes."

"As Fred's wife," Nandria completed the image.

Bodie turned. "Mr. Minnick, you is a fair man. Tough, Lord knows, but fair. But I don't think even you'd believe me if'n' I wasn't dyin'."

"Ah, Bodie," Will begged, "don't."

But Bodie kept his eyes on Grover Minnick's face as he continued. "We was drunk, the boy and me. I didn't give it to him. You gotta believe thet. Not to a kid."

"Fred was good at sniffing out liquor. Not just yours, Bodie," Will told him.

"What are they sayin', Mr. Minnick?" Doris asked him, her hand clutching his arm.

"Truth," he told her, shifting the baby to be able to pat his wife's hand.

"I was drivin'," Bodie continued when he could. "Freddy was battin' at mailboxes."

Minnick nodded. "There'd been a bunch smashed up, even out toward Fox Haven."

"It weren't our first night out."

"Fred hid his bat when it got too beat up." Will sat forward, his hands clasped between his knees, his eyes closed, remembering.

"Told me he was done with baseball," Minnick nodded. He, too, remembered.

"Freddy? Is my Freddy coming, Mr. Minnick?"

"No, Mother. Freddy isn't coming. Never again."

"We'll hafta go to him, Missus," Bodie whispered. "I'm so sorry."

"They hit a pothole, pa. I was on my bike behind them. Couldn't catch up, couldn't stop them, but I saw it all. That box was homemade. No curled edge on the front cover thing." He lifted his face, staring at his father, begging with his eyes to understand that it had been just a crazy, stupid accident. "Fred leaned out. The truck hit that pothole… swerved . . . That front cover . . . came off, slicing the air . . ."

"Beheaded," Nandria breathed, nauseous just picturing what had happened and wishing to Heaven that her husband had not seen it at all.

Will shuddered and she wrapped her arm around his shoulders, rocking with his grief.

"They said our boy'd lost his head, but..." Doris slowed and went silent.

Minnick's anguish drove his chin to his chest. Nandria found she was holding her breath until he squared his shoulders and lifted his head to peer at Will.

"But you was the one drove him to Dr. Marburger's, Willard," Minnick finally looked up at Will.

"I was too busy retching into tall grass by the side of the road. Couldn't do nothin'," Bodie groaned. "Your boy picked up thet head and drove off like there was somethin' could'a been done to fix things."

"But there wasn't," Doris whispered, eyes closed.

"I blamed you," Minnick said gruffly to his remaining son.

"You'd just lost your son, Pa."

"And then I lost it all. Everything. Too quick to blame; not quick enough to see. Did you try to tell me, son?"

Will searched his face. It was evident he had tried, but each time his father simply would not be approached. Now, Grover Minnick lowered his face again and sat unmoving for a long while. Not until he at last raised his head did Will speak again.

"How could I, Pa? If you had known, you'd have killed Bodie and been hauled off to prison. I couldn't keep up this farm or take decent care of Ma here, either. We needed you. And when you were functioning again, I..."

"You joined the Army. Was it because you knew I couldn't stand the sight of you? Did you know that, boy?"

"Pa, I was never cut out to be a farmer. We both knew that. It was better I just went away."

But Nandria shook his arm. "Tell him, Will. Tell him we love him and Mother Minnick. Say it. He has not lost us, or Rose, or the new baby coming."

Bodie, lying back, closed his eyes, smiling.

"Grammam. I ain't no Mother Minnick," Doris declared. "I'm Grammam Minnick."

"To pickaninnies," Minnick said, shaking his head in wonderment. "Who'd've ever thought a darky could be a beautiful woman?"

"I knew," Will smiled. "From the first minute I knocked her over in the grass and fell for her."

Amid the low chuckles, Nandria's face reflected the emotions of every battle of her war. Smiling, she looked up at her husband and this family to which she finally belonged.

Nancy's Scones

395 degrees for 10-12 minutes or until
bottom and tops are lightly golden

Ingredients:

3 ½ cups all-purpose flour

1 tablespoon baking powder

1 teaspoon baking soda

½ teaspoon salt

¾ cups granulated sugar

½ cup butter (1 stick)

½ cup buttermilk

2 eggs lightly beaten

For Fruit Scones: to buttermilk/egg mixture
add 1 tablespoon grated orange zest (or 1 tsp extract)
or 1 cup currants/raisins or both
(I add orange zest and currents, cranberries or raisins)

Also butter, preserves, clotted cream or whipped cream
to put on top if you like

— Continued on next page —

Directions:

1) Preheat oven to 395 degrees

2) Butter and flour baking sheet
(or parchment paper is the best!)

3) Mix flour, baking powder, baking soda, salt and sugar

4) Cut butter into dry ingredients until mixture consists of fine crumbs

5) Whisk buttermilk with eggs
(add zest and cranberries now for fruit scones)

6) Add milk mixture all at once to dry ingredients

7) Stir to mix

8) As soon as mixture holds together, turn out onto floured surface to knead slightly

9) Take large orange- or grapefruit-sized clump of dough, knead gently to form a ball.

10) Flatten each ball to a thickness of ½ to 1 inch. With a sharp knife, cut each round into 8 triangles

11) Arrange on prepared baking sheet and bake until golden brown
(395 degrees, 10-12 min)

12) Cool on rack – *Enjoy!*

Nancy Danielson, Forest Grove, Oregon

Christine's Ham Loaf

Heat oven to 350 degrees

1 ½ lb lean ground ham

1 ½ lb ground pork

¼ lb veal (or ground chicken)

1 egg

1 cup milk

1 ½ cup ground bread crumbs

¼ cup finely chopped onion

Make into loaf and baste with following sauce:

½ cup vinegar

2/3 cup brown sugar

1/3 tsp dry mustard

cook until dissolved

Bake at 350 degrees for 2 hours

Serves 12

Christine Davie – circa 1935

Mushroom Coconut Curry

Fill half crockpot with diced vegetables

(potatoes, sweet peppers, onion, garlic, beets,
red cabbage, carrots, corn from the cob, etc.)

Add 2-3 Tb of Mae Ploy Curry Paste

Turn crock pot on low for 6+ hours

Add about ½ to 1 lb. Chanterelle or other mushrooms plus 1-2 cups Coconut Milk. Simmer for about an hour.

Just before serving, you may add more mushrooms, if desired. Warms up yummy for several meals.

{note: the color from the beets and red cabbage melts after the first couple hours and there is no bloody mess at all}

Susan Schmidlin – Schmidlin Angus Farm, Vernonia, Oregon

Alice's Ranger Joe Oatmeal Cookies

Preheat oven to 350 degrees

1 cup shortening

1 cup granulated sugar

1 cup brown sugar

2 eggs

1 tsp vanilla

2 cups flour

½ tsp salt

1 tsp baking soda

½ tsp baking powder

2 cups rolled oats

1 cup coconut

Mix, add dry mixture and shape into walnut-sized balls.
Set on greased cookie sheet.

Bake ~ 15 min at 350

Alice Pritchard – circa 1939

Mary Jane Nordgren, a retired family practice physician raised in the Midwest, now lives in the Pacific Northwest. Author of ***EARLY: Logging Tales Too Human to be Fiction***, MJ branched into fiction with ***QUIET COURAGE***.

NANDRIA'S WAR is the first novel in her series depicting challenges of the 1940s to loved people of her youth.